Maggie's Dream

Leslie Tall Manning

ISBN: (Mobi) 978-0-9961306-7-7
ISBN: (Paperback) 978-0-9961306-8-4
ISBN: (Audio) 978-0-9961306-9-1

Cover layout and typography by J. Kenton Manning Design.
Copyright © 2017.
Original illustration by Johnny Linder, used with permission.
Book formatting by Polgarus Studio.

Available at Amazon.com and other book stores.

This book is dedicated to my grandmothers, Lena Argenti and Helen Tall, who forged unconventional paths while rising above the din of inequality.

"The dream is the small hidden door in the deepest and most intimate sanctum of the soul, which opens to that primeval cosmic night that was soul long before there was conscious ego and will be soul far beyond what a conscious ego could ever reach."
~ **Carl Jung**

"The great question that has never been answered, and which I have not been able to answer, despite my thirty years of research into the feminine soul is,
'What does a woman want?'"
~ **Sigmund Freud**

Prologue

April 2, 1944

My Dearest Samuel,

Twenty-two letters have now traveled between us. It is incomprehensible that we've been apart for over a year! I can only hope you are as entertaining to the soldiers as you were to the children you left behind at the hospital.

Things at the plant took an interesting turn. No more greasing engine parts six days a week. You are now looking at the first woman in our division to operate a drill press! Who would know to look at me that I could handle a job of this nature? Mr. Sanders has also decided I will head a taskforce to collect more scrap metal in downtown Baltimore. What a wonderful opportunity. If I'm not home enough to cook Campbell's Soup, I may as well be collecting their cans!

I hope you don't think me vain to share how proud I am of myself, and how I long for us to be together so we can celebrate my promotion with a glass of champagne. After all, we hardly had a chance before you left to finish the bottle from our honeymoon.

My eyes are trying not to close at the moment as I am exhausted by eight o'clock every night. I barely have the energy to make it through my favorite radio shows. I suppose Bob Hope and Dinah Shore will have to wait until this war is over to share our evenings again.

Another dream came to me last night. Like the others, I heard your voice, but still your face escaped me. You were lost. Everywhere I searched, but your voice drifted away, disappearing into a fog. When I awoke, I felt as though you weren't the only one lost.

I have made a warm cup of Ovaltine to calm my nerves for a sound sleep tonight.

If only you were next to me in our bed, so in the morning your eyes would be the first to gaze upon me. My darling, I love you and pray that this war doesn't keep us apart much longer.

Maggie

June 10, 1944
My Little Magpie,

Do not fret about my being lost. I am right here—not in your arms directly, but perhaps soon.

We get word almost daily of the Allies advances. All looked as though we were making headway when US troops landed in Normandy. But with Soviet forces storming Finland yesterday, it is anybody's guess what may happen next. There are now three million men fighting for England's cause—I hope we don't get a large percentage of the wounded here. Italy has certainly had its share of unnecessary destruction.

Please keep President Roosevelt in your prayers. He is only one man, after all, and his ideals hardly compare to Hitler's dangerous ways of thinking.

How proud I am that your boss has given you such a prestigious placement within the company. But do not despair about dragging through that dirty job for very long, for soon you can take your place again as a doctor's wife, and all you will need to worry your sweet head about is raising a brood of wonderful children and making a comfortable home. Two things you will handle with finesse!

You are my wife, and I adore you. I count the minutes of each day until we can be together again.

My Love Forever,
Sam

September 15, 1944
My Dearest Samuel:

Days are long at the plant. The Andrew Sisters and Cab Calloway make time pass more quickly, but it is the news in between the music that most of us listen for. The factory echoes with reports of countless deaths and troops moving ahead with their secret plans. Why doesn't Germany surrender? England will not rest until Hitler and his regime are destroyed. But at what cost? All those young boys flying to their demise, leaving behind families at the hands of a fanatic. It seems so senseless. I thank the Lord you are on the ground rather than among the bullets and bombs. I am thankful to be a doctor's wife.

Please don't think I complain about working to help the war efforts. On the contrary, I rather like packing a lunch and heading into the grind, united with other women for the same cause. It is surprising that I should be so good at this everyday routine and rather efficient at handling the drill press for hours at a time. There are now forty-two of us. The women and I seem to fit right in. Some of the men even include us in their political conversations during our breaks. I am learning so much from them.

But I am still tired. And not from the long factory hours, or keeping the can drive going, or spending Sundays weeding the neighborhood victory garden. Even though I fall asleep easily each night, I do not awaken in the morning feeling rested. Your voice follows me into my dreams, but the harder I try to find you, the more distant your voice becomes. I've heard that taking a tranquilizer before bed may help, but I am hesitant to try such things.

I keep reminding myself that as soon as this awful war comes to a close, our lives will return to normal. As soon as you are beside me again, this nervous energy will wither away. I am sure of it.

With All My Heart,
Maggie

December 19, 1944
My Little Magpie:

Imagine my surprise to hear that my darling wife has a sudden penchant for politics. Your coworkers are merely humoring you, my love bird. I do hope you haven't decided to become one of those female radicals.

Good news: We haven't lost one boy in three days. That means we've saved seventy-two this week alone; seventy-two young men who can go home to greet their families, or to start one. Many are missing limbs or have burns like road maps spread across their bodies, but that can't be helped. War is destructive.

Do not take tranquilizers, my love. They are only supported by the new brain-digging enthusiasts who believe that a pill can cure anything. Here, we doctors dispense morphine like bartenders serve martinis, but it only masks the true scars these men have acquired; scars they will have to deal with once the physical pain dissolves.

Your sleeping difficulties can be blamed entirely on this damned war. My nerves are frazzled as well. Of course, being near an air-strip doesn't help. The endless vibrations of transport planes seep through the hospital floors, shaking the surgical instruments as well as our nerves.

Trust me. Once I am home, your emotions will return to those of a happy, healthy wife. For now, try soaking in a hot bath. Or perhaps delve into a lady's novel, one with a troubled but courageous debutante, or a sordid love affair plaguing the upper class. Those stories always seem to calm you.

Enclosed is a photograph of myself in a rare moment of relaxation, seated with another captain at an Italian gentlemen's club. I know you do not like the smell of cigars, but there is not much else to do here to keep my mind off the woman I adore.

With All My Love and Christmas Wishes in Your Stocking,

Sam

March 6, 1945

Dear Sam:

Mother passed away ten days ago. Please forgive me for not writing sooner. There were funeral arrangements to be made, and I had to take time off from work to manage her financial affairs. She had a secure nest egg, but there were still so many things to do. Documents had to be signed, papers I had never seen the likes of before. My sister did not arrive from New York until the day of Mother's burial, but the funeral director helped me through much of the process, as did one of my coworkers.

It hasn't hit me yet that Mother is gone. It seems like only yesterday we held hands as we walked along the shore, placing seashells in her skirt to take home. How could it be she was so sick and I never knew? The doctor said her heart was weak, that it had been for a long time.

Sleep has been my enemy for three days, and the dark shadows beneath my eyes prove it. My thoughts are of Mother and you and death. Each and every day, the war inches closer to home. We are bombarded with stories of soldiers killed. Beautiful buildings destroyed. Museums blown apart. Statues toppled. Russia's pact with China and Mussolini's assassination hardly give Americans reason to celebrate when there is so much ruin. Even the president's conference with Churchill and Stalin should encourage me, but it does not. I am weary, my darling husband. Lonely for the comforting arm of a loved one.

My sister has her busy life up north. The gals at the plant are exhausted, some with children to care for on top of working their shifts. There is no one here to support my emotions. If there is any way for you to come home—even for a brief leave of absence—I would be forever indebted to Uncle Sam. I know this wish is futile, but still I pray for it. Knowing you are coming home one day is the only thought helping me function.

Love,

Maggie

May 19, 1945

My Darling Maggie:

I am so sorry to hear of Mother's passing. She was a sweet woman and will be sadly missed. I wish I could be there for you, but, of course, I do not make the orders, only follow them. I am with you in spirit, my love, and will have my arms around you before you know it.

It is rumored we are to test a new bomb somewhere in America's desert, bringing much debate, even here in Italy. I thank God you are safe on the east coast. The last thing I need to worry about is my little Magpie.

Hitler is dead and so is Germany. Our country is strong, and freedom will remain our constant star. It is only a matter of time before the world sees the power of the red, white, and blue. Being a part of this mess has its ultimate rewards.

I have enclosed a little extra this month so you can treat yourself to a permanent. That should help perk you up.

You are the love of my life.

Sam

July 28, 1945
Dear Sam:

Happy Birthday, my darling husband. Enclosed is a photo of me wearing a new dress, standing near the statue on Federal Hill. If only I could wrap my body in pretty paper and mail myself overseas!

Love,

Maggie

August 11, 1945
Dearest Maggie:

Things are rather chaotic at the moment. The Hiroshima-Nagasaki situation has created a wide gap between the military men here, Europeans and Americans arguing over whether the bombing was ethical.

Because of Japan's imminent surrender, there is a good chance I will be home before the New Year! I didn't want to tell you as you may work yourself up. But I can't contain my excitement of seeing your freckled face again.

Yours Forever,

Sam

November 3, 1945

Dear Sam:

I am feeling a bit like my old self again. Sleep has finally come to me like an avalanche! I'm sure it is the weight of the war being lifted from my shoulders, and knowing you will be safely returning to me in a matter of weeks.

But the dream still comes, and your voice still calls to me, though I do not know why. I read an interesting article in *Redbook*. It suggested that with psychotherapy treatment, a person can get in touch with the root of their feelings, often exposing the truth behind their worries.

I keep reminding myself, now that the war is over, my anxiety will wither away. Soon, when you call to me, I won't have to look very far because you'll be right beside me.

Love,

Maggie

December 10, 1945

My Dearest Maggie:

Psychotherapists are fools, every one of them. We do not need a stranger asking us whether or not we love one another, or offering a more appropriate way in which to do so. Our marriage has merely been tested by the miles that have separated us. There are babies to raise, a home to nourish, and my career to get back to. These are the only things we need to be happy. Once my job here is finished, then so will be your temporary life at that dreadful plant. Once I am back in your arms, then so will your nightmares vanish. And once we are together again, then so will our life begin.

Nearly three years have been stolen from us, but in a matter of weeks, I am yours forever.

With All My Love,

Sam

Chapter One

"Go back to your real lives," Mr. Sanders told his employees after the six o'clock whistle ricocheted through the factory, momentarily drowning out "String of Pearls," sounding through the speakers. "Back to what it is you were meant to do."

Maggie glanced at the other sixty or so anxious women crammed into the narrow hallway outside Mr. Sanders' office. Underneath the dim glow of the bulb, they hardly differed from the men. Sweat stains had appeared under their work jumpers the first day worn and were too stubborn to disappear, even with an extra scoop of Rinso. Goggles were pushed up on top of twenty-five-cent scarves bought at Woolworth's, which in turn covered hair that hadn't been consistently curled or color-rinsed in months. Their black boots were scuffed. A number of assorted engagement rings, for those who were lucky enough to hook up before three quarters of Baltimore's men had shipped out, hid beneath uniforms on chains around their necks. Nails were chipped and caked with grease. Biceps flexed with a defined hardness Maggie didn't know could exist in women's arms until she'd witnessed her own firm muscles in her floor-length mirror.

These women were living testimony that they had supported their men and nation for months or, for some, years. Breaking their backs until the war ended, until the government informed America's Rosies that their shift was permanently over. It was time to get back to neglected kitchens, modern appliances, creative casseroles. Time to redo hair and nails, shave legs and underarms, shop at Sears for new garters and the latest in stockings. After all, the GI's deserved a grand homecoming.

One gal, whose name Maggie couldn't remember, a mousy thing with a nose so thin Maggie wondered how she breathed, pale skin pulled tightly over her delicate bones like a lamp shade, spoke up.

"I don't want to leave."

The crowd was split. Some nodded in agreement while others cast their eyes toward their boots or canvas high-tops.

"Mr. Sanders," the gal said, "I don't know about these other ladies, but I've gained a lot of pleasure working for this company. I'd like to stay, sir. You can pay me half what I'm making now. You can even put me on swing-shift. But I'd like to stay. If you don't mind, sir."

Some of the women discussed the possibility among themselves, their subtle murmurs gaining strength as they weighed the pros and cons.

"Now, now, ladies," Mr. Sanders said, scratching the stubble on his jaw. "Let's settle down. That's kind of you to offer, miss, but there won't be any jobs left to give you. The men you replaced will be storming through those doors the second they get home. The non-crips, anyway. It wouldn't be fair after fighting for your country to tell 'em they don't have jobs no more, now would it?"

The mousy gal nervously readjusted the scarf on her tiny head, and her lips quivered. "I don't have nothing to go back to, sir. It's almost Christmas time." She whispered, "I don't have no husband."

An older woman placed an arm around the gal's shoulders.

Mr. Sanders smiled. "There'll be plenty of boys coming home who'd sell their purple hearts to have you cook his meals and make him feel nice. Once you change back into your girly clothes, you'll have no problem gettin' yourself a swain."

He winked, causing her to smile.

"Now," he said, twice clapping his hands. "We got twenty-six men coming in tomorrow morning, seven o'clock sharp. Look at the chart hanging next to my office to see whose last day is today, whose is tomorrow, and whose is Friday. We'll be high-tailing it to get this factory back to the way it used to be. Oil and blood stains need to disappear. Equipment needs to be cleaned so machines can be reworked or sold. Your floor managers will tell you what needs to be done. Take them aprons and jumpers home and bring 'em back clean with any holes sewed up. If you have your own shoes, so be it. If you borrowed boots, I want 'em spit-shined. Once you've done all that, you'll hand your time card to me prompt-like. Final pay'll be given to you at that time. Those of you chosen to finish out the week will do the same on your last day."

Mr. Sanders disappeared behind the wooden door and locked it. His shadow stood still behind the ribbed glass before slowly retreating.

Maggie crowded against the cork board with the other women to see where her name was in the line-up. As she inched her way closer to the list, she noticed the dock foreman, Jonathan, nicknamed JD by his cohorts for his love of whiskey, standing outside the restroom at the end of the hallway, observing the women as they mobbed the bulletin board. An only son whose father had been killed at the beginning of the war, JD, along with a handful of other men at Eastern Weapons, had narrowly escaped the draft.

He raked his fingers through his dark hair and smiled at the collection of women in his usual soft and kind way, but there was also the presence of sympathy beneath that smile. The mousy girl glanced hopefully in JD's direction. How lonely she must be, Maggie thought, spending nights by herself, wondering what was to become of her life once she no longer had a place that needed her; a place that gave her—and all the other women—a sense of purpose.

Maggie thought fondly of the many discussions JD included her in and felt a searing pang of sadness. She had learned so much about economics, the political reasons for the war, the truth behind the bombings; had been an integral part of those conversations, even coaxed to interject her opinion. She was regarded by JD, as well as a few of the women who joined in on the lunchtime chats, as an intelligent person with more to offer than a shapely pair of gams and freckled dimples.

She offered JD a wilted smile before he disappeared into the stairwell, and then her body was pushed up to the wall. She scrolled down the list with her finger and found her name near the bottom, squinting to read it better under the dim lights, pushing wisps of auburn hair from her forehead. The words had been scratched onto a piece of paper in dark, sloppy handwriting:

LERNER, MARGARET D.

LAST DAY: FRIDAY.

A sigh slid between her lips.

Two more days before being forced to trade in her drill and boots for her iron and heels; digging her cookbooks out from under the flour sacks in the pantry; becoming reacquainted with her Hoover vacuum and lemon furniture polish.

Two days Margaret Diana Lerner, drill press extraordinaire, would savor.

Chapter Two

On Friday afternoon beneath an overcast sky, Maggie sat on the chilly cement steps with two other gals from the line, her open lunchbox beside her. She wrapped her coat more tightly around her, then pulled out her daily SPAM on Wonder Bread and placed it on her lap, spreading out the wax paper until it became a smooth placemat.

Their lunch-time chats used to be filled with interesting discussions and exciting debates regarding the war. Now, with most of the women dismissed and the men working through their lunch hour to gear up for the stampede of post-war arrivals, their group of more than twenty had shriveled down to a mere threesome.

"Who knew the world could change so fast?" Jocelyn said, her usually olive cheeks rosy from the cold. "It seems like Pearl Harbor happened just yesterday."

"I feel like I've aged ten years," Colleen said. She poured milk from her thermos to the lid and sipped it, wrapping her gloved hands around the cup.

"Did you see those eager beavers over on Lombard?" Maggie asked. "They're already lining up for the parades."

"I read the economy's going to bounce back fast," Colleen

said. "'Post-war Optimism', the paper called it."

Jocelyn played with a dark loose curl falling from beneath her head scarf. "Well," she said, "at least they have jobs to come back to."

"Thanks to us," Maggie said, looking at her sandwich. She wasn't feeling very hungry.

"I'm perfectly happy to spend some time in my little ole kitchen," Jocelyn said, folding her hands together under her chin in dramatic thankfulness and letting her eyelids flutter. "To cook with mushy canned vegetables. Experience the thrill of dish pan hands!"

The women laughed.

"Truth is," Jocelyn went on, "I'm grateful they gave us the shaft. I can't wait to get out of this place; sit at a typewriter or work a switchboard. I'll get to wear a lemon-fresh dress every day instead of smelling like a man, and buy silk hose again, too, instead of drawing that black line up the back of my legs. I was beginning to feel like a zebra. And I'm dying to buy a brand new pair of kicks and go dancing, with all those desperately single men on the loose." She splayed the backs of her hands. "My only worry is whether or not this grease will ever come out from under my poor nails."

Colleen leaned back on an elbow against the steps and stretched out her long, jumpsuit-covered legs. "My Mitchell doesn't come home from Poland until well after the New Year. Post-war clean-up or something. He's forbidden from talking about it."

"Hmmm…" Jocelyn said, narrowing her dark eyes and donning a Russian accent. "Perhaps he is in cahoots with a Communist regime."

"Joss!" Colleen said, slapping her coworker's arm. "This Cold War is nothing to joke about. Trust me. In a few years, they'll be finding Reds all over the country, hiding in places you'd never suspect. So just don't joke about it."

"Sorry."

"Anyhow, Mitchell not coming home right away is fine with me. Gives me more time to get myself back to that BYT I was when we first met. Get my hair done." Colleen lightly touched the ends of her frizzy brown curls. "Mitch loves my hair. Or, at least, he did. Before the war. And I need to prepare the kids for their daddy's homecoming. I'm not sure they remember what he looks like."

"I've scrubbed and dusted until my hands are raw," Maggie said. "I'm done with the house. Now I can concentrate on me. Get a henna rinse, buy some new bras, drive the car instead of taking the bus. And what I wouldn't give for a nice cup of Maxwell House."

"A-men," Jocelyn said.

The back door opened. JD and one of the dock workers, Norman, stuck their heads out and sang, "Goodnight ladies! Goodnight ladies! Goodnight ladies, we're sad to see you go!"

"Thanks, fellas," Jocelyn said, laughing. "But you don't know how sad you'll be until we're gone. Having to run those machines by your sad little selves. How will you ever survive without us?"

Norman opened the door the rest of the way, pressed it to the wall, and leaned against it. He pulled a pack of Camels out of his pocket, tapped one out, and lit it.

"Well, Jolly Joss," Norman said, blowing a long stream of smoke into the chilly air and flicking the match over the metal railing. "Without those pretty peepers lighting up the place, we might just fall apart at the seams. But I'll say one thing, it'll be nice making household appliances for a change, instead of those crummy weapons. If I have to give any more blood, sweat, and tears for that goddamned war, pardon my French…"

The group nodded in unison.

"Still got a lot to get done," JD said as he leaned against the railing. "Dragging the old equipment out of storage, setting the line up the way it used to be, taking inventory, making sure no one accidentally takes off with a riveter in her pocketbook. Probably working through the weekend. Monday's gonna be a big day, and she's gonna come quick. Thank God we've got holiday time to look forward to."

"I plan to get me a week's worth of shuteye," Norman said, the edges of his Dumbo ears a bright pink. He hopped from one foot to the other to stomp out the winter chill.

"Vacation?" Colleen asked.

Norman blew a couple of smoke rings into the air. "Yessiree. As soon as the plant is back on her feet and the boys get reacquainted with their old jobs, most of the crew gets some time off. With pay. For good behavior."

"We girls get a little vacation, too," Jocelyn said. "A permanent one."

"Is that resentment I hear in your voice?" Norman asked.

"Are you kidding?" Jocelyn snickered. "I'm watching the second hand until that damned rooster screeches in my ear for the last time. Then it's off to the undergarment sale at Macy's and a root beer float at the Double T."

"A bunch of us are heading down to Fell's Point tonight," JD said. "Some from the line, some from the warehouse. Like a last supper."

"Or a last binge," Norman interjected.

"Anybody interested?" JD asked.

"I'll take a rain check," Colleen said. "I've got the kids…"

"Joss?" Norman said. "Think Macy's can wait one more day

before you buy 'em out of all their stockings and slips?"

"You could twist my arm. I'll take a stiff drink over a float any time."

JD eyed Maggie. "There's always a first time," he told her.

"I don't know…maybe…" Maggie said, casting her eyes toward her scuffed boots, knowing that her ambiguous reply more than likely meant no. She enjoyed sharing discussions with JD and the other men during lunch, but an evening get-together? She should wait for Sam to come home before stepping out. She should celebrate his homecoming, not the loss of her job.

"Well, think about it," JD said, rubbing his hands together then blowing into the center of them. "One o'clock bell's about to ring…"

"You guys eat any lunch?" Colleen asked.

Both men shook their heads.

The women rounded up bits and pieces of their lunches: an apple, an untouched SPAM sandwich, a hard-boiled egg, and four oatmeal cookies.

"Boy, we sure are gonna miss you gals," Norman said, dropping his cigarette to the stoop and squashing it under his boot. He grabbed the apple and bit into it.

"Ditto," JD said, pulling a comic book out of his bib pocket to make room for the cookies.

"Which one is that?" Maggie asked.

Entertainment was a commodity at Eastern, and she and the other gals had often been amused by the *Captain America*, *Human Torch*, and *Superman* leftovers scattered about the break room.

JD held up the magazine. Wonder Woman stared out from the cover, donned in her high red boots and strapless armor, her face in a permanent scowl.

"Get a load of JD," Norman laughed, pointing a thumb in JD's direction. "A few years working with the ladies and he's convinced they have special powers."

"Maybe some do," he said, offering a crooked smile.

"I'd say JD is a smart man," Colleen said.

"What a sap," Norman told JD. "It's a good thing they didn't send you off to Europe. You would've had the girls throwing grenades from a foxhole before we had a chance to yell, 'Hitler is kaput!'"

The steam whistle blew. Lunch time was over.

"Ladies," Norman said, saluting.

JD tossed the *Wonder Woman* comic book to Maggie. A colorful parrot tattoo peeked out from under the edge of his rolled up sleeve, then hid again. "I think you'll appreciate this one," he said.

He followed Norman back into the plant, letting the heavy door swing closed behind them.

"My keister's freezing," Colleen said, standing up and stretching her long arms into the air. "You all coming?"

"Right behind ya," Jocelyn said.

Colleen picked up her lunch pail and disappeared inside.

"Step out with us tonight, Maggie," Jocelyn said. "It's probably going to be the last time we all get together."

"I don't know…"

"Come on. Everyone's going to be there."

Maggie rolled up the comic book and shoved it under her arm. "I suppose one night won't hurt."

The two women stood up and collected their trash.

"You haven't said anything about the pills," Jocelyn said, scrunching her nose as she picked up Norman's cigarette butt and wrapped it in a tissue.

"Oh," Maggie said. "I'm sorry. My mind has been so muddled lately."

"Have they helped?"

"Absolutely," Maggie said.

"I'd never have given them to you if one of the warehouse gals hadn't bragged so much."

"You got them from someone here? I thought you said they came from a doctor."

"Well, the original prescription did. We've shared a lot more around here than casserole recipes, you know."

Maggie was relieved to hear that she was not alone in her quest for a good night's sleep. "Who else takes them?" she asked, curious.

"Well, let's see," Jocelyn said. "Colleen…"

"Colleen?"

"How else could she keep her children on track while working over forty hours a week?"

Maggie hesitated, then asked, "Who else?"

"Tina, one of the secretaries…Ada May, out in the warehouse—"

"Which one is she?"

"Used to be on swing shift," Jocelyn said. "The tall blond with the huge…you know…"

"Oh. Yes."

"And Percy."

"Percy?"

"That little scarecrow with the long bird nose."

"Somehow I always manage to forget her name," Maggie said.

"She hangs out with the other wallflowers. The ones who polish and sort out nuts and bolts in the back. I can't think of a more tedious job. But that doesn't mean she doesn't have her share of anxiety."

"True."

"And there's Barbara, Bonnie, Lora Lee…"

"So many," Maggie said, leaning against the railing. She pulled a stalk of celery from her lunchbox and thoughtfully chewed on the end. "Can I ask you a question, Joss? It's of a personal nature."

"Shoot."

"When you take one of the pills, do you find that your dreams are…more vivid?"

"To be honest with you, kiddo, I don't remember dreaming at all. I conk out like someone hit me in the head with a baseball bat. My neighbor swears she can hear me snoring through the apartment wall."

Jocelyn's voice suddenly turned breathy, like Lauren Bacall sharing an intimate moment with Bogie. "Isn't your sleep the most amazing ever? And don't you feel like a new person in the morning? I have so much energy, Maggie, and it lasts all day. I'm never on edge anymore. Six weeks ago, I thought I was headed for the funny farm. But now I'm floating from morning till night. And I'm happy all the time, too. Aren't you?"

"Yes. Of course. It's just that when I dream…well, my dreams tend to—"

The back door flew open. An angry face appeared in the doorway.

"Tea time is over, ladies," Mr. Sanders said. "Steam whistle blew three minutes ago. Last day or not, you're still on the clock."

He held the back door open as the two women gathered up the rest of their belongings, swiftly sidestepped him, and headed back to their last day on the line.

Chapter Three

"Aren't you going to miss anything about Eastern?" Maggie asked Jocelyn as they stepped off the bus in Fells Point.

The dull smell of fish and Maryland blue crab leftover from autumn rode on the cold wind, picking up speed and moisture as it blew across the Chesapeake and spilled onto the downtown streets. Friday night people huddled on the sidewalks as they moved in tight-knit clusters, heads down to brave the wind, wrapping their coats more firmly around them like Eskimos trekking across the tundra.

"Let me think," Jocelyn said, holding up a gloved hand and counting to three with her fingers. "No. Heck no. And hell no."

"I feel let down," Maggie said.

"Let down how?"

"It's like a strange Christmas," Maggie explained. "You get all these wonderful gifts. Ones you had hoped for all year. Then the day after Christmas, there's a knock at your door, and these awful store clerks come into your house and take all the gifts back because it turns out they weren't yours to begin with. They take back your new dresses and cashmere sweaters, your new mixer, your new sterling silver tea set, your new jade earrings. Just take them all away."

They stood shivering on a street corner, waiting for the light to change. "You're comparing that hell-hole to Christmas?" Jocelyn asked.

"What I mean is I don't want to give the gifts back. I want to keep them. I want to keep what was given to me."

"Why don't you ask Sanders if you can stay? Maybe he'll let you do some secretarial stuff. Or go over the books or something."

"I don't want to do those things," Maggie said. "I want more."

"Like what?"

Maggie shrugged. "It's hard to know what I want when I haven't had it yet."

"Now I've heard everything." They stood waiting for the light to change, their sides up against each others' for extra warmth, their heads nearly touching. "You have more than most girls, Maggie," Jocelyn said. "You know that, don't you? You don't *have* to work. You don't *have* to slave at a job you hate until the right guy comes along. You don't *have* to do anything."

"But I want to."

The light turned green.

"Yeah? Well, I want a lot of things." They walked across the street and stepped carefully onto the uneven cobblestones. "I want a man to come home to. A crib to fill with babies and blankies. An apartment that isn't one block from a smelly factory. An apartment that isn't empty."

They hurried down the walk in between rows of bars and dive restaurants, varied sounds of music and laughter crossing their path each time a front door swung open. In a few minutes, they stood beneath a blinking green neon sign which told them to "COME-ON-IN!"

"But you know what I want more than anything?" Jocelyn asked, pushing the door open.

"What?"

"A stiff drink."

***

Cigarette smoke and loud Friday night voices collided. An old upright piano with a silver-haired pianist wailed a Fats Waller tune from a dark corner. Maggie didn't think the piano player was a bona fide musician, but his hands seemed ambitious as they pounded the keys in an effort to surpass the clatter of the growing crowd.

"There's Norm!" Jocelyn shouted, moving at lightning speed through the mob. She pulled her hat from her head and tossed her dark spirals over a shoulder, cocking her head in her usual flirtatious way. "Hi-de-ho, Norm!" she called again. "Over here!"

Norman turned in their direction.

"JD!" Norman said, punching his buddy in the arm. "Look what the cat dragged in!"

Maggie couldn't believe how many people from the plant were packed into the tiny pub. She started to count heads but lost track when JD grabbed her by the elbow and pulled her to the crowded bar.

"What'll it be, Maggie?" he shouted. He wore a pressed white shirt and a pair of slacks. She pictured the parrot tattoo hiding beneath his sleeve.

"What are you drinking?" she asked.

JD held up a tumbler filled with three inches of whiskey. "What else?"

"Do they have any wine?"

"Awe, come on, hon. Live a little. Have a gin and tonic."

"Yes. All right. Why not?"

She scanned the bar to see where Norman had dragged Jocelyn off to, but she couldn't tell the face of one woman from another. The room was only lit by a row of schoolhouse lights dangling over the bar and a bit of lamplight squeezing through a stained glass window. On the dance floor, dozens of men spun their partners in crazy circles, each gal a blurry mixture of freshly permed curls, bright skirts, and gay smiles as they twirled past.

JD handed Maggie a clear drink with a lime floating among the ice cubes. He clinked his glass against hers.

"Here's to the end of a war and the beginning of a new era!"

"You sound like a politician," Maggie said, hiding a grimace as she took her first sip.

JD said something else, but his words were buried beneath the music as the piano player had a sudden burst of energy. "Ain't Misbehavin'" was traded in for the old hat "Maple Leaf Rag." Maggie tapped her ear and mouthed the words, "Can't hear."

JD took her wrist and led her through a door in the back of the bar. In the second room, two long fluorescent lights dangled over a pool table. A man bent over the table aiming up his next shot while another leaned on his cue. Two pretty women stood on the sidelines watching and giggling secrets to each other as the man concentrated on making his shot. There was no live music in the room, but the beat from the bar could still be felt, the thumping of piano keys and stomping of feet penetrating through the wall.

On the far side of the room, Jocelyn and Norman sat on folding chairs at a long ratty table, talking to a few coworkers. *Ex*-coworkers, Maggie reminded herself. As Maggie and JD approached the table, they were acknowledged by more than a dozen people, sitting or standing in the small but crowded room. She smiled and held up her glass in salute as she made her way. A young man offered Maggie his chair. She thanked him while JD found an empty spot on the other side of the table.

The conversations were varied as one topic smoothly, almost undetectably, melded into another. Talk of guns became talk of war. War became Communism. Communism became spy. Spy became traitor. Traitor became Benedict Arnold. And around and around it went, opinions and rants traveling up one side of the table and down the other. Maggie chatted with some of the plant's dock workers, secretaries, even the janitor, who smelled like onions and cigars as he breathed into her face.

Jocelyn and Norman eventually made their way down to Maggie's end of the table, Jocelyn politely kicking the janitor out of his chair so she could sit next to Maggie. Norman sat next to Joss. JD left the other side of the table and pulled up a chair behind the group. They turned their chairs to face one another in a tight circle.

For over an hour they sat in their huddle, laughing at corny jokes and recalling funny incidents at the factory. Like the time Sanders wore a shiny black toupee to work, and when he tried to fix one of the switches on a machine that had gone haywire, the toupee suddenly leapt from his head and wrapped itself around a cog. The machine smoked and strained as Sanders did everything he could to save the wig without losing his fingers in the process. Finally, he called in some mechanics with steel brushes and other tools to pry the bristly hairs from the contraption. To make matters worse, Sanders decided to put the ratty thing back on his head. In the weeks that followed, each time Sanders passed the workers, his fake hair heaped on top of his head like black barbed wire, they had to look at their shoes and hold their breath to keep from snickering.

Stories like that one, along with more serious ones, wound their way around the circle: the man whose hand was shredded to bits during a maintenance check; the young gal who went into labor during her shift, her twins delivered right there on the shard-covered floor. They talked about nothing in particular, things that ordinary blue collar workers are likely to talk about in bars after a long week at the grind: baseball, unions, flying saucers, the latest in automobiles, and so on.

As the wife of a surgeon, Maggie's home life was far from the world of blue collars. Most of her coworkers lived in tenements near the factory. Only a handful were privileged enough to live in the tree-lined suburbs like Maggie, in large brick houses with paved driveways and even sidewalks and neighbors who shared their cookie and casserole recipes, miles away from the smells of diesel and fear of inner city crime. But she was cozy and happy here with these people, no matter how different they were, and she tried to ignore the fact that she would probably never see them again, either at work or socially.

They ordered another round. Then another. It was nearly midnight before the crowd in the back room started to thin. Maggie was tipsy. Her lips felt tingly and her eyes seemed to witness movement and conversation in slow motion.

JD held up his empty glass. "Where'd that waitress get to?"

"I'm going to the bar," Jocelyn said, her words slurred.

"I'll tag along," JD told her. They stumbled their way across the room and through the door.

Norman chugged down the remainder of his beer and let out a loud belch. He told Maggie, "Rumor has it your soldier doctor hubby comes home soon."

"Two more weeks."

"Hot dog. He's one lucky fella."

"I'm a lucky woman."

Maggie felt as though her words were coming from far away, no longer a part of herself. She tried to picture Sam's face, but the gin had erased it.

Norman sat backward on the metal chair. He leaned toward Maggie, his arms folded in front of him over the chair's back, the empty mug dangling from his hand. With his long arms and legs and face, he resembled a cartoon monkey.

"We've been asking you to step out for over a year," he said. "Why now all of a sudden?"

"To celebrate."

She twirled her finger in the air, feigning enthusiasm. She was tired. Any earlier excitement had waned by the time she'd finished her second drink.

"Ah," Norman said, nodding his head. "The last hoorah."

Voices from the front seeped into the back room again as the door opened. Three women from Eastern walked in: a masculine-looking gal Maggie had seen out on the basketball court behind the factory; the tiny one with the long nose, whose name Maggie kept forgetting, her eyes darting from one person to another like a baby bird afraid of being abandoned; and the buxom blond named Ada May, who, even though she had what Maggie believed was potential, dressed like she lived in a depression-era Shantytown, her worn scarf and dirty coat like she'd stolen them from a sleeping bum.

Wallflowers from nuts and bolts, Maggie thought tipsily, thinking it sounded like the name of a jazz band, pressing her lips together to keep from saying it out loud.

The masculine woman made her way to the opposite side of the table and sat across from Norm and Maggie, flattening her palms on the table top. The skin on her hands was peeling off in thin translucent strips; the tips of her fingers were covered with tiny cracks, thin black fissures created by time spent on the assembly line.

"Hey, Norm," she said. "What's cooking?"

"Hey, Roberta." He nodded his drunken head to her and then her friends over by the door. They returned timid smiles and looked down at their flats.

Maggie did not know these women personally, only from seeing them at the plant as she clocked in or out, or used the john in the back of the factory if the toilet at her end was on the fritz. Sanders didn't like the different departments to fraternize and demanded that each stayed in their own sections. After all, an efficient factory was a happy factory. "Straighten up and fly right!" he had reminded them daily.

"You seen Joss?" Roberta asked Norman. She toyed with a bobby pin that held a homemade curl in place.

"In the bar somewhere."

"Oh."

For a moment no one said anything.

"So," Roberta finally said, taking a moment to chew the inside of her cheek. "Last day for us at Eastern." Her right eyebrow twitched. She seemed worried she may say the wrong thing as though casual conversation was something completely foreign to her.

"So I hear," Norman said.

"You staying on at the plant?" she asked.

"As long as they'll have me."

"Yeah?"

"Yeah."

"Okay," she said after a pause. "Well, don't call us. We'll call you."

"Yeah. Right."

Roberta went back to her friends. Together they disappeared back into the bar.

Norman shook his head and laughed.

"What's funny?" Maggie asked.

"Those gals," he said. "I don't think this is their scene." He held up his empty mug and turned it upside down. "I'm dry. You want another drink?"

"No. Thank you. Three's my limit."

Actually, one was her limit, but after the first two gin and tonics caused her to ignore this rule, she had allowed someone along the way to buy her a double shot of some syrupy liquid that made her tongue go numb. Her brain felt slippery, out of joint.

"Awe, come on," Norman coaxed. "It's a celebration. You said so yourself." He stood up, nearly knocking over the chair as he rose. "Come on, Maggie. Have a little fun."

A cup of Ovaltine and her comfy bed were suddenly all she desired. The next day was the first Saturday in months she'd be able to sleep past sunrise, and she planned on doing just that. Besides, she thought sadly, there really wasn't much else to do. The neighborhood garden was buried beneath winter soil, the house was spotless, and her job no longer existed. The only thing she had to look forward to until Sam came home was sleep.

She grabbed her coat and followed Norman, reminding herself that this was the last time she'd kick about with the men and women who had stood beside her while Sam was at war; who, for the last two years, had been the closest replication of family she could think of.

Back to the front they shuffled, Norman absently bumping into people and Maggie quickly apologizing after. The bar had quieted down considerably, and for that, Maggie was grateful. Only half the crowd had stayed past midnight. The piano player's hands seemed to have worn out as they slowly tinkered with the keys, like a piano tuner tweaking his instrument.

"JD!" Norman shouted, Maggie trailing behind. "Buy a fella a drink!"

JD and Jocelyn stood at the bar, each holding a shot glass filled with liquor. Next to Joss stood the nuts-and-bolts gals, laughing as they clinked glasses together and downed their shots.

Not so shy after all, Maggie thought.

JD shouted to the bartender who lined up seven shot glasses, then filled each to the top with Jack Daniels. The bartender passed them to JD who passed them down the line, first to Norman, then to Jocelyn, then to each of the wallflowers. He kept one for himself and handed the last one to Maggie.

"Now's the time," JD said, "because this is our last time."

In a flash they tilted their heads back, downed their shots, then slammed their glasses upside down against the top of the bar—everyone except Maggie. Six faces waited with drunken grins. Roberta wiped her mouth with the back of her sweater sleeve. Jocelyn actually swayed on her feet, a few inches to the left, then a few inches to the right, as if trying not to fall off a rocking boat. The three other women smiled stupidly, like mentally incapacitated children waiting for a bedtime story.

JD stared at Maggie with his eager face and lighthearted smile. Good ol' JD. He had always been so patient, listening to her views of the war, coming to her defense when a male coworker condescendingly shook his head at Maggie's naiveté regarding current events. JD was the one who had guided Maggie through all that daunting paperwork when her mother died; sympathized with how much she missed her husband;

recommended her to Sanders for the can drive; put in a good word to help her advance from cleaning engines to running a drill press. And he was the only one who never laughed when Maggie disclosed how much she loved her work.

Didn't she at least owe him a thank you?

"Here goes," she said, offering a smile of surrender. She toasted the air, placed the glass to her lips, sucked down the liquid, and slammed the glass upside down on the sticky bar. She puckered her lips and shifted from one tired foot to the other as her new fans pounded fists against the bar for her to down another. The room began to spin clockwise and counter clockwise simultaneously. Maggie closed her eyes, hoping to make the feeling go away, but the darkness only made the spinning worse. Her stomach lurched. It occurred to her that she hadn't eaten dinner, and she had only nibbled tiny bits of her lunch that afternoon.

When she finally opened her eyes, Norman was talking to a soldier on his left, JD was headed toward the men's room, and Jocelyn was holding up a small glass bottle which she shook in front of her like a castanet.

"What's that?" Maggie asked, her voice floating a few feet in front of her.

Jocelyn said, "I was just telling the girls here how much they've helped you."

The nuts-and-bolts gals smiled at Maggie like they were best pals. But Maggie was embarrassed. She didn't want others knowing she had taken tranquilizers. She didn't even want Sam to know. How she handled her nerves was personal. Taking pills was a private activity, one that all of a sudden made her feel like a coward. A *drunken* coward.

"Don't be a fuddy-duddy, Maggie," Jocelyn said. "It's a new

age. You make it sound like it's a big secret that only you know about." She unscrewed the cap and sprinkled a pill into her own hand. "Here," she said, holding out the white tablet. "By the time you crawl into bed tonight, you won't even feel your feet."

"I can't," Maggie said.

She had already made up her mind to stop taking them. Sam would be home soon; the pills were no longer necessary.

"Hogwash," Jocelyn said. "You need to keep up with the Joneses. Half the people in this bar are high on something. It's a Friday night. No one's running a press. No one's punching a time clock. They're just out having a good time. Letting everything go for a change. The damned war is over, Maggie."

She pressed the pill into Maggie's palm and handed her a glass of water that appeared out of nowhere. Maggie felt like she had just been dared to do something unspeakable, like start a fire in the woods or bash in an old lady's mailbox with a baseball bat.

The war is over.

With her eyes shut, she placed the pill on her tongue and downed the glass of water. When she opened her eyes again, JD stood across the room speaking to the piano player. He dropped a bill into the man's jar. A contemporary version of "By the Light of the Silvery Moon" filled the room, charming the crowd, as each man grabbed the nearest available woman and pulled her to the floor. Norman had the masculine Roberta in a deep embrace in the center of the floor, and JD was pulling Maggie by the hand in the same direction.

"I really shouldn't," Maggie said, her feet moving without her help, her mind wobbly but eager.

"Shouldn't what?" JD asked, his dark eyes shimmering. "Have fun? It's called a dance. We're not doing anything wrong. Just stop your gobbledygook."

His grip was gentle but enticing as he glided her onto the tiny dance floor. Soon they were crammed in the middle, one dancer pressed up against another, different colognes mixed with sweat passing under her nose each time a couple passed by.

JD's singing spilled into her ear, like a cheerful tipsy Bing Crosby: *"By the light…of the silvery moon…"* He spun her around, and she laughed.

"I haven't danced since my wedding," Maggie said, barely able to recollect that day at the country club.

"Then you're overdue." JD's hand was soft on her waist as he sang, *"I want to spoon…to my honey I'll croon love's tune…"* He pulled her to him, lightly, not with the brute strength she would have imagined him possessing. *"Your silvery beams will bring love dreams…"*

She was spun around again, and when she faced forward, her partner had been replaced. Norman now swung her in slow circles, his movements less graceful than JD's, though all the more earnest. Dancing with Norman was like dancing with Art Carney. As she tried to keep up with his clumsy, syncopated movements, she searched for JD and spotted him swaying with Jocelyn a few feet away. Norman twirled Maggie around until she felt like a spinning top, then dipped her. By the time she caught sight of JD again, he was dancing with Roberta. On Roberta's left, blond and buxom Ada May held tightly to a skinny pimply man, dressed in a pressed GI uniform, her chin resting on top of the young fellow's head. Maggie glanced at the bar and saw the third companion, her sharp nose buried deep in a glass of liquor that she held between spinster hands. Sorrow flooded Maggie, the alcohol magnifying her emotions as she watched the girl swaying next to the bar alone, waiting for Mr. Right, Mr. Somebody, Mr. Anybody to come and whisk her away.

The tempo suddenly quickened and bebop traveled through the crowd like a surge of electricity. Soon, JD was twirling her again.

"Go dance with her," Maggie said when the twirling was over, nodding toward the bar.

JD let go of Maggie and pulled the sad sack onto the dance floor. From where Maggie now stood at the bar, she could see the young girl's face flush as if she hadn't considered any form of exercise in a long time, and for a moment Maggie thought the idea a poor one, that the tiny thing would pass out right there on the dance floor. But JD's partner kept up with the quickening pace of the music, her ratty hair falling across her face when JD dropped her back in an arch. She giggled like a prom queen until partners switched again, the girl falling into the arms of some other man who whisked her away and into the core of the crowd.

"I saw you take one of those things earlier," JD said. He was suddenly standing next to Maggie at the bar. "You shouldn't have. Especially with alcohol."

"But I didn't." Maggie dipped a hand inside her skirt pocket. She held out the pill for him to see. "I stuck it up here," she said, pointing to her cheek. "Like a kid does with overcooked peas."

A passerby inadvertently bumped into Maggie, knocking the pill to the floor. It rolled onto the dance floor and under a man's heel.

"Good," JD said, taking her hand and pulling her back to the dance floor. "No one needs those things to have a little fun. Jocelyn's just trying to make some extra lettuce. Times are hard for women right now."

"Have you ever taken them?" Maggie asked.

He nodded.

"And?"

"Let's just say the only way you could force another one of those down my throat is if you tied me down."

For the second time that night, Maggie felt like a coward, knowing she had once taken those little tablets as if they'd change her life in some profound way. She didn't need the pills; she only needed Sam, a home, a family. All of the things she believed would bring her to where she ought to be. Bring her to real life.

The music corralled them as Maggie and JD rocked together, the rhythm entering her bloodstream and keeping beat with her racing heart.

JD whispered in her ear as they rocked, "Do you miss him?" Before she could get her lips to reply, he said, "Wish I'd met you sooner, Maggie. Before the damned war. But, like they say in the dugout, nice guys finish last."

"You are a nice guy, JD," Maggie said, wondering if he could understand her slurred words. "One day, you're going to make a woman very happy."

Her eyes closed again, but this time her head spins remained buried beneath a calm floating sensation. She let the melody pour over her, imagining ten deft fingers as they rolled up and down the ivories, shiny black shoes as they worked the pedals. A part of her drifted to a faraway place. Her feet turned invisible. Her arms and hands tingled as if they were covered with tiny butterflies.

When her eyes opened, Norman again held onto her, his lanky arms wrapped securely around her waist, his warm beer breath in her ear like Sam's during baseball season. She looked up into that smiling monkey face. Funny Norman, always the comedian, liked by everyone, even those at the plant who weren't too keen on socializing. Maggie closed her eyes again, giving in to his dead hoofer's dance style.

The music fell beneath the building and settled there, muffled by the floor boards, as Maggie drifted up and away. Smells of cigar smoke and spicy aftershave turned into something indefinable and sweet; a smell so strong and inviting she could nearly taste it.

Someone else held onto her now, but she didn't know who it was nor did she care. As they shimmied back and forth, the floor slid away from the bottom of her feet. The walls melted into each other, then into nothing. The music slid deeper into the earth. She found herself gliding, moving forward without knowing how, warmth wrapping around her like a blanket. *Contentment* was the only word she could think of as she began to fall, ever so gently, like a baby bird's lost feather on the wind, until the falling became wonderful; falling became the way she always wanted to be.

Chapter Four

Maggie rolled the smooth white tablet between her fingers and let it fall into her palm. She regarded it as though it were a miniature child curiously staring up at her.

Just one more time, it coaxed.

Sam will be here in the morning, she rebutted.

The thought filled her with courage.

"No," she told the pill, dropping it into the toilet where it floated for a moment, then slowly sank. Smiling, she shook the remaining pills from the bottle and watched as they, too, sank to the bottom. "Tata, my friends," she said, pressing down on the handle. She watched the pills as they swirled together briefly in a tiny whirlpool, then disappeared down the hole.

The task complete, she threw the empty bottle into the wastebasket under the sink but just as quickly plucked it out again. What if Sam should discover it? She stepped into the bedroom and looked around, then went to her closet and tucked the bottle inside one of her pocketbooks.

The new sheets felt cool as she slid into bed. Only one more night without her husband.

Her husband.

Picturing Sam next to her was like crawling around inside a

surreal painting. He had been deployed only two weeks after their honeymoon, and she had lived as the wife of an absentee husband for as long as she'd been married.

But now Sam was coming home. Maggie's worries would disappear. Her fears of death and abandonment would vanish.

Watching that pill get crushed under a stranger's foot two weeks before had helped her gain control. That same night, the pleading voice from her dream began to fade like the tail end of a song on a record. Since then, each night before bed, she had continued to open the medicine cabinet, uncapping the bottle and peering inside at the little white pebbles, testing her own willpower. Even though she resisted the temptation, the bottle had become an odd sort of security blanket, one she continued to believe she needed. But things would be different now that the pills were sliding through pipes on their way to the waste plant. Probably a mile away by now.

She turned out the light and drifted off to sleep.

I don't need them anymore. All I need is Sam.

One final night without the tangible comfort of her husband, and the first night in weeks without the pills calling to her, enticing her, trying to convince her how much she still needed them.

***

She almost missed seeing him at the train station and kept eyeing him in the cab on the way home. He had just a touch of gray at his temples, and his moustache was thick. Tiny crows feet joined at the corners of his eyes and fanned outward. Her husband looked nothing like the man she had married.

Neither did she, apparently.

"Your hair is different," he told her as they stepped through the front door.

"You're just now noticing?" She lightly patted the curly red wave which rested high on the front of her head. "It's the *New Look*."

The cab driver brought the dolly into the foyer and carefully slid the trunks onto the floor. Sam tipped the cabbie, then attacked Maggie as soon as the front door closed.

Maggie arched her back as he kissed her lips, her cheeks, her neck.

"Hey! Your moustache tickles."

He grabbed her hand and led her up the steps.

"Not even a drink first?" she asked, feigning surprise.

He laughed. "You are my drink!"

They stayed in bed for hours, swiftly becoming reacquainted with each other's tender spots and fulfilling each other's wishes.

It was nearly two in the afternoon. Against the pillows they lay in bed nude, Sam holding his wife against him, breathing in her ear.

"I missed you more than I can describe," he whispered. "I can't believe we're finally together again."

"I can't either."

"Are you ready for this?"

Maggie gently reached between his legs. "Again?"

He moved her hand and held it tightly. "Ready for us, Maggie. Our marriage. Starting a family. Taking care of each other."

Maggie closed her eyes and snuggled against him. Her husband was lying beside her now. No more searching. No more pills.

"Yes," she said, feeling his hardness once again press against her. She gently positioned herself on top of him, rotating her hips in smooth circles, carving out the number eight. "Yes," she said again, biting her husband's lower lip and presenting an Academy Award performance as the most contented wife in the world.

Chapter Five

Hello? Hello?

Maggie heard the voice but wasn't sure from which direction it was coming.

Sam? Is that you?

All she could see was the familiar fog filling the space around her. As she moved forward, the mist moved with her; stopped when she stopped. It was as if the fog was connected to her. Belonged to her.

She screamed as a hand reached from behind and firmly grabbed her shoulder.

"Maggie!"

Her eyes flew open. The fog was sucked away. In bed she lay on her right side, facing the tall cherry dresser. The sheets had tangled themselves around her ankles.

Sam, on his knees in the middle of the bed and wearing only his boxer shorts, leaned over his wife. His hand gently moved her damp hair from her forehead. Shadows from the early morning rainclouds deepened the wrinkles above his eyebrows and around his mouth. He looked like an old man.

"You were shouting in your sleep," he said. "You scared the hell out of me."

Maggie sat up. "What time is it?"

"Barely five o'clock. You were dreaming."

"You were calling to me," she told him. "I…was trying to find you. You're lost, and I have to find you before you get…"

But how could that be? Sam was home now.

"Oh, Maggie, honey," Sam said, pulling her to him. "Nothing bad can happen now. There's no more war. I'm home. You see? I'm right here." He placed her palm against his chest. "There's no need to worry anymore. I won't leave you again. I'm here forever. You know that, don't you?"

Maggie nodded, but Sam's soothing words couldn't vanquish the insistent voice which had called to her from the depths of her dream. Nor could she shake the feeling that something still waited for her out there, hidden in the fog, and would patiently continue to do so, whether or not she found her way back there again.

***

"Married how long?"

"Almost three years. But my husband was in Italy for the first two years and ten months. He recently returned home."

Maggie watched the doctor's hand jerk as he scribbled on the pad.

"Your husband does what for a living?"

"He's a surgeon. At Saint John's Children's Hospital."

"Happily married?"

"Of course."

"How did you meet?"

"About five years ago, a neighbor's little girl got stung by a bee. She was allergic. My mother and I rushed her to the hospital. Sam was the first person to greet us when we entered the emergency room."

"What did you think when you first saw him?" Dr. Germaine asked.

"That he was very good looking for an older man."

"Older?"

"I'm twenty-five," Maggie explained. "He's my senior by nearly ten years."

"He wasn't yet married?"

"No. He came from very little and had to work his way through medical school. It took him longer than most. He wanted to establish himself as a surgeon before he got married."

"You were engaged for how long?"

"We courted for almost two years. He wanted to get married right away, and with my mother's blessing. But I wanted to wait."

"Why is that?"

"To be sure it was what I wanted. When Sam got his orders, well, we both felt getting married was something we should do. He was about to leave. We had courted two years already."

"So you've said."

Maggie waited while Dr. Germaine looked over what he had written.

"Parents?" he asked.

"My mother passed away last year. I haven't seen my father since I was two."

Scribble, scribble.

"Siblings?"

"I have a younger sister, but…"

Dr. Germaine waited.

"We don't see each other often," she said. "She's lives in New York."

"Brothers?"

"No."

"Is that it for your immediate family?"

"Yes, I suppose it is. Sam is my family now."

"Children?"

Maggie touched a red curl with a manicured finger. "One day. Of course."

She noted the objects on the doctor's desk: a blue glass paperweight holding down a pile of papers; a pile of thick folders stacked on the opposite side; a large black telephone sitting next to a silver beer stein filled with pencils and pens and letter openers; a photograph of a finely-tailored woman with a small child on her lap, turned just enough for Maggie to see the child's smile.

"My wife and son," Dr. Germaine said. "He's three."

"Oh." As if caught looking at something forbidden, she moved her eyes away from the photo. "They're both lovely."

"So, no children at the moment?"

"No. Though Sam plans for us to have at least two."

"Sam?"

"He wants the perfect-sized family to raise in our perfect-sized house."

The doctor scratched more than one sentence on his note pad.

"Did I say something wrong?"

"Not at all." The therapist smiled at his new patient. "I like to write down anything that strikes me as interesting."

"Wanting children is interesting?"

Dr. Germaine didn't explain. Instead, he continued with his questions. "Hobbies?"

"I'm a good baker. And I like to read."

"Magazines?"

"And books."

"Cookbooks? Romance?"

"Adventure stories, mostly. Jack London and the like. The occasional comic book, just for laughs. A little fantasy. And history. I especially enjoy stories about the early Greeks. I just finished *Zorba*. It's fiction but a good read."

"What else do you do to occupy your time?"

She thought a moment. "I tend to the house. Make sure we're comfortable. Shop. Cook. Clean. Garden. Nothing else, really. I mean, nothing I can think of…off-hand…"

Her voice drifted away as Dr. Germaine's pen scribbled away.

"Sex before marriage?" he asked.

Maggie blushed. No one had ever asked her about sex before, except her closest girlfriend.

"Everything you tell me in this room is confidential," Dr. Germaine said. "That's why you're here. To talk to someone in private about things that are just that—private."

"Yes."

"Sex before Sam?"

"With a high school boy," Maggie said. "We were both seniors."

"Consensual?"

"Of course. Though I didn't know any better at the time."

"Was it enjoyable?"

"Is the first time supposed to be?"

"Tell me, Mrs. Lerner—"

"Please, call me Maggie."

"Maggie. Do you tell your husband each time you have one of these dreams?"

"I don't have to. He hears me in my sleep."

"What do you say?"

"As far as I know, I only call his name."

"Sam's?"

"Yes."

The doctor flipped the notepad over and continued onto the next page.

"Marijuana? Cocaine? Alcohol?"

"I've never taken illegal drugs. I drink wine or champagne now and then. I prefer hot tea. Or heated Ovaltine."

"Barbiturates? Tranquilizers?"

"Tranquilizers…yes. For a time. Though not anymore."

"Who prescribed them?" Dr. Germaine asked.

"My mother had died. Sam was away. I couldn't sleep. I bought them from a coworker. It was only one bottle."

"Where do you work?"

"*Did*. At Eastern Weapons." Maggie fiddled with her wedding ring. "I lost my job just before the holidays. When our men came home."

"And this caused you distress?"

"Distress?"

"To lose your job. What did you do for a living?"

"I operated a drill press."

Maggie smiled with pride at the thought of sweat dripping into her eyes, JD's proud hand patting her and her coworkers' backs at the end of each day.

"Did you take all of the pills?"

"All but a handful."

"And why is that?"

"Sam came home," Maggie said.

"And so you thought—"

"That the dream would end."

"But it did not?"

Maggie shook her head. "It only ended for a short while, a

few weeks I think, then it came back again."

"What's the name of the tranquilizer?"

Maggie opened her pocketbook and pulled out the empty glass bottle. She handed it to the doctor who read the handwritten name on the side.

"It can be dangerous business taking pills that aren't prescribed," Dr. Germaine said. "If it really is as the name suggests, it's a relatively common one. What does your husband think about all of this?"

When Maggie didn't answer, Dr. Germaine looked up from his notepad.

"As I mentioned, he's a surgeon," Maggie said. "He doesn't believe in magic pills or—"

The doctor waited.

"In *you*," she explained. "In psychotherapists. Psychoanalysts. He thinks they're—you're—"

"Quacks?"

Maggie nodded and stared at her folded hands.

"That's all right," Dr. Germaine told her. "Many people are frightened at the thought of having a person dig through their brain. And their past. It can be an unsettling experience to have a stranger discover things about you that perhaps you didn't know yourself."

"I'm not afraid to tell you anything."

"That's good, Maggie. That will help us progress nicely. Having you trust me is key to treating you."

"What is wrong with me?" Maggie asked. "Am I mentally unstable? I had a great-aunt who was institutionalized—"

"What I think we're dealing with is a simple case of melancholy. Some people refer to it as depression."

"But I don't feel depressed."

"Depression often wears a mask," the doctor explained. "You may not recognize your depression right at this moment or in your daily routine. You may be too busy to notice it, or unconsciously escaping from it in one way or another. But during sleep, well, that's when things really get going. Dreams are the windows to the subconscious. Our subconscious minds won't allow us to get very far without trying to show us there is something amiss. Our subconscious doesn't lie."

"What if the dream never goes away?"

Or, her mind countered, *what if it never comes back again*?

Tears fell unexpectedly, and Maggie lowered her face to her hands.

Dr. Germaine pulled a starched white handkerchief from a drawer and walked around his desk, holding it out to her. She took it and dabbed at her eyes.

"Maggie," he said, leaning against the desk's front. "There are many things as a therapist I can honestly admit I don't know. Every day, I discover something new about the human mind. The human condition. Things that change the way I view the scientific world. The way I look at others and myself. The way I look at religion, at God even. But there is one thing I do know: You will be fine. Let's get to the crux of what troubles you, and together we will work to eradicate it."

Maggie nodded, hoping to show her therapist that she would work hard to be a worthy patient.

"However," Dr. Germaine said. "The honesty held between these four walls should find its way into your marriage, too."

"You want me to tell Sam."

"If you're seeking help for emotional pain, your husband should know it. Wouldn't you want to know if Sam were suffering?"

"Yes."

"Then start thinking about the how and when." Dr. Germaine went back to his chair and sat. "In the meantime, I'll write you a prescription for the same tranquilizer you have presumably become familiar with."

"I didn't think you'd want me to take them again."

"Why not?"

"Because Sam is home now. I shouldn't need them anymore. I should be happy—I mean, I *am* happy. What I mean is, I should be able to sleep better now that he's home. I should be able to be a good wife, a proper wife, without this feeling of apprehension getting in the way. Why does the voice still call to me? Why can't I let go of my anxiety?"

"That's why I'm here, Maggie. To help you figure out exactly where your anxiety stems from. The dream may still come, but in the meantime, the tranquilizers will at least help keep you calm, both while you're awake and while you sleep."

Maggie's heart thumped loudly. She didn't realize until that moment how much the dream had become a part of her.

She kept the excitement from seeping through her voice. "Do I start taking them right away?"

"That's up to you."

"What do you mean?"

Dr. Germaine folded the piece of paper and placed it in a desk drawer. "You can have the pills as soon as you've told your husband."

Chapter Six

"I don't like those slacks on you," Sam told Maggie, kissing her on the cheek. "They make you look like a boy."

"At least I'm still thin enough to wear them."

He patted her stomach. "I'd say it's time we lost our childish figure."

He grabbed his hat and sailed through the kitchen door. He jumped into their brand new Pontiac Silver Streak, started the engine, and blew a kiss through the windshield as he backed down the driveway.

Babies.

She couldn't utter a word these days without the connotation somehow burrowing its way into the equation. Almost daily, Sam brought home magazines from the hospital with photos of infants or toddlers on the cover. He'd been leaving photos around the house of cribs and bassinets torn from the new Sears catalog. On the inside of the pantry door he'd tacked up a list of his favorite names: Kelly, Catherine, Elizabeth, Howard, Thomas, Milton.

Maggie and Sam were trying, weren't they? How much more could they make love without it becoming as routine as doing the dishes?

Melancholy. Depression.

For days those two words hovered over her like vultures as she tried to find a way to tell her husband of her recently diagnosed disorder. Where would she begin? She hardly compared herself to one of those crazy poets she'd heard about, drinking vodka for breakfast, clicking away at a typewriter for hours upon end in a mountain cabin, threatening suicide every time writer's block took over. Or one of the debutantes she often read about in her books, the ill-fated heroine who falls in love with the wrong man, then predictably dies of a broken heart.

Was she really *depressed*?

The reflection in the kitchen door window held no answers.

Sleep held no answers either.

The dream had changed over the last few nights. Evolved, a psychotherapist might tell her. Now, in the dream, she can feel her feet. She glides along a soft floor, like moss, only it's thicker and greener than any moss she's seen before. The fog still drifts in, but only in the beginning. Then it clears. What she sees when the fog lifts is a door. A massive, wrought iron and wood door, like in a Shakespeare play. She walks confidently to the door, but as soon as she reaches it, she freezes. Her hands try to make contact but cannot. The voice floats to her from behind the door, but her own vocal cords have frozen. She awakens feeling anxious and frustrated, yet at the same time she yearns to go back; aches to see what is behind the door.

It was wrong to feel this way, Maggie knew, and yet there was nothing she could do to squelch the desire.

In less than a week she would meet with Dr. Germaine again, and he would expect her to have done what he had asked.

But not today. Today Sam was talking about babies. She would come clean tomorrow. Or the day after.

Then Dr. Germaine would give her what she needed to become right again.

***

Susan cackled in her hearty way.

"What's so funny?" Maggie asked her best friend, surprised by how much she'd missed that laugh while working at the plant.

They sat in Maggie's kitchen drinking hot tea while fresh sugar cookies baked in the oven. It was the first time since the middle of the war that Maggie had been able to buy sugar instead of that awful molasses.

"You and your ideas of going back to work," Susan said.

"What's so crazy about that?"

Had she just said the word *crazy*?

"In case you haven't noticed, Maggie, your life is gravy. You're married to a doctor. A *surgeon*. Jiminy Cricket. What happened to you in that joint, anyway?"

"Nothing happened."

"It sure seems like something did."

"Don't you miss working?" Maggie asked.

"I spent my days counting two by fours at a lumber yard."

"Don't you miss getting out of the house?"

"No."

"Or a paycheck?"

"Now, look here," Susan said. "My Charlie may not be a doctor, but he's no ditch digger. He makes plenty of dough as an accountant, I can tell you that. Oh! Get a load of these! From Charlie. Just for being me!"

Susan tucked a handful of silky blond curls behind an ear. Glassy pink flowers with silver trim were clipped to her earlobes.

"Pretty," Maggie said.

"And expensive."

They sipped their tea.

"You know," Susan said, "you seem sort of different. Are you sure nothing's wrong?"

"Don't be silly."

"Hey, kiddo, I'm the first one to make a joke in a crowd. But if something's wrong, you can tell me."

"Well," Maggie said, holding the tea cup in front of her mouth as though it were large enough to hide behind. "There is something—"

"Hot Dog! Mother told me the first sign of pregnancy is being uppity."

"Suze, I'm not pregnant."

"Oh. Rats."

"I'm…depressed."

"What?"

"I have depression," Maggie said for the first time. "You know, melancholy."

"If I know you, and I must say I do, I can tell you as your best friend and number one secret-keeper since grammar school, you are not depressed. Depressed people give me the heebie-jeebies. Moping around in a robe all day, looking for rocks to put in their pockets. Who put that idea into your head anyway?"

"My doctor."

"Sam?"

"Sam isn't my doctor, silly. You think he takes out an organ every time I have cramps?"

Susan laughed. "Then who?"

"My…" Maggie lowered her voice. "Psychotherapist."

"Holy Mackerel. Did you just say what I think you did?"

Maggie nodded.

"You're seeing—"

"I am."

"Maggie! I know we go a little nuts sometimes, but a psychotherapist? What's next, electroshock therapy?"

Maggie shuddered at the thought. "I just needed someone to talk to."

Susan exaggerated a pout. "Your best friend's not good enough?"

"You can't help me with—with what I have."

"What do you have?" Susan whispered, looking around the room as though a Red might be hiding in the pantry.

"I told you. Depression."

"Let me get this straight. You're married to a good-looking doctor who adores you. You live in the suburbs. You plan to build a garage. Your new coupe is the envy of the neighborhood. You're baking cookies in a gas-operated Magic Chef, and you're depressed?"

Hearing Susan say those things out loud made Maggie pause. After all, she didn't feel sad at this very moment, sitting here with her best friend of nearly twenty years in her cookie-warm kitchen.

"Maggie," Susan said, her voice growing serious. "What if he's wrong? What if this psychotherapist is like that guy they arrested up in Canada? The one who hypnotized women and… well…you know…"

"He doesn't plan to hypnotize me."

"Not yet, anyway."

"You listen to too many radio mysteries."

Maggie got up and grabbed the warm tea pot from the stove. She refilled both cups before sitting back down.

"Suze," Maggie said, "Sam doesn't know."

"Where does he think you go every day?"

"It's not every day. I've only had one appointment so far."

"At the sanitarium?"

"Of course not. He has a private office about a mile from JC Penney."

"How are you paying for it?" Susan asked.

"I cashed in an insurance policy my mother started for me years ago. I also managed to sock away a little from Eastern. For a rainy day."

"Aren't you worried Sam will find out?"

"My therapist wants me to tell him."

"Jiminy Cricket."

Susan stirred some sugar into her cup and placed the spoon on the dish. "What does it feel like to be depressed?"

"I don't know. I'm tired a lot."

"Oh."

"And I don't feel…" Maggie took a moment looking for the right word to describe how she felt. It was close. So close she couldn't see it clearly. "Satisfaction," she finally said, tasting the word on her tongue for the first time.

"What's that supposed to mean?" Susan asked. "When you've got a husband who takes care of you and babies are just around the corner, who needs satisfaction?"

"Do you really want them?" Maggie asked quietly.

"What?"

"Children."

"Are you out of your cotton-picking mind, Maggie? Of course I want children. Who doesn't? What do you think all the lipstick and garters and sex is about? Geez. I can't imagine another friend asking me that question."

Maggie said nothing, only stared at the loose grounds of tea that had managed to escape the bag and settle on the cup's bottom.

"Don't you want babies, Maggie?"

"Maybe."

"What woman on this green earth doesn't want at least two kids?"

Maggie looked at her friend. "Me?"

Susan let out a sigh that was loud enough for both of them. "That's just hogwash. Every woman wants her own children. It's what God intended us to do. And now that the war's over, well, I can't think of a better time to propagate."

Maggie said nothing, suddenly ashamed.

"You're all-nerves about motherhood, that's what it is," Susan said. "Lots of women are. I'm not, of course. I plan to have four. Two boys and two girls, if I have any say in the matter." She reached across the table and touched Maggie's hand. "You'd make a wonderful mother. A perfect mother, if you want my two cents' worth. Your kids would be happy and healthy, and you'd never have to worry about them getting sick or hurt with Sam around."

"I'm not afraid."

"Then why, Maggie? Why don't you want them?"

Although Maggie was a relatively happy child, and a normal one from what she could gather, she was never overly stimulated by playing with her doll collection—their pin-holed heads filled with bristled hair and tiny mouths that a baby bottle's nipple would never fit into—though her mother bought her a doll each birthday and Christmas. The same intuitive way Maggie knew not to share her dislike for sewing, she understood that her indifference toward babies would deeply sadden her mother, perhaps even shock her, having a daughter who didn't crave to become a mommy one day, as well as spend countless hours practicing. In front of her mother she pretended to love her dollies, holding and rocking and cooing them, placing them in their wicker carriages and wooden cradles and covering their disproportioned bodies with tiny blankets. But as soon as she was alone, her mother busy in the kitchen cooking dinner or working a few evenings a week as a secretary at their church, Maggie would abandon the dolls and turn to the wonderful collection of books which sat on the shelf between her bed and her sister's. The countless fairy tales and *Young Readers* and mysteries she'd purchased with birthday money at the general store kept her happy for hours at a time.

Glancing up from her reading to see the dolls discarded haphazardly throughout her young girl's bedroom, their bottles lost under a bed, their bonnets and booties scattered about, she realized she was not like other girls. It wasn't that Maggie disliked the dolls; she just didn't feel a connection to them. She had never made a conscious decision not to desire children, just as she didn't choose to have red hair and freckles. It was simply who she was.

"I don't know," Maggie finally told her best friend, shrugging off the topic as if it had never been broached, then casually steering the conversation in other directions: the recent robbery at Anthony's Fish Market; the fear of Communism; Europe trying to rebuild; Susan's mother-in-law coming in town for a week-long visit. Maggie was quite skilled at pointing their discussions toward local news and gossip, the same way she did with Sam. Perhaps it was all that pretending during her childhood that had gifted such expertise in the art of deception. Or maybe it was her fear of causing waves that made her so proficient at sleight of hand.

Whatever the reason, it seemed that lately she had become quite the master magician.

Chapter Seven

Sam kissed Maggie on the neck before zipping up the back of her black gown. Together they stood before the full-length mirror in their bedroom.

"We really are an amazing couple," Sam said, putting his face closer to the mirror to examine the knot in his silk bow tie.

Maggie clipped on her dainty diamond and pearl earrings and wrapped a shawl around her shoulders. "Do you think so?"

"I know so," Sam said, facing his wife. "And we finally have a chance to show each other off."

Within twenty minutes they had left the house and were handing their car keys to the valet in front of the Belvedere Hotel. Arm in arm, Sam and Maggie spun through the revolving doors and glided with other admired doctors and dolled-up wives down the hallway to the Charles Room.

The New Year's decorations were dazzling. Nearly every inch of wall and ceiling space glittered. Silver streamers hung like magically spun spider webs from chandeliers. Elaborate center pieces constructed of roses dipped in silver coating and deep red candles had turned each table into a work of art. All around Maggie posed beautiful women in gowns of black velvet, dark blue satin, ruby red silk, taffeta and ruffles, and low-cut backs.

Swirled hair sat on top of heads in high buns decorated with small tiaras or flowers. Each man wore a black tuxedo, some with tails, others in top hats and white gloves. Nearly every guest held onto a martini or wine glass, heads tilting gracefully back with laughter, or slowly shaking back and forth with sympathy in response to a tragic ER or OR story.

Maggie knew she hardly stood out in this mixture of ballroom beauties, but still she glanced around her, believing there must be a fairy godmother hovering close by, waving a magic wand over her head.

Sam and Maggie each enjoyed a glass of red wine as they meandered around the room, greeting various doctors and their wives or fiancées, shaking hands as introductions were made, nibbling finger food which appeared in front of them on a silver tray.

Hundreds of guests eventually drifted to their assigned tables. Four handsome couples dotted the round table along with Maggie and Sam. The loud hum of conversation in the room died down as dinner was served: prime rib *au jus* piled high on clean white china, carrots coated in brown sugar, sliced potatoes swimming in a buttery cream sauce. Dessert came shortly after: a large truffle, dark chocolate coating covering a light creamy center. Another glass of wine for her. Three more for Sam.

Conversations picked up among the various doctors at their table, the sparkly women smiling politely at one another, gazing at their water glasses, daintily readjusting hair pins.

Sam was speaking to another surgeon on Maggie's right, a man whose face was unusually tan for late winter, his skin as smooth as a Tupperware lid.

"So," Sam was telling the man, his words clearly marked by four glasses of burgundy. "After so many young boys coming across my table with their blown off body parts or melted skin, I nearly felt like a plastic surgeon myself."

The other man nodded. "I've had a few soldiers come in for reconstructive surgery, but most never seem to make it past the initial consultation. Not afraid to fly through enemy bullets, but frightened to hell by a little scalpel. It's the women who keep me hopping!"

He looked at his perfectly sculptured wife as he said this. Then he turned to Maggie. "I can do something about those freckles if you'd like, Mrs. Lerner," he said, speaking loudly over the other conversations at the table.

"He really is a wiz," his mannequin-wife told Maggie as she caressed the large diamond pendant hanging like a fancy cowbell around her neck.

"Her freckles?" Sam said. He put his arm around his wife, inadvertently knocking the shawl from her shoulders onto the floor. He placed his lips near Maggie's ear, but spoke at the top of his voice. "Don't you dare let this man touch one sweet dot on that pretty face, my little Magpie!"

"My shawl," Maggie said as she dipped out of Sam's crook and reached toward the floor.

Sam continued. "The ones who repair injuries, who make lives better through the challenge of science, those are the *real* doctors."

All clanking of silverware and china at the table ceased. Maggie grabbed her shawl from the floor and sat up.

Sam downed the remainder of his wine and added, "It takes a different kind of doctor to choose tummy tucks over healing the sick."

The plastic surgeon across from them spoke so softly that Maggie, who pretended to rearrange her stole, could barely hear him.

"It doesn't take a scholar to explain that humans *feel* better when they *look* better," the man said, his lips pursed. "I will have you know that the last surgery I performed before getting dressed tonight happened to be on a fourteen-year-old boy—a *child*—born with his nose on the right side of his head, eyes on the left, and ears that stuck out like a pair of kites in the wind."

"There's no need to be defensive," Sam said. "I was merely explaining the difference between us." He stood up. "I'm going to get another glass of wine."

Maggie watched as her husband left her sitting at the muted table, disappearing into the crowd of people who were once again strolling around the room or dancing on the illuminated dance floor.

"I should follow him," Maggie said, standing. "Looks like we may be taking a taxi home tonight." She smiled apologetically at the group, but no one returned the gesture.

She only searched a moment before spotting Sam across the crowded ballroom, leaning against the bar, a fresh glass of wine in his hand. He was already engaged in another conversation, his jaw stiffening as he spoke to a man whose back was turned away from Maggie.

She stopped.

The dream had never come to her while awake; certainly not among strangers. But now, while surrounded by the white noise of conversation, clarinet music, and the general hum of people gathered together, the urgent voice from her sleep made its way to her ears. Gone was the room around her. High and low octaves of laughter and dialogue disappeared, replaced by the desperate, incessant voice of her dream.

Maggie…Maggie…

Underneath her velvet dress, trickles of cold sweat slid

between her breasts and pooled there.

Maggie shook her head and closed her eyes. When she opened them again, Sam's own dark eyes unexpectedly darted toward her like an eager hunter reacting to the first deer of the season.

Chills moved through her center and out the top of her head. People revolved around her, too busy mingling or too tipsy to notice that a woman was frozen in her tracks by the sudden and unquestionable glare of her husband.

Maggie had barely got a chance to know all of her husband's temperaments before Uncle Sam had dragged him off to war. But she could sense the anger, even from this distance, and without ever having experienced it.

With a hand, he motioned for her to come.

Like the good wife she so desperately wanted to be, worked hard to be, she obeyed.

Maggie approached Sam just as the gentleman he'd been speaking to stepped away and tunneled through the thickening crowd. The man offered his profile as he pushed through a cozy foursome. His cheek shone with redness, like he was angry or embarrassed.

Then Maggie realized who the man was: Dr. Germaine.

"Coincidence, don't you think?" Sam asked Maggie, his words slicing through her, his eyes staring at Germaine's back as he disappeared into the mob.

Maggie's stomach threatened to bring up all that rich food. She said nothing, laboring to keep her dinner in its place.

Sam's words were loud, but the clusters of guests talking and laughing and dancing their way to the midnight hour were too wrapped up in their private *tête-à-têtes* to care about one man who'd had too much to drink.

"What's a coincidence?" Maggie whispered.

"That out of all these doctors, I would wind up talking to two jack asses in the same evening. Two quacks who call themselves medical professionals. Two men, if they are indeed men, gaining wealth at the expense of their patients!"

Maggie realized with relief that Dr. Germaine hadn't disclosed anything—Sam was merely responding to his own cynicism regarding plastic surgeons and psychiatrists. But she still had to get her husband to calm down. She tried to take the wine glass from his hand, but he pulled it back. Red liquid splashed to the floor.

"Darling," Maggie tried. "Maybe we should—"

"They will never know what it's like to stitch up a child's cracked skull. To remove an apple-sized tumor from an intestine. To hold a dead heart in a tired fist. To tell parents their child is going to die. That their child *has* died!"

Guests within hearing range shot uncomfortable glances at the man splashing his wine and waving his arm through the air like an amateur orchestra conductor.

"Samuel?" A short, balding man appeared from the crowd and touched Sam's wrist. "Let's get that glass out of your hand before you stain someone's pretty clothes."

The man gently pulled the glass from Sam's hand and placed it on the bar. Bits of different conversations became muddled in Maggie's ears:

"Do you think *The Bells of Saint Mary's* or *Mildred Pierce* will take home more Oscars?"

"Jackson Pollock? Brilliant artist."

"A toast to higher speed limits!"

"Simply shocking, the recent totals on war casualties."

The man shook Maggie's hand and spoke over the cacophony.

"I'm Ted Warner. "Sam and I recently started working together. Isn't that right, Sam?"

Sam nodded.

"Let's get you some coffee, buddy. Bartender, black coffee, pronto!"

The bartender immediately set a hot cup of coffee on the bar.

"What's the matter, Sam?" Dr. Warner asked, carefully placing the coffee in Sam's hands. "Not having a good time? Your wife here—she certainly looks like a catch." He winked at Maggie who smiled a thank you. "She's dressed to the nines, you're dressed like Fred Astaire. It's New Year's Eve for Chrissakes. Whatever you have going on in there—" He tapped a stubby finger against Sam's temple. "You need to let it out."

Sam shouted, "Are you saying I should see a PSYCH-O-THERA-PIST?"

The mob near the bar collectively took a step away from Sam and his hot cup of coffee.

"Come," Dr. Warner said, taking the cup from his hand. "Let's go outside for a bit of air."

Maggie followed quietly behind as the kindly older man took Sam by the elbow. He led him through the crowd, across the lobby, and through the front doors.

Sam and Dr. Warner shared a bench next to the valet stand. For a few moments neither man said a word as Sam sipped from the coffee mug and handed it back to Ted. Maggie leaned against a nearby pillar, wrapping her shawl more tightly around her against the winter chill.

Sam looked up at the starless sky. Finally, he said, "I lost one."

"I know, Sam," Ted said, patting his coworker on the back. "It happens to all of us."

"She was four, Teddy. Four. She had soft, baby-blond curls—

a perfect Macy's doll. Her parents had just bought her a pair of ice skates for Christmas. She was supposed to learn how to skate—"

Sam's body suddenly folded, his head falling into his hands, his sobs tumbling across the sidewalk and onto North Charles Street.

"Her liver was gone before she was ever admitted," Ted told Sam. "You had nothing to do with that. Nothing."

"For nearly three years I saw things you can't imagine, Teddy. As many as twenty boys a day. Most of them barely old enough to sport a moustache—arms and legs blown off, heads split open so far you could see through to the table beneath, faces melted like cheap candle wax. Boys calling out the names of their wives or girlfriends or mothers, just before the death rattle shook what was left of their ravaged bodies. But this isn't war, Ted. This is home. I'm home now. This shouldn't be happening."

"We only have life because we have death, Sam. You can't have one without the other. First thing you learn in medical school. Maybe you went back to work too soon. Maybe you need a break."

"A break?"

"You and your pretty wife could go on a trip together. A vacation. Re-do that honeymoon you told me you barely had time to enjoy. What do you say, pal? Another honeymoon?"

"Yes," Sam said, wiping his face with a tuxedo sleeve. "Another honeymoon. With my sweet Magpie."

Behind the column, Maggie smiled.

"Okay then," Ted said. "Let's sit out here a little while longer then get you a fresh cup of coffee. I know a woman who deserves to have a sober husband dipping her as the clock strikes twelve."

"Yes," said Sam. "Another honeymoon. For Maggie and me."

Chapter Eight

"I think time spent alone together will do you both good," Dr. Germaine told Maggie from behind his desk.

Maggie nodded in agreement. "Thank you for not saying anything at the party."

"My ultimate decision is only because I witnessed Sam's display firsthand. This is not my usual practice. In most cases, I insist upon the spouse's involvement. Keeping our sessions from your husband goes against more than just my principles."

"I understand," Maggie said.

Dr. Germaine opened a folder. "Are you still having the dreams?"

"*Dream.* Yes."

"Let's begin then. See if we can get into that subconscious mind of yours to discover what lies at the root."

He reached into a bottom drawer and placed a small metal contraption on top of his desk.

"Is that a recorder?" she asked.

"This makes it easier for me to take accurate notes."

"Oh."

"Please—go to the couch and make yourself comfortable."

"Should I lie down?"

"Some of my patients feel it helps them relax. Helps them retrieve hidden feelings or memories more easily."

Maggie left her pocketbook on the chair and went to the couch. She noticed the pretty floral print and how out of place the feminine sofa looked in the dimly lit room decorated with dark wood furniture. She sat down in the center of the couch and smoothed out her pleated skirt.

"I'd prefer to sit," she said. "If you don't mind."

"Whatever makes you most comfortable."

Dr. Germaine opened the recorder, fiddled with something on the inside, and pressed a button. He spoke clearly into the machine which he turned halfway in Maggie's direction. "January 4th, 1946. Patient number 4403." His voice turned smooth and low. "Close your eyes, Maggie, and relax. Take a deep breath and let the air out slowly."

She did as he asked.

"Again. That's it. Good. Keep breathing. Very good. You are feeling completely relaxed."

The room filled with silence as she concentrated on her breaths.

After a while, she heard his voice again: "I will soon be asking you some questions that I'd like you to answer without thinking too much. Just say the first thing that comes to your mind. While we speak to one another, I want you to keep your eyes closed. That's it, now. Keep breathing. Relax your shoulders, your back, your jaw, your hands. That's right…very good…"

After a few moments of silence, Dr. Germaine resumed speaking, his voice gentle and calm, nearly void of inflection.

"Your nightmare began when?" he asked.

"It's not a nightmare."

"I thought the dream is what brought you here."

"It is."

"It doesn't frighten you?"

"Yes. No. I mean, it did. Before. Now it's a little of both."

"Can you elaborate?"

Maggie paused, took in another deep breath, and let it out. It was good to keep her eyes closed while speaking of her dream. It helped her see it more clearly.

"It feels very pleasant there," she said. "Safe. Happy. Even the fog feels warm and velvety against my skin. I can't hear my footsteps, or even see my feet. Maybe I don't have any. I can see the ground. It's green and mossy. Then the other night I realized I can smell."

"What do you smell?"

"I'm not sure. Something summery. Whatever it is, it's very strong. And getting stronger all the time."

"Let's again discuss when the dream began," Dr. Germaine said. "It was while your husband was in Europe, correct?"

"Yes."

"How long had he been away?"

"A few months? A year? I'm not sure. The dream evolved slowly."

"How so?"

"When it first came to me, I was able to wake myself up before it went too far. But then, as the weeks and months wore on, I had a more difficult time waking up, and it became—more detailed. But Sam's voice…"

"Yes?"

"His voice was there from the beginning."

"How else has the dream, as you say, evolved?"

"At first, it was more of a feeling, not anything tangible. The fog was just the *thought* of fog. Like thinking about London but not actually being there. Even the smell was just a *sense* of smell. But now…"

"Go on."

"Now, the dream is so vivid. Bright colors. Magnificent blues and greens. Fog I can almost sieve through my fingers. And the smell…"

Dr. Germaine waited.

"Lemonade maybe?" she asked herself out loud. "Or lemon pie? Whatever it is, the scent is very strong."

"Perhaps a smell of a childhood memory. Those can often trigger intense feelings."

"Oh."

"How often does the dream occur?"

"Every night. Well, every so often it stays away. Or maybe I'm dreaming but just can't remember. But it always comes back. The same exact dream."

"Are you sure that it's the same?"

"Yes," Maggie said. "I always move in the same direction. See the same things. Lately I've been able to stop myself from shouting out in my sleep."

"How have you managed that?"

"I don't know. It's strange that I can control this. I've become quite good at hiding it from Sam."

"Why would you want to hide your dream from your husband?"

"I don't want to worry him."

"I see."

"But it's getting harder to do," Maggie explained. "The more I have the dream, the more defined everything becomes. I *want* to see things. Smell things. Touch things. Like the door."

"Door?"

"That appeared most recently."

"What kind of door?"

"A large one."

"Is it in a wall or is it suspended alone?"

"It could be standing alone, though I sense that it's part of a wall. I don't have any peripheral vision in the dream. I can only see what's precisely in front of me. I think that's why, when I look for Sam, I can't find him. I can't see anything other than what's directly in my path."

"Can you describe the door in detail?"

"Thick rustic wood, with a long handle and large iron hinges. I know this sounds silly, but it looks like a castle door. The kind you'd find at the end of a drawbridge."

"What does it feel like?" Dr. Germaine asked.

"I've never touched it."

"Why not?"

"My hands stay locked at my sides."

"Does the door frighten you?"

"I'm not afraid of the door itself," Maggie said, "but rather of what I'll find when I open it."

"*When?*"

Pause.

"If."

"What do you think you may discover?" he asked.

"I don't know."

"If you don't know, then why are you afraid?"

"It's the voice behind it that frightens me."

Another pause.

"You didn't mention that before," Dr. Germaine said. "Why would Sam's voice frighten you?"

"In the beginning, I believed he was hurt. You know, the war and all. When the door appeared, I thought I'd find him on the other side, injured. From a grenade or a bullet. Dying or…dead. But now…"

"Now, what?"

"I don't feel that way anymore."

"Please explain."

"In the beginning, I was sure the voice was Sam's. But right around the time he came home, the voice started sounding different. Now, I'm not even sure it's Sam's voice at all. Or that it ever was. I'm not sure of anything. It's the change in the voice that frightens me. Yet, at the same time, it attracts me to it."

"But you are no longer afraid Sam is hurt?"

"That's right."

"Could that be because he's home now, and you are no longer worried about his welfare?"

"Maybe. But if it's not Sam, then whose voice is it?"

"You mean, who or what does the voice represent? That's what we're here to find out. What does this voice say to you?"

"He calls me. Calls *to* me. He needs me to open the door."

"He has asked this of you specifically?"

Maggie thought about this.

"No."

"Then how do you know this is what he wants?"

"I just do."

"Is it the voice or the *request* that frightens you?"

"I'm not sure…"

"Is there anyone else in the dream?"

"No."

"Can you tell me what you look like?"

Maggie thought a moment. "I don't know."

"Tell me what you see besides the door. Tell me more about the smells, the sounds."

"It's fading away…"

"Just relax and let your mind go."

"I can't grasp it…"

"Think of yourself moving through the fog, see the door, listen for the voice…"

"I can't. It doesn't come." Maggie opened her eyes. "I can't," she said again. She pulled a handkerchief from the sleeve of her sweater and wiped her wet cheeks. "I'm sorry."

Dr. Germaine smiled. "Why are you sorry? We've made some wonderful progress."

"We have?"

"Absolutely. This is the first time you've shared your dream with another person, yes?"

Maggie nodded.

"Just talking about it should offer some relief. You do feel better, don't you?"

"Yes."

She did. A little.

"Good," he told her. He pressed the stop button on the recorder and stood up. "When we discover who is behind that door, I think we'll have a real breakthrough."

Dr. Germaine came around the desk, sat next to Maggie on the couch, and handed her a folded piece of paper.

"Let's see how these work this time, with Sam home. Start tonight before bed. You can get it filled at any drugstore."

"Thank you," Maggie whispered, gripping the piece of paper between her perspiring fingers.

"Now," Dr. Germaine said. "Since you have that second honeymoon next week, we'll have to resume our sessions when you get back. Where are you headed?"

"Cape May."

"One of my favorite summer spots."

"It'll be freezing in January," Maggie said. "But that's where Sam thought we should go. He's dead set on an uninterrupted week of snuggling."

Dr. Germaine stood up and held out his hands. Maggie let him help her up from the couch.

"Don't hesitate to call me while you're away if you need to," Dr. Germaine told Maggie as he walked her to the office door. "When you get back from your well-deserved respite, we'll see what progress you've made. The tranquilizers will help you relax. Getting a week's worth of good sleep should make all the difference in the world."

Chapter Nine

The Chalfonte Hotel was nearly abandoned, the northeasterly gusts either driving the locals south or keeping prospective travelers at bay. But Maggie was happy to be in a quiet place only three blocks from the smells of taffy and fudge drifting along the boardwalk, the Atlantic waves crashing nearby, the sand swirling in tiny funnels along the water's edge.

Both Dr. Germaine and Dr. Ted Warner were right: A respite was just what they needed.

The day before, while packing her suitcases, Maggie had found a perfect hiding place in the pocket of one of her makeup bags, a place in which Sam would never show an interest. After checking into their hotel room, Maggie gave her husband an Eskimo kiss and excused herself to wash, shave, and primp in the pretty bathroom. After slipping into something sexy and comfortable, she plucked the pill from the *cloisonné* pill box she'd bought at the drugstore, placed it on her tongue, and sipped water from the tap.

When she stepped into the room, Sam was already under the covers in the king-size bed, his arms folded neatly behind his head. Candlelight flickered on the walls. Both windows were open a crack, letting in a thin stream of damp ocean air and the sound of surf in the distance. A glass of champagne sat on each end table.

"Mr. Romantic," Maggie said.

"*Doctor* Romantic," Sam said, leaning up on an elbow and tossing back the covers on Maggie's side of the bed. He was nude.

Maggie let her pale green chiffon robe collapse to the floor, revealing a *charmeuse* nightgown which clung gracefully to her slim hips. She pulled the pins from her hair as she walked slowly toward the bed, her red curls falling and bouncing along her shoulders. She picked up her glass of champagne, leaning over just enough to expose her small breasts beneath the lace bust.

"To a perfect vacation," she said, raising her glass.

"To my perfect wife."

"To my perfect husband."

"To our perfect life."

They laughed in unison at the silliness of the rhyme.

Maggie sipped from her glass and placed it back on the end table. "Just what the doctor ordered." She climbed in beside him.

Sam took his wife into his arms and placed the back of his hand gently against her face. His hardness pressed against her thigh.

Within minutes her nightgown was pushed up to her belly. He was on top of her, then inside her, his breath warm and gentle in her ear, his lips everywhere from her cheeks to her neck to her breasts.

"I love you," he whispered, exhaling each time his hips moved forward, inhaling each time they moved back.

"Oh, Sam. I knew this was all we needed." Little puffs of air escaped Maggie as her hips tilted up to greet his. "You and me and this." Her orgasm was so close, just below the surface. She couldn't wait to give in to it, to let herself fall completely. "This is all we need," she whispered, for the moment believing her words. "Each other."

"And a family, Maggie. Let's make a family. A collection of little me's and little you's."

The orgasm that was just within her reach suddenly slipped from her grasp. In frustration, she slid her hips from side to side, hoping to achieve the same position from moments before. She twisted her lower body and forced her pelvis higher, wrapping her legs around Sam's buttocks. But it was no use. The possibility of release drifted away, leaving her with feelings of disappointment and desertion.

"Oh, Maggie," Sam said, his voice cracking as he teetered on the verge of his own climax. "Babies…will…complete us. Make… us…perfect…"

His lips pressed hard against hers, his tongue darting around inside her mouth, his body taut, his groans vibrating through his ribs and into hers. The shaking lasted nearly twenty seconds before subsiding. His body relaxed, grew heavy.

"God, how I love you," Sam told his wife, nuzzling his face into her neck and kissing her lightly.

Soon, his dead weight became too much for her, and she nudged him off. He rolled onto his side, breathing deeply, legs twitching, already dreaming.

Maggie listened as Sam's snoring found its familiar rhythm. In the dark, she disregarded the emptiness she felt, and instead prayed that what Sam so desperately wanted she could convince herself to want as well. That her therapist would help her discover what was preventing her from being a proper wife. That the tiny pill she had taken less than an hour before would purge the notion that she was somehow defective.

As she prayed for these things, her mind turned fuzzy and

exhaustion quietly seeped into her bones, dragging her off to sleep.

***

It was neither day nor night. Neither cold nor hot. The smell of lemons was everywhere, like she had just soaked her hair in dish liquid. The door stood before her without her ever having walked there. First it wasn't there—and then it was.

Maggie tilted her head to the side, regarding the door.

It seemed different. Larger? Richer in color? Perhaps it was she who had changed, she thought without really thinking.

She glanced down at her hands. For the first time, Maggie noticed her fingers. She held them up and smiled to see their movement, then looked down toward her feet. There they were, long thin toes wiggling in a pair of pretty flat sandals. What else was she wearing? She started to move her eyes up her body when she heard the muffled voice.

"Maggie?"

Her focus snapped back toward the door.

"Maggie? Is that you?"

In the back of her mind she heard another man's voice: *Is the door in a wall? Or is it suspended alone?*

Who had asked her those questions? She tried to remember but could not. She only knew she was expected to find the answer.

Her eyes took in either side of the door. To the right and left, a high stone wall continued into the fog as far as she could see. She cast her gaze upward. The wall disappeared into the low clouds which hovered above. Her arms moved away from her sides, no longer frozen in place. She placed a hand against the wall. It felt like granite. Very old granite. Dampness touched her palm.

Maggie took a deep breath, the lemony air entering her sinuses and lingering there. Her forehead touched the wooden door.

"Hello?" she asked.

"I can barely hear you," the voice said.

She spoke a little louder. "Hello?"

This time, only silence greeted her.

Maggie tried again.

"Hello?"

A noise came to her from beyond the door. A shuffling sound, like someone dragging a bag of sand across a floor.

"Sam?" she tried, knowing that saying his name meant nothing.

The shuffling continued a moment longer before fading away.

In front of her feet, a thin beam of yellowish light seeped through the crack at the bottom of the door. She stepped back and stooped down, the soft earth reaching up to greet her knees. She placed a cheek against the ground and peeked under.

There, on the other side of the door, was a pair of sandals much like the ones she wore, and in those sandals stood a pair of feet much larger than her own, and much more masculine looking. Feet that did *not* resemble Sam's.

As Maggie placed her face closer to the opening, the feet quickly stepped back.

"Don't go," she said.

The feet stayed where they were, and Maggie smiled. This was like a game, though what kind of game she wasn't sure. She only knew it intrigued her.

She spoke through the narrow gap. "Why don't you open the door?"

The owner of the feet remained silent.

"Open the door," she said as sternly as she could without trying to intimidate. "I won't hurt you. I want to see you."

After a moment, a voice drifted through the crack.

"I cannot."

Maggie stood up and tried to reach for the handle, a simple gesture to work a simple mechanism, but suddenly her hand would not move. She had moved her fingers only a moment before, so why couldn't she reach out her hand?

Because I'm not allowed to. The thought lingered a moment before vanishing.

"Pull on the handle," she ordered.

"What?"

"Pull on the handle."

"There is none."

"Of course there is," Maggie said. "How could there not be?"

"There is none!"

The unexpected panic startled her. "All right," she said calmly. "Don't get upset."

"The handle has been removed," the voice told her.

"Why?"

"For my own good."

"Did you do something wrong?"

Another voice, one that didn't belong to the man on the other side of the door, snuck up behind her.

"Maggie!"

She flew around but only silent fog greeted her.

"Maggie!" the voice called again.

"Sam?" she said, guilt-ridden heat rising to her cheeks.

Why would I feel guilty?

"Maggie, wake up. Wake up, my darling."

Maggie opened her eyes to see Sam towering over her in his silk robe, shaving brush in hand, thick white cream pasted to his face like a frothy beard. Bright streams of blinding light tore through the room.

With Sam's free hand he yanked the covers from her body, her nightgown still crumpled up above her waist, causing her to feel exposed.

"Rise and shine, my magpie!" he sang. "Today is ours to do as we please!"

"I was sleeping," she muttered, wanting to pull the covers back up but not finding the energy to do so.

"We can't have you sleep the entire day away. It's already half past seven. You've been dead to the world." He continued the conversation from the bathroom. "I'd never hear the end of it if I didn't give you enough time to ready yourself. We have a wonderful breakfast awaiting us downstairs. Columbian coffee, eggs Benedict, fresh strawberries shipped all the way from California…"

Maggie sat up. The dream was gone, but the damp fog still clung to her skin, and the mysterious voice still echoed in her ears. Sitting on the edge of the bed, she looked down at her feet, half expecting to see a pair of sandals. But her feet were bare, her toenails a pretty shade of winter red. She closed her eyes again, trying to recapture the lemon scent from her dream, but all she could smell was the hint of Chanel No. 5, dabbed on her wrists and in between her breasts the night before. Her mind struggled to picture the heavy wooden door, but it had already melted away, just as the voice and the fog were also melting away.

"Did you sleep well, my darling?" Sam asked cheerily.

She turned toward her reflection in the vanity mirror, catching the dark circles under her eyes, the small worry lines that invaded her forehead. Had she slept? She felt as though she'd been the first woman to run the Boston Marathon, and yet, at the same time, she yearned to lie back down on the pillow and do it all again. Not for the rest she knew she needed, but to see who was behind—

"Maggie?"

Sam stood in the bathroom doorway. His face was clean shaven, save for the groomed moustache, and his hair was slicked back with Brylcreem.

If we were strangers, I'd still know he was a doctor.

"What?" Maggie asked.

"How did you sleep? Was your side of the bed as magical as mine?"

"Yes," she said, standing up and plucking her robe from the floor. "Magical."

As Maggie slid into her robe she thought, *There isn't a better word to describe it.*

Chapter Ten

Just as Sam had predicted, their vacation moved along flawlessly. By the second night, she found comfort while she slept, her dreamscape once again returning to that of the normal variety, with snippets of the day's events and simple plots flashing and disappearing again before she had a chance to wittingly participate. She rose from bed refreshed, awake, and ready to seize the day, content to read her novels while Sam went to the indoor pool for a swim, or ride to dinner in the back of a taxi with her arm hooked comfortably in his.

For nearly a week there was snuggling through chilly nights, dining in the hotel restaurant every morning for breakfast, relaxing with the paper while sipping afternoon tea. They splurged on fine dinners in a different restaurant each night, feasting on roasted pheasant, lobster tail, baked brie, and desserts extraordinaire. Maggie could feel herself calming down, her heart slowing to a steady pulse; she could feel the tension in her neck dissolve with each walk on the beach, each stroll down the boardwalk, each glass of wine before dinner.

The tranquilizers were doing their job, her doctor would tell her, pleased. Working exactly as they were supposed to in order to get a good night's sleep. And for this, Maggie was immensely grateful. But within a few days of the dream's departure, she discovered an emptiness she couldn't define; a craving for something that had yet to be discovered. A type of withdrawal, she surmised. She mourned the loss of her dream as though her sense of purpose had died along with it. In her dream, there was something she was expected to do. She was needed. She was sure the person standing on the other side of that door—the door which was slowly fading from her memory like the words to a senseless poem—still stood there, awaiting her return.

She didn't know the complicated answers, if there were any, to her psychological queries. Maggie only knew one thing with certainty: She missed her dream and wanted it to come back again.

***

Instead of going out to dinner their last night in Cape May, Maggie and Sam ordered room service: a final bottle of champagne, a plate of international cheeses with crackers and fruit, and a sampling of decadent pastries. They turned the radio to a station playing some of the swing band tunes Maggie had loved as a teenager: Jimmie Lunceford, Count Basie, Duke Ellington, Chick Webb, and her all-time favorite, Benny Goodman.

Sam took Maggie's hand and kissed it gingerly.

"Would you care for a final dance, my lady?"

Together they swayed to Benny's clarinet, one cheek against the other, their breath warm in each other's ear.

"Maggie," Sam said, hugging his wife, "I want you to know how sorry I am for what happened on New Year's Eve."

It was the first time Sam had mentioned that night.

"I know," Maggie said.

Sam stopped rocking and held her out at arm's length. "I

think it was a culmination of so many things. Dealing with all those wounded soldiers on a daily basis. Coming home and believing there'd be no more death, which of course is ridiculous, but I wished for it nonetheless. Coming home and—knowing you were so sad while I was gone."

"But I'm not anymore."

"Are you sure?"

"Of course," she said, smiling wide to prove it.

"And the bad dreams? They are behind you now?"

She paused. "Yes."

"Sometimes you seem so sad to me, Maggie. Do I make you happy? Is our marriage everything you'd hoped it would be?"

"Sam—"

"I know you liked working."

"I worked hard for our country like all the other women. We did what we were asked to do."

"And that's commendable."

Sam took Maggie by the hand and guided her to the edge of the bed.

"You were highly regarded at the plant, weren't you?" he asked, sitting next to her.

"I don't understand why you're bringing up—"

"You need to put those ideas away, Maggie."

"I have."

"Have you?"

"Of course."

"No notions of getting a job outside of our marriage and our home? No fancy ideas about being independent? I can take care of you, Maggie. It's what I want to do. It truly is."

"I know that."

"Then you're ready? Genuinely ready?"

"Sam, why are you acting like this?"

"Do you want children, Maggie?"

"Yes."

"Do you?"

"I've told you, yes. Why do you keep making me say it?"

"We've been trying since the day I came home," Sam said. "You haven't conceived yet."

"You're a doctor. You know these things can take time."

"I also know that if a couple truly wants a family, they are blessed with one."

"What are you saying? That I'm not getting pregnant on purpose?"

"Maggie—"

She yanked her hands from Sam's and stood up.

"How could I possibly prevent myself from conceiving? I've never dreamed of using one of those awful diaphragms, and you haven't put on a condom since before our wedding day. That's the most ridiculous thing I've—"

"Maggie, stop. I didn't say those things to upset you. I just want to make sure that we're both in this together."

"We are."

"All right, then. I only wanted—"

Maggie suddenly pulled her cashmere sweater over her head and threw it to the floor. "You want babies? I'll give you babies." She undid her buttons and dropped her pleated skirt to the floor, revealing her thigh-high nylons underneath. She kicked off her heels. Her eyes never left the surprised look on Sam's face as she peeled off her stockings, slowly rolled them down to her ankles, picked them off, and arranged them across his shoulders.

She turned around, her back to Sam. "Unhook me."

He did as his wife asked.

After tossing her bra to a corner chair, she placed her hands against the waist of her underwear. "Pull them down."

Sam slowly slid down her panties, pausing to kiss her buttocks. She kicked the panties away and again faced her husband.

"I'll show you who's ready to make babies."

For the next hour, she and Sam were wild in their lovemaking, devouring one another until they fell asleep on the floor, wrapped up in a blanket that had followed them there, lights on, radio blaring, the expensive champagne turning warm and losing its fizz.

Afterwards, Maggie slept without dreaming, the mystical door left to its own devices in another world, the smell of lemons buried deep beneath her conscious memory, the fog as far away as the moon.

Chapter Eleven

"So," Dr. Germaine said while leading Maggie to the sofa, "did you enjoy the Jersey shore?"

"Yes," she said, sitting in the couch's center.

"And your husband?"

Maggie thought of all the food and drink and sex. "I think he gained five pounds."

Dr. Germaine laughed. "And you got the rest you needed?"

"I'm fine." Maggie straightened out her skirt and then patted her hair.

"Fine?"

"Cape May was splendid. For both of us. Just what the doctor ordered."

Dr. Germaine walked behind his desk, sat down in his large leather chair, and clicked on the recorder. "January 20th, 1946." He leaned back. "So tell me, Maggie, have the tranquilizers—"

"Yes."

"And the dream?"

"Gone," Maggie said.

"Gone?"

"Yes."

"Completely?"

"Yes."

"How do you feel about that?"

Maggie fiddled with the enamel brooch on her blouse. "Fine."

"Are you sure?"

"Yes."

"Maggie, the first day we met we talked about honesty. It's important that you are as open with me as possible, but more than that, you need to be open with yourself."

"I'm sure I don't know what you mean."

"I think you do."

Maggie fought to hold back tears as she whispered, "I don't understand why it stopped. It didn't stop when I took the tranquilizers before."

"The mind does what it needs to, when it needs to."

"But why now?"

"Perhaps you don't need the dream anymore," Dr. Germaine offered.

"But I do. I want it to come back."

"Want and need are two different things."

"*Need*," Maggie said. "I *need* it to come back."

"I see."

"You told me we'd find out who's behind the door. How can I find out if the dream is gone?"

Maggie unconsciously twisted her wedding ring, but stopped when she saw the rise of her therapist's eyebrows.

"How are things with Sam?" he asked.

"I told you—we had a splendid time on our vacation. A splendid time."

A long pause fell between them.

"Maggie," Dr. Germaine finally said. "You can discover who

is behind the door without having the dream. As long you have the desire to know the answer."

"How can I figure that out if I can't see it anymore?"

"Just close your eyes and relax, and if it is still there, we can get to it again. Together."

She was suddenly feeling agitated. "I need the dream to see it."

"A dream is merely a manifestation of your subconscious mind. We can get to the door without it."

"But…"

"But what?"

Maggie didn't answer.

Dr. Germaine leaned forward, his elbows on his desk, his fingers folded in front of him. "What else is troubling you?"

"Nothing."

"As your doctor, I am inclined to disagree. You have never seemed so out of sorts before."

"I need to see it," Maggie whispered, ashamed of the admission.

"I understand that."

"I…I miss it."

"Why do you suppose that is?"

Maggie thought a moment. "I don't know."

"What else do you miss?"

"What do you mean?"

"In your life," Dr. Germaine said. "What else do you feel is missing?"

"I can't imagine. I have everything I've ever wanted. More than I've ever dreamed of."

"Everything?"

"Yes."

"Do you miss your mother?"

"Of course," Maggie said. "But that's to be expected, isn't it?"

"And your father?"

"I never knew him. I wouldn't know what to miss."

"And your sister? The one in New York?"

"Not particularly."

"And your husband being away," he said. "Do you miss that?"

"Of course not."

"Are you sure?"

"What are you implying?"

"I'm not implying anything. I just want to get to the crux of why you miss something that once caused you torment. Your dream's absence should bring an element of relief."

Maggie was silent. She thought about the last time she'd had the dream. The sweet odor, rising to her nostrils like a fresh batch of lemon cake mix. The stone wall under her fingers. The handsome feet. But the dream hadn't returned. She even took a nap the day before in the afternoon, when Sam was called to the hospital for an emergency. For two hours her subconscious mind worked to locate the door. She slept hard, but later awoke without the memory of having dreamed at all and feeling groggy and cross. *Depressed*, her doctor would likely declare.

"Maggie?"

"I know who's behind the door," she whispered.

"You do?"

"Our first night in Cape May. I had the dream one last time. It was extremely vivid."

"What did you see?"

"A man."

"Sam?"

Maggie lowered her eyes as her cheeks warmed. "No."

"This makes you feel guilty, the fact that you encountered another man in your dream?"

"I haven't quite met him. He's there, but…"

Dr. Germaine waited as she gathered her thoughts.

"He's still on the other side of the door," she said finally. "He still calls to me. And I saw his feet."

"You're positive the feet do not belong to Sam?"

"Yes."

"Did he speak to you, aside from calling your name?" Dr. Germaine asked.

"Yes."

"What did he say?"

"He explained that he was unable to open the door from his side. I wanted to help him, but…"

"But what?"

"I couldn't."

"Were your hands still frozen?"

"No. This time I could feel the wall under my hand. But…"

"Don't stop now."

"I *can't* open it."

"Are you afraid to open it?"

"Maybe…"

"What do you think would happen if you did?"

For some reason, as many times as Maggie had analyzed the dream, she had never questioned what would happen if she were to succeed.

"I don't know."

"Take a guess."

"I really don't know. I only know that I want to. Desperately. I want to see who's behind it. I want to open the door and look the person in the face and ask him who he is."

"What do you think he would tell you?" Dr. Germaine asked.

"I haven't any idea."

"None at all?"

Maggie shook her head.

"Does he frighten you?"

"If he frightened me, I wouldn't want to open the door."

"Let's not forget the dream frightened you back in the beginning."

"That's when I thought the voice belonged to Sam."

"Maggie," Dr. Germaine said. "I still believe we're getting closer to what's troubling you, even though the dream has stopped."

"But I want it to come back. I want to open the door."

"As I've explained, you don't need the dream to help you get there. We can see what's behind the door together in the safety of our sessions. Wouldn't you rather have someone beside you as you take this journey?"

"I suppose…"

Dr. Germaine unfolded his hands and leaned back again, causing his leather chair to squeak under his weight. "Let's go a little while longer on the tranquilizers. If we don't see any noticeable progress during our sessions, then we'll take a different course. The most important thing right now is getting the proper amount of sleep."

***

On the way home, Maggie stopped at the market for some odds and ends, the dry cleaners for Sam's shirts, and the library for a new novel Susan had recommended. When she got home, she hung up the pressed shirts on the back of the kitchen door, tossed the book onto the table, preheated the oven, dumped eggs and milk and sugar into the mixing bowl, and set the mixer on high.

The billboard slogan bounced around in her head as she rotated the mixing bowl with one hand and used the other to scrape the rubber spatula against the inside: "If you can use an electric mixer in your kitchen, you can learn to run a drill press!"

Once the bunt cake was in the oven and the mixing utensils cleaned and put away, she pulled out the small calendar in the drawer by the telephone and placed it on the counter. She flipped to the previous month and stared a moment at the red circle around the date: December 3rd. Next, she counted days with the point of a pen until she landed on December 31st, even though she could have done it in her head. She did this twice, just to be sure. She then placed a finger tip against the current date's square: January 20th.

As she sat in her warm kitchen waiting for the cake to rise, she picked up the library book and read the title: *The Goddess and the Moon*. The kind of story she enjoyed most, being thrown into other worlds with their legends and magical lives. But she read the first page twice, unable to concentrate, the numbers from the calendar storming through her mind.

Not just a little late, those numbers warned. *Three weeks late*. For the very first time, ever.

Chapter Twelve

Maggie's gynecologist, the same man who had been her mother's doctor, though much older than when her mother had gone to see him, took blood and urine and told her to go home and relax, not to lift anything heavy, and to eat extra vegetables and drink plenty of orange juice. If Margaret Lerner was pregnant, she would have to prepare for it. Eat right. Sleep well. Share the news with her girlfriends.

Tell Sam.

But not until she had to.

Mother to be. With child. In a delicate way.

She would have to learn to express her condition with dignity, excitement, pride. She'd have to beam in public; cast the rosy glow of an expectant mother; enjoy the weight on her hips and thighs. Baby pamphlets, baby magazines, and baby books would be stacked high on her bedside table. For the next eight months, there would be shopping for blankets and booties in the infant's department at Sears, receiving baby gifts, gabbing with girlfriends and the older ladies at church about the joys of incubating a miracle.

An unsuspecting Sam left for work that morning, kissed his sleepy wife on the forehead, and backed the coupe down the slushy driveway.

Maggie went into the bathroom and opened her makeup bag. First a little powder to cover her freckles, some brown mascara to give her light lashes a lift, and a pale rosy lipstick. She changed out of her nightgown and pulled a brassiere and panties from her top drawer. As she stood in the bathroom hooking her bra, she noticed something on the tile, just inside her left foot. She stepped back and peered at the speck, stooped to touch it, then held up her red finger for closer inspection.

Blood.

She pulled some toilet paper from the roll and dabbed between her legs.

More blood.

Sitting on the toilet, Maggie watched as a stream of crimson poured into the bowl, and followed it as the dark cherry dissolved in the water like food coloring. She grabbed a belt from the vanity drawer, clipped a sanitary napkin into her underwear, and got dressed.

She telephoned her gynecologist.

"Mrs. Lerner," he said. "I was just getting ready to call you."

"I think I miscarried. I don't have cramps, but the blood is heavy."

The sound of ruffled papers came through the line. "You're not miscarrying," her doctor said. "You were late."

"Three weeks?"

"Sometimes stress or an abrupt change can alter a woman's cycle."

"I wasn't pregnant?"

"Not this time. But there's still plenty of time. If this news upsets you, you can make an appointment to come in and talk—"

"No," Maggie said, smiling. "Thank you, though."

"You're sure?"

"Yes. I am."

"Very well," he said. "There is something I'd like to suggest."

Maggie waited.

"Sam should get a physical."

Maggie silently laughed at this. Her husband, a leading surgeon at one of the finest hospitals in the country, having his blood pressure checked, bending over for the icy thermometer, opening his mouth to say, "Ah."

"Why would Sam need a physical?" Maggie asked.

"Because your tests came back normal. There's no reason why you shouldn't conceive. You're a healthy woman in her prime."

"You think Sam is the reason—"

"I see many cases where it isn't the woman who is having difficulty. Sometimes it's low sperm count, sometimes the sperm are just too lazy to do the job. Whatever the reason, I do think Sam should be tested."

It had never for one moment crossed Maggie's mind that Sam could be the reason. How would she tell him? And how would he react?

Then the question came to her that crushed the others: Would she tell him at all?

She thanked her doctor and hung up the phone, then doubled over with an odd sort of happiness as a wave of familiar cramps surged through her gut.

***

"What are you talking about?" Sam asked his wife over dinner that night, a dollop of spaghetti sauce fringing the edge of his moustache.

"I…I thought there was the slightest chance I could be pregnant. But I'm not."

"When were you planning to share this with me? After the baby started crawling?"

"There's no need for sarcasm, Sam. I would have told you the second I knew anything. That's what I'm doing now. Telling you. I didn't want to say anything until I knew for sure, one way or the other." She added, suddenly, as an afterthought, "If I had been pregnant, I thought it should be a romantic moment. You know, with our song playing in the background, and your favorite beer on the table next to your favorite meal."

"Why aren't we getting pregnant?" Sam said. "Did your doctor tell you what could be wrong? Did he run tests to see why you aren't conceiving? You're not ill, are you?"

"Everything is fine. I'm as healthy as ever."

"I just don't understand," he said, sipping from his glass of milk and wiping a napkin across his mouth.

He seemed so desperate, the way his eyes stared at his half-eaten dinner, his hands clutching the round corners of his plate.

She would have to be delicate.

"Sam," Maggie said. "You're a doctor. I'm sure that what my gynecologist explained to me you will understand better than I…"

"What did he tell you?"

"Something about…oh, I'm not exactly sure how he said it. But he recommended that you get tested, too."

"For what?"

"Sperm count, or something like that. He can discuss it with you in medical terms."

"Your doctor informs you that you aren't pregnant, then in the same conversation puts the blame on me?"

"No one's blaming you, Sam, least of all me. He just wanted to let us know that there are ways to treat you—if treatment is needed—to help you. Us, I mean."

"I see."

Maggie wasn't sure what Sam did or did not see. He wound his dinner napkin around his hand like a tourniquet.

"I'll see my urologist next week," he said quietly.

"You will?"

"If it is me, then I'll just have to deal with it. I'm not above getting tested. Especially if it helps us start a family."

***

The urologist's words lingered in Maggie's ears like the echo of a bittersweet melody long after the radio has been turned off: *too low…*

They sat in leather chairs, facing the urologist's desk. The man was young but considered one of the best in his field.

"What now?" Sam asked.

"Well," the urologist said. "I suggest a balanced diet and exercise. Eat extra greens. Stay away from booze and cigarettes. Play eighteen holes once the weather allows."

"This is ludicrous. I already do those things." He stared at the urologist as though one magical word would align his spiraling universe.

"I'm sorry, Sam. We're relatively limited on both data and resources regarding male sterility."

"I am not sterile."

Maggie touched Sam's arm but he jerked it away.

"I'm sorry," the doctor said again. "I didn't mean to sound insincere."

"What's next?" Maggie asked.

"Go back to your lives. Keep trying. After all, in this line of work, miracles happen every day."

Chapter Thirteen

Maggie pretended her life was normal. Pretended that her marriage moved along as always. Acted as though she didn't feel relief at not having to deal with Sam's daily inquisition regarding her menstrual cycle, a part of her that until lately had been personal and sacred. She was also sickened by her own genuine lack of caring; at her inability to allow childlessness to turn her life upside down like it did Sam's.

Instead of coming home at six, Sam began arriving after eight-thirty, just in time to eat alone at the kitchen table, his meatloaf or tuna casserole warming in a Pyrex dish in the oven, his glass of milk chilling in the refrigerator. After dinner, he listened to *The Adventures of Ozzie and Harriet* or *Ellery Queen* on the radio. He worked in the ER on Saturdays and spent Sundays after church washing and waxing his car if the weather permitted. Each night, after secretly taking a tranquilizer, Maggie waited for him in bed with the end table light on, reading one of her novels. He'd undress in the bathroom, slip between the covers, and kiss her goodnight on the cheek before rolling onto his side. Maggie would fall asleep soon after her husband, her mind prepared for the dream to return.

But it did not.

Maybe the man behind the door had represented Sam after all. Their voices were somewhat the same, and without seeing his face, how could she be sure?

But Maggie was sure. She was positive that if she passed those mysterious sandaled feet on the beach or boardwalk, she would immediately recognize them as belonging to the stranger in her dream, and not her husband.

Nighttime wasn't the only time Maggie invited the dream. Twice a week for more than a month, she tried to bring it back during her sessions, closing her eyes, relaxing completely, like Dr. Germaine had taught her. But it was no use. No matter how hard she worked to locate the door, to smell the citrus, to see those perfect toes, reining in the dream was futile.

"Perhaps you have discovered a solution to the problem lying within you," Dr. Germaine explained. "We often gain answers to our deepest questions when we least expect it."

Constantly thinking about Sam's inability to get her pregnant made it impossible for her to concentrate.

She opened her eyes to find Dr. Germaine intently looking at her.

"Something you would like to share?"

"No."

"Maggie." He sounded disappointed. The way a father might sound at the discovery of his teenaged daughter's lost virginity.

"Well," she said, "there is something…"

Dr. Germaine folded his hands and waited.

"There won't be any babies," she said at last, relieved to have finally told him.

"This is something you have both agreed upon?"

Maggie explained the situation in detail.

"I see," Dr. Germaine said. "I'm sorry."

Maggie did not respond.

"You, however, are utterly relieved."

Still, she said nothing.

"It's obvious that a weight has been lifted from your shoulders, do you not agree?"

She shrugged.

"I find this coincidental," Dr. Germaine said.

"What?"

"Let's take a closer look at what's happened: You find out that your husband can't give you children. This causes you relief, which in turn—"

Maggie started to speak but Dr. Germaine put up his hand to stop her.

"Please, let me continue. You are relieved that you won't be burdened by what society dictates you should do. Instead, your life will move along swimmingly, the fear and frustration of bearing children taken away. That's the first part. The second part is your dream. Which has stopped."

"But I didn't want it to stop."

"Evidently, you did. If you wanted the dream to move forward, or to become self-explanatory, it would have done so. There is no reason now for the dream to continue. Maybe it had to do with you not wanting children."

"Your theory is wrong," Maggie blurted. Then, "I'm sorry. That was rude."

"Not at all. Only you know the truth. I merely offer suggestions to get you thinking. Your beliefs are much more important than my speculations."

"I don't think one has anything to do with the other," she said. "The tranquilizers are preventing the dream from coming back. Maybe the ones I got from work weren't the same ones after all."

"That's possible. But don't you think it's ironic that your mysterious dream ended as soon as you found a solution to your problem?"

"It wasn't my fault that Sam—"

"Of course not. I just meant I find it interesting that you've harbored your secret of not wanting children throughout your entire marriage. Then the dream began. Even after Sam came home, the dream continued. It wasn't until you discovered that children would no longer be an issue that the dream stopped."

"No," Maggie said, after analyzing the suggestion. "And I'll tell you why."

Dr. Germaine allowed his patient to collect her thoughts.

She sat up a little straighter to show her confidence regarding her theory. "The dream stopped *before* I found out that Sam was infertile. Weeks before."

"Often times, dreams border on the intuitive," Dr. Germaine said. "It's more likely the dream disappeared because *you* had already come to the conclusion that you weren't getting pregnant. *You* had already made up your mind. The fact that Sam is infertile is a fluke."

"But I still feel the desire to have the dream." It was more of a thirst, really, like yearning for a glass of water while hiking in the desert. "Why would I continue to have this desire if my so-called problem has found a solution?"

"Before we answer that question, let's look at the reasons as to why you don't want children."

"I've asked myself that question for a long time," Maggie said. "I don't know why."

"We all know why we make the decisions we do. Sometimes we just don't want to see the answers."

Maggie said nothing.

"Do you fear you wouldn't be a good mother?" he asked.

"I like children enough, enjoy hearing them laugh, enjoy seeing them play in the park on a Sunday afternoon. I just don't want any of my own."

"Is it because of something in your childhood? An overbearing mother, perhaps?"

"My mother was a saint," Maggie said. "After Father left, she became two parents rolled into one. And she never complained. Never once showed shame that she was destined to grow old alone."

"And your father?"

"As I've told you, he left when I was very small. I don't know anything about him, except that he enjoyed most of his amusements outside the home."

"He was unfaithful?"

"Yes."

"Your mother shared this with you?"

"Not in so many words."

"Have you ever seen a photograph of him?"

Maggie shook her head. "My mother either threw them out or hid them. Or maybe she never had any to begin with. When I cleaned out her home after her passing, I found nothing regarding my father. It's as if he never existed."

"And your sister?"

"Caroline."

"She's younger than you, is that right?"

"By two years."

"Does she remember him?" Dr. Germaine asked.

"Probably not, since she was just an infant when he left…though I don't know for sure what she remembers. She and I don't talk but once a year."

"By choice?"

"We just don't have anything in common."

"Maggie, even though you don't consciously remember your father, is it possible that somewhere deep within you do remember him and miss this vague memory? That you may be experiencing a void in your life because of your father's absence?"

"I've never thought about it before."

"Is it possible that the man in your dream represents your father, or, rather what you imagine your father to be? The paternal relationship you were never able to realize? And now that your husband can't help you conceive, you no longer need your father's image—you no longer need the dream—because the issue of whether Sam will make a good father or not no longer matters."

"Sam would have made a wonderful father," Maggie told him, feeling the need to defend her dejected husband. "Having a family is all he cares about."

"I understand that. But we're not talking about Sam, are we? We're talking about you. About a dream where you are inches from encountering a male figure, with a door standing between you that you can't seem to open yourself."

"I don't understand."

"Is it possible this door represents the wall between you and the man who abandoned you? The dream started while Sam was away from home. He had deserted you."

"He was called to war."

"He deserted you *emotionally*. Like your father did so many years ago."

"But Sam is home now."

"Right. Sam came home. Time to start a family. Your father left when children came along. Your subconscious may want you to believe that Sam would leave, too. Now we have a new conflict. This conflict caused the dream to shift. The voice changed around the time that Sam came home?"

Maggie nodded.

"And the last time the dream came to you, you were able to see the feet of the man behind the door. For the first time ever. It may have only been a glimpse, but it was there all the same. Who's feet were they?"

Maggie hesitated. "My father's?"

"And now, since you've discovered you aren't destined to have children, the dream has no reason to continue. The fear of getting pregnant and the thought of your children being abandoned is eliminated. No more fear, no more conflict, no more dream."

"If the man in my dream represents my father, shouldn't I take the opportunity to speak to him?"

"What would you like to tell him?" Dr. Germaine asked.

Maggie had to be careful. She knew the man in her dream was not her father, the same way she knew it wasn't Sam.

"I would tell him I had a hole in my life because he left."

"You mentioned in an earlier session that you didn't miss him."

"Well," she said, tilting her head down slightly so he wouldn't see her swallow hard. "Maybe I could tell him how angry I am."

"You are angry with him?"

"Maybe. A little."

Maggie never did like lying, but lately it had become a part of her she couldn't control. She sucked on her bottom lip and squeezed her folded hands together. She tried hard not to appear desperate, but this was her last chance. She had only come to a therapist with the hope that he would help her get to the crux of her dream, not celebrate its departure.

She moved forward, the craving taking over.

"Is it possible for you to give me something else?" Maggie asked. "Something like what I'm taking now but without the foggy memory afterwards. Something that will get the dream to come back. Then we can see for sure if this man is my father."

"How can you be positive your dream hasn't left for good, with or without help?"

"Maybe it has. But at least let me find out for sure."

"The pills you have taken are the most effective in the industry, especially regarding sleep."

"There must be something else," Maggie said. "They're always coming out with something new and better, aren't they? Isn't that what those large companies do? Come up with better pills?"

Dr. Germaine paused a moment. When he spoke, the degree of his voice lowered to half its normal volume. "There is something…it's about to change the Australian psychiatric field…"

Maggie's heart fluttered. "Yes?"

"But it hasn't been used in enough trials in Australia or here in the States to prove its effectiveness—"

"I'd like to try," Maggie said. "I could be—like part of an experiment."

"There may be side effects."

"Like what?"

"Sleepiness, sleeplessness—"

"I already have those."

"A few studies reported episodic psychosis, delusions—"

"You can hover over me like a G-man."

"We'd have to keep a watchful eye on your blood pressure, your thyroid—"

"Needles don't bother me."

"Maggie, the only information I have is from charts, graphs, vague statistics."

"Please, Dr. Germaine. I need to understand why the dream came to me in the first place. Let me try. If it doesn't come back, then so be it. I will dump the pills forever and move on with my merry life."

Oh, but it will come back, she thought to herself as her heart pulsated within her slender frame.

Dr. Germaine regarded Maggie a moment. He let out a small sigh, one that an average person walking by wouldn't have noticed.

But Maggie noticed. Her stomach rumbled with excitement as she watched her doctor scribble on a piece of paper.

"Let us treat this as an experiment, as you said," Dr. Germaine told her. Then his voice grew stern. "You will not go to the drugstore. Hand this to my secretary on your way out and come back tomorrow. She will have it ready for you. Any side effects—dizziness, hypersensitivity, anything out of the ordinary—you contact me immediately. Do you understand?"

Maggie nodded as she got up from the couch and controlled her shaking hand as she reached for the slip of paper.

She chose to take the stairs instead of the elevator down to the lobby, anticipation seeping through her pores as her low heels echoed through the stairwell. Once outside, she held her palms up toward the sky as the first pre-spring raindrops tickled her hands. She remained in that position a moment, ignoring the umbrella hooked over her arm, then nearly skipped across the street to catch a cab home.

Chapter Fourteen

Maggie had already gone to bed by the time Sam got home. She could have waited up for him—she had done so in the beginning, when they'd first found out about Sam's problem. But not anymore. The night after her last conversation with Dr. Germaine, Maggie told Sam she wanted extra beauty sleep, then headed upstairs before nine o'clock while Sam ate a late dinner and listened to the radio. She slipped into her nightgown, tapped the first new pill into her hand, swallowed the large tablet with a full glass of water, and crawled between the cool sheets.

The house was silent except for the scratch of the large oak's branches sliding its tips across the bedroom window, a sound which crawled into Maggie's subconscious as she instantly fell into twilight, and then a deep sleep.

Voices and images came and went.

Dr. Germaine, sitting at his desk: *The door represents a wall between you and the man who abandoned you...*

Sam, holding Maggie in his arms: *My little magpie...*

Her gynecologist, saying the words as though there had been a terrible accident: *I understand how you must be feeling...*

Sam's urologist, staring out his office window: *Miracles happen every day...*

And then another voice, one that prevailed over all the others; a voice that poured over her with a mixture of joy and apprehension: "Maggie?"

The door was there, only steps away! Maggie ran to it, the fog at her sides curving up and outward like land masses making way for a new volcano.

"Yes!" she shouted. "I'm here!"

"I knew you'd come."

Maggie placed the side of her head against the door. "Can you open it?" she asked.

"I cannot. But you can."

"No, I can't," Maggie told him. "I've tried before."

"Try again," the voice pleaded.

Maggie placed her palms on the door in front of her. The backs of her hands looked remarkably young as they slid along the surface. The wood was both warm and cool at the same time. She watched as her right hand attempted to travel toward the latch.

"I can't," she said.

"Yes, you can."

She slid her hand a little farther. Her thumb touched the flat top of the wrought iron handle.

"Do it," the voice whispered.

Maggie nodded as though the stranger on the other side of the door could see through it. Before she pressed her thumb on the latch, she knelt down on the ground and peeked under.

A pair of handsome feet in leather sandals stood there, waiting.

She stood up again. The latch grew warm under her fingers as they wrapped around the handle. Her thumb pressed down, and she heard the loud "click" as a hidden mechanism released.

"Quickly," the voice said. "Pull."

Maggie placed both her hands on the door handle. She pulled hard. Then harder. The door wouldn't budge.

"Open it," he said.

"I'm trying."

"Try harder."

Maggie planted her feet squarely on the ground, the tendons in her arms and back rigid as she yanked until her muscles ached. The door remained stuck in its frame.

"Why don't you push at the same time?" she asked, slightly irritated at having to do all the work herself. If he wanted the door opened so badly, shouldn't he at least show a little effort?

"I cannot help you," he told her. "You must do this part by yourself."

His words sounded like a therapist's.

"Why should I care if this door opens or not?" Maggie asked, dropping her throbbing hands to her sides. "This is only a dream."

"Dreams are the key to life," the man said, his voice as smooth as Crosby's or Sinatra's. "Dreams are what make the intangible tangible. Dreams give us hope."

She placed her hand back on the latch, suddenly unsure of what to do.

What if she did open it? What if the man behind it was her father, as her therapist had speculated? Would she hug him? Indulge in a regular father-daughter conversation as though they were relaxing on a park bench or taking a stroll beside the ocean?

"Who are you?" she asked.

There. That was simple enough. Why hadn't she done that before?

The voice didn't answer.

She stooped to the ground and again peered under to see if he'd had enough; if he had finally walked away.

But there he was, waiting.

Exhaustion pulled at her mind. She never knew before this moment that it was possible to grow weary in a dream. Being tired was for real life, shopping for groceries, following busy schedules, dealing with everyday trials. Sleep was supposed to help a person unwind; help let go of all the stresses of the day. But Maggie felt as though she'd been running up a steep hill, her legs weakening like a pair of overused rubber bands.

Maggie grabbed the handle to help her stand and leaned against the door. The latch rested between her fists as she once again wrapped her hands around the metal, her body prepared to deal with the weight of the door, her mind prepared to meet in person the man on the other side. It didn't matter how difficult opening the door would be. It's what she'd been waiting for; what she knew she was supposed to do. She thought of the milestones over the last year that had led her to this moment: Sam's extended absence during the war; the opportunity to work in a man's world for a time; the pressure of child-bearing removed from her life; and now, finally, coming face to face with the voice that beckoned.

Grunts navigated through her breath. With the last bit of energy she drew from the depths of her psyche, Maggie pulled hard enough to make the thin blue veins in the backs of her hands bulge beneath her peach-white skin. She bent her legs at the knees, her feet shoulder width apart, her head down.

The door budged. First one inch. Then two.

"That is the way," he told her.

She felt as though she were freeing herself as well as this stranger, as the door painstakingly crept another few inches.

"Isn't this exciting?" the voice said. "To open a door one has been trapped behind for so long?"

"Yes," Maggie grunted.

"To open a door that liberates," he said.

"Yes."

Another inch.

"To open a door that I have not been allowed—"

"MAGGIE!"

Maggie froze. It was Sam. Sam was in her dream!

How did he get in?

Her hands released the handle as she turned around, expecting to see her husband glaring at her through the fog. But there was no one.

"MAGGIE! WAKE UP!"

"No!" she shouted into the fog which now swirled around her, filling her mouth and leaving a film across her eyes. A sour taste entered her throat.

She again looked toward the door. It was closing. Maggie flung her hands out in front of her and grabbed onto the door handle.

"Do not let it close," the voice on the other side begged. "Please."

A man's sandal suddenly entered the space between the door and the frame.

"MAGGIE! WAKE UP!"

The massive door would smash the stranger's foot. Maggie tried to keep it from shutting, but it was no use. The man pulled his foot back just before the heavy wood slammed back in place, the hinges squealing out in pain, the door clicking loudly as the bolt moved back into position.

Maggie shut her eyes and began to cry. "No. Please. I don't want to…"

When she opened them again, her eyes darted around the lamp-lit bedroom, tears streaming down her cheeks and onto her pillow.

"Oh, Maggie."

Sam stood beside the bed in his robe, observing her without emotion, like a doctor examining a white spot on an x-ray.

Maggie sat up and wiped her eyes. She pushed her hair back from her sweaty forehead. "Why did you wake me?"

"I'm not supposed to stop you when you cry out in your sleep?" Sam said angrily. "I'm not supposed to do anything while you thrash about in our bed? You almost socked me a good one. For Chrissakes, Maggie."

She pulled the covers up to her chin as though a stranger were gawking at her.

"What is the matter with you?" he asked.

"I was dreaming."

Sam shook his head. "There's something wrong with you. It doesn't take a doctor to see that."

"There's nothing wrong—"

"It's midnight. I'm tired. I can't afford to lose sleep because something troubles you that can't be shared with your husband. I'm going downstairs."

He walked around to his side of the bed, grabbed his pillow, and closed the bedroom door behind him. Maggie listened as his footsteps descended the stairs before disappearing into the wall-to-wall carpet of the living room.

She turned off the light and waited for sleep to come. For two hours she changed positions, praying that the man's voice would again come to her, coax her, bring her back to where he stood waiting behind the door. Just after three o'clock, Maggie finally fell asleep. The dream she prayed for never came. It lingered just below the surface, like a hungry fish reaching for the lure, but never quite succeeding.

Chapter Fifteen

For forty-five minutes she sat on the flowered couch, staring at her unpolished nails, readjusting her hairpins from time to time, barely contributing to her doctor's idle chitchat.

"You seem drained," Dr. Germaine said. "We can stop the pills—"

"No," Maggie said, exhaustion buried beneath her angst. For the last few weeks, even though she was sometimes able to enter her dream, the voice had stopped calling to her. She would stand in front of the door for what seemed like hours, tapping a white knuckle against the wood, pulling on the handle, waiting for his voice, but to no avail. "I can handle being tired. It's not as if I have anything important to do during the day."

The sound of resentment in Maggie's voice permeated the room.

"Does this anxiety have anything to do with your dream?" Dr. Germaine asked.

Maggie said nothing. She suddenly felt repulsed by her doctor's obsession to snoop around inside her. To analyze her like she was a defendant under cross-examination in a courtroom. She had done nothing wrong; she merely wanted to be left alone. After all, it was *her* dream. She didn't have to share it with anyone, and she told him so.

"I see," he said. "Well, if you've had a bit of a breakthrough and you don't share it with me, who else will you share it with?"

She certainly couldn't share this with Sam. And she'd been avoiding Susan's phone calls for weeks, especially since sharing with her best friend Sam's inability to give her children. Maggie was hardly in the mood for Susan's relentless optimism or personal questions regarding the not yet filled baby's room upstairs.

"It doesn't always have to be about the dream," he continued. "You can talk about anything you want. Just relax and tell me whatever is on your mind."

The dream was the only thing on her mind, but she didn't want to share it with Dr. Germaine, she decided. Not right now. Just this once she needed something to call her own.

Maggie chose to turn to conversation toward her husband instead. "Sam has decided that sleeping with me is no longer an option."

"Is he still sleeping in the house?"

"On the sofa."

"Are you speaking to one another?"

"Only formalities. But I think that's because…"

Dr. Germaine waited.

"He's angry with me," she finally said.

"What about?"

"For not having children."

"It's no one's fault—"

"Sam needs to blame someone other than himself," Maggie said. "It may as well be me."

"Communication is very important at a time like this. Have you tried to explain how you feel?"

She hadn't. Avoiding Sam altogether made it easier for her to sleep. With him downstairs instead of next to her in bed, she didn't feel as guilty trying to get back to that other world.

"This isn't a good time for Sam and me to talk," she said.

"Why not?"

"He's getting ready for a conference in Chicago. As a guest speaker. He has a lot to prepare on top of work. The last thing he needs is to discuss what he knows can't be fixed. He's a man of diagnoses and cures. If Sam can't fix it, it's better left alone."

"How are things outside the marriage?"

"I don't have a life outside—" She cut herself off.

"Perhaps you need to rediscover it, Maggie."

"How?"

"You tell me."

"I've never thought of doing anything other than being Sam's wife. I wouldn't know where to begin."

"What about before Sam came along? What were you doing then?"

"I was enrolled at Goucher College. Some of my classmates became teachers or nurses. I had thought about becoming a school teacher…"

"That's a wonderful profession."

"But only because that's what some of my friends were doing."

"What were your other interests?" Dr. Germaine asked.

"I enjoyed playing tennis and volleyball. And I liked my math professor a lot. He said I had a great mind for numbers."

"You see, you do have outside interests. You aren't just Maggie-the-wife."

"I'm not?"

"Did you think you were?"

Of course she did.

"Sam would never talk to me about these things," Maggie said.

"Perhaps he feels threatened."

"By what?"

"By a woman with more on her plate than meets the eye. Many men are insecure about their wives making their way in the world independently. It makes them feel inferior. In most societies, men have an innate need to take care of the family structure. Today, men obtain much of their security by doing this financially."

"Oh."

"Have you had any more thoughts about working outside the home?"

"I've never thought about that."

"Never?"

"Only while Sam was in Italy," Maggie said. "But that was temporary. It's silly to think about doing that now. I'm not meant to work in a man's world. I'm much better suited as a doctor's wife."

"Why is that?"

"Because…I'm not sure."

"Maggie, the world is changing at a rapid pace. We've proved how strong our country is. We no longer believe the moon is made of cheese. There are medical advances which allow us to cure diseases like tuberculosis and certain cancers. We can now watch current news and family programs and comedy shows, spilling into our living rooms at the touch of a switch. Our cars are faster, our children are smarter, and the family dynamic is changing as rapidly as the world that guides us."

"But women are supposed to be—*women*."

"What does that mean to you?" he asked.

"I suppose it means raising children, keeping a clean house, making sure our men are well fed, taken care of, happy."

"And this socially accepted view of womanhood gives you satisfaction?"

Maggie shrugged.

"Maggie, we all have thoughts about what it would be like on the other side of the fence. Do not be ashamed that you have desires—ones that don't include your husband; that have to do with you, and you alone. Having desires doesn't mean you can't be a good wife or have a strong, healthy marriage."

"But I don't know what those desires are."

"Yes, you do."

"No," Maggie said, "I don't."

"Were you sad while Sam was in Italy?"

"I missed him immensely."

"Missing him is one thing. Were you sad?"

She shook her head.

"Why not?" Dr. Germaine asked.

"Because I was—I don't know how to say this without sounding awful and selfish."

"There is no such thing in this room. You can say anything you wish. I am not here to judge, only to guide."

"When Sam was away, I was—free."

"How so?"

"I could come and go as I pleased, take the bus into town without putting on my makeup and high heels. Have dinner in or out, early or late. I had a purpose."

"Ah. A purpose. And what was that purpose?"

"Running a press at the plant. Heading up a can drive."

"Did these things fulfill you?"

"Yes."

"The same way your marriage fulfills you?"

Maggie glanced at her watch. "I think my hour is up."

"Don't worry about the time," he said. "Please answer my last question."

"I can't."

"Of course you can."

"No," she said, her voice lowering to a whisper. "I can't."

"Very well. Let us end for now." Dr. Germaine turned off the recorder. He stood up and walked to the couch. "We will get to this again. Perhaps not right away, but sometime." He helped her up from the couch. "Try to get some rest this weekend. *Real* rest. Be sure to take your pill at the same time each night to offer the best benefit."

"I will."

"And start communicating with your husband. It takes two."

"I will," she said again.

But she knew she was just saying the words to placate her doctor. Sam was preoccupied with his upcoming conference, a blessing in disguise. Beginning Sunday, Maggie would have the house and bed to herself. She could thrash about all she wanted, kick the covers to the floor, lash out in her sleep without anyone getting in her way.

God willing, she may even get the man behind the door to call her name again.

Chapter Sixteen

Maggie looked forward to Sunday night like a first date after Sam left for Chicago, his lips barely brushing against his wife's forehead before getting into the waiting cab. She took a long hot bath, dabbed Chanel No.5 onto her wrists and slipped into her favorite spring-time nightgown. At seven-thirty, she downed a pill with a large glass of water. A little earlier than usual, but that didn't matter. The only thing that mattered was that she was free to do as she wished. Free to dream whatever she pleased; make her way to that other world; remain there as long as she liked. By eight o'clock, Maggie lay in bed with the lights out, a mask covering her eyes, the bedcovers tucked comfortably around her. There was something liberating about Sam's absence, about knowing he wasn't there to interrupt her, judge her, scold her. Within seconds she was sleeping soundly. Within minutes, the dream was hers, as tangible as the vanilla batter on a mixing spoon, as real as the freckles on her face.

The fog reeled her in and carried her like a pod of dolphins piloting a diver to their mysterious part of the sea. The door was before her without having to wish it. Her hands reached out without having to force them. She moved automatically, intuitively, the same way a robin digs for the earthworm just before a rain, or a butterfly settles on the rose instead of the thorn.

She listened but heard nothing. Her toes wiggled about beneath the straps of her sandals. She bent down and touched the soft, smooth leather straps, stood up again and stretched her arms outward, splaying her fingers in front of her. Her nails were clean and short, the freckles which had once been strewn across her arms and hands like a map of stars faded into specks of watered down cinnamon, the tiny dots barely noticeable. Her right palm rubbed against the back of her left hand, feeling the smoothness of her skin, the bones within the knuckles—and then stopped. The ring finger on her left hand was bare, a band of smooth white skin in place of the half-carat diamond set in white gold. She stared at the unadorned finger with confused wonderment and looked to the ground in an artificial attempt to find it, knowing that the ring was not lost; it was never meant to be a part of this world.

As if the dream knew that Maggie was truly on her own without disruption, the voice whispered to her from behind the door.

"Maggie?"

"I'm here," she responded with eagerness, pressing her hands and forehead against the door. The tangy scent of lemons swirled around her.

"Is he with you?" the voice asked, a hint of fear beneath the words.

"Who?"

"Sam."

Had she mentioned Sam's name before?

She quickly reminded herself that this was a dream; she made up the questions, and she controlled the answers. The voice asking her about Sam could very well be an element of her subconscious mind and nothing more.

"Is he?" he asked again.

"No. Is that why you stopped calling me? Because of Sam?"

Her question did not receive an answer. Instead, he said, "Open the door."

There was no pressure this time. No one would stop her from moving the dream forward; no one would interrupt her the moment she began to shout out in her sleep. There was no one but Maggie deciding what to do or when to do it.

The power she held was quite satisfying.

Maggie smiled as her graceful hands slid down the wooden grooves to the lever and wrapped around the handle. Her thumbs, side by side, pressed firmly against the latch, her legs bent at the knees to prepare for the burden.

As soon as she did all of these things, Maggie knew this wasn't like the last time. This time would be tremendously easy, just as it had been easy to return to the dream. The clasp within the handle released, and the door seemed to exhale with relief as it swung outward.

Maggie stepped back.

The man did the same.

For a moment neither said a word. His remarkable blue eyes met with hers as they took each other in.

He was a thing of beauty, a flawless creature that only a dream could create. Shimmering blond locks fell across his head to his shoulders in waves of perfectly spiraled curls. His face was smooth and hairless like it had been chiseled from marble. His nose began between his eyebrows and descended steeply in a straight line to just above his full upper lip. He stood before her like a Michelangelo or Rodin sculpture; a monument of a Greek or Roman god come to life.

The man let out a small laugh. He stepped through the doorway and held his lean athletic arms out to his sides. He then turned gracefully in a circle, his short white dress showing off a pair of beefy thighs and calves.

"You look like me," he said.

"I do?"

Was Dr. Germaine's theory correct? Could this man be Maggie's father?

"I do not mean like *me*," he told her. "I mean our clothing."

For the first time, Maggie noticed what she wore besides a pair of sandals. Her body was barely covered by the same daringly short tunic, only hers had a fabric sash belt around the middle and his a leather one. Her sleeves were gathered with gold braided thread at the shoulders, exposing a pair of long shapely arms. Facing one another, they could have easily been mistaken for actors in an early Greek play. She reached her hands to her head.

The man laughed again.

"No ivy," he said.

Maggie smiled as she dropped her arms to her sides.

"Thank you for opening the door," he told her. "That was a difficult task for me."

"Difficult how?"

"You are the most beautiful woman I have ever seen."

Maggie had no idea how to respond to this stunning creature, who most definitely was not her father, who was nothing remotely like Sam, who represented a part of her mind she had no idea existed until now.

He took an enthusiastic step forward.

Maggie warily took a step back.

"Do not be afraid," he told her. "I only want to touch your hand."

He leaned forward, took a hold of the thin fingers on Maggie's right hand, and brought them to his lips. "Beautiful," he whispered.

She dropped her hand back to her side. "Who are you?"

"I am who I am."

"What shall I call you?"

"Names are not needed here."

"You called me by my first name."

"Then call me…how does John sound? That is a simple name; as easy to pronounce as it is to remember, yes? John. *John.* Yes, I like that."

"Why am I here?"

John's grin grew wider. His teeth were straight and brilliant.

"Is there somewhere else you would rather be?" he asked.

"No," she said, telling the truth.

"Of course there is not." He glanced toward the doorway. "Let us get away from here so we may talk in private," he said, his voice dropping to a whisper.

"You're not alone?"

He didn't answer as he pushed the door until it slipped back into its frame, and the latch locked it in place.

"How will we open it again?" she asked.

"You did it once. I am sure you can do it again."

They moved away from the door and into the rolling fog, Maggie's temptation to look back squelched beneath her yearning to see what lay ahead.

"It feels so good, so right, to finally be outside," he said as they floated together.

"Who are you? Why am I here?"

"There are a lot of things you do not yet understand. I cannot tell you everything at once. Let us take our time."

Maggie glided with him along a path that was just becoming visible through the fog.

"Where are we going?" she asked.

"You tell me."

As soon as he said the words, Maggie spotted a clearing. A cluster of thick lively oak trees bordered a meadow, filled to the brim with clover and jonquils and daisies. A path through the center led to a gazebo a few yards in the distance.

"I knew you would take me someplace amazing," he said.

Maggie thought it was the other way around.

"This is *yours*." He spread his arms wide. "*All of this*."

They walked to the gazebo and up the steps as if they had done so a million times before. From the center of the porch they gazed around them. Straight ahead, the swaying flowers continued into the distance until the shades of their petals blurred together. A bright beam of sunlight spilled across the field, but even though Maggie looked directly at the sun, it didn't make her squint. In the distance, barely visible through the fog, stood the large fortress, two long narrow windows she had not noticed before peering out of a high tower through the clouds. She could barely make out the outline of the wooden door beneath.

"Is that where you live?" she nodded toward the castle.

"So I am told."

"What do you mean—"

"Look over there!" John shouted cheerily. "How wonderful that you would give us a rainbow!"

Sure enough, there stretched before them a marvelous rainbow, filled with vibrant hues of yellows and reds and blues, magically suspended over the field.

"You are quite creative," he told her.

Maggie glanced at John as he stared up at the sky, his eyes sparkling, his head tilted slightly upward, like a young boy experiencing his first set of fireworks. The light blond curls wound in ringlets on his head like a doll's, falling along the back of his neck and extending past his shoulders. His skin was a perfectly seamless landscape for his stately jaw line and high cheekbones. No five o'clock shadow. No moles. No freckles. It seemed he was without pores of any kind. His physique was neither too muscular nor too skinny. He was more handsome than Gary Cooper and Gregory Peck put together. More handsome than anything she could have imagined.

He seemed to be designed from the best parts of different men.

Perhaps he is your father and Sam rolled into one, her inner psyche offered.

This man looked nothing like Sam, but since she never knew her father, it was possible her imagination had taken the liberty of convincing her that they resembled one another. Of course, in real life, her father would be much older now, if he was even still alive. John appeared to be Maggie's age, though his skin seemed so youthful it was possible he was even younger.

Dozens of questions flooded Maggie's mind. She sifted through them quickly, hoping to reach for the most important ones first should she suddenly roll over in her sleep, spilling her dream into nothingness, or awaken to the sounds of early morning commuters warming up their engines before heading off to work.

"You can stay as long as you like," John told her as she sorted through her queries.

"I don't even know where I am."

"Where you are does not matter. This place is simply where

you are right now. And where I am right now. The rest is easy."

"The rest of what?" Maggie asked.

"Life in here."

"Are you saying that you're alive?"

"Of course."

"You're only part of my—"

"World?"

"Part of my imagination," Maggie explained.

"You do not think the imagination is a world unto itself?"

"Is it?"

"What do you believe?"

"I don't know what to believe," Maggie said. "Here I am, standing in the middle of a gazebo—"

"You chose this place."

"Wearing a tunic—"

"Your interpretation."

"And speaking to a man stuck behind a door he can't find a way to open himself."

"Of course I cannot open it," he said. "It is not my world."

"Where is your world?"

John said nothing as he looked toward the castle, his smile as far away as Maggie's other life.

"Can I come there?" Maggie asked. "To your world?"

"No," he said firmly, his eyes leaving the castle and moving back to meet hers. He reached for Maggie's hand. "Sit down with me," he said, pulling her to the step. "We have much to discover."

Maggie sat beside him, her hip pressed against his. A warm breeze drifted across her face and arms, entered her body, and tucked itself cozily beneath her skin.

"Ask me anything you like," John said. "I'll do my best to make you feel at home."

She looked out over the field of flowers, her eyes following their synchronized movement. "How long have you been here?" she finally asked.

"I do not know. There is no time here, so I have no need for keeping track of it."

"Why is it that you can come to my world, but I can't come to yours?"

"I only know that is the way it is. No one has ever opened the door before you."

"I'm the first?"

John's eyes drifted toward the meadow. "You make beautiful flowers. I do not have these where I come from."

"I made these?" Maggie asked.

"Of course you did."

"Did I make up the sunbeam?"

"Yes."

"And the breeze?"

"Yes."

"And you?"

John was silent.

"John?"

"You are in control out here. You can have anything your heart desires."

"How is that possible?"

John shrugged his shoulders. "I only know it is so."

"What about you?" Maggie asked.

"What about me?"

"Can you make up anything your heart desires?"

"Of course not," John said.

"Why not?"

"Because this is not my dream."

A dream, Maggie remembered with a sudden fill of despair. At any moment it could end. At any moment she could be forced back into the real world. And there was always the chance she wouldn't find her way back here again. It pained her to think this could be her last time. Anytime could be her last.

"If this is my dream," she continued, "why can't I come into your world if I choose to?"

"It is not allowed."

"Says who?"

"Maggie," John said, "you have control over what goes on out here. Not in there." His face turned abruptly forsaken as he glanced toward the tower in the distance.

"Did I…" Maggie began. "Did I create the door?"

"I am afraid not."

"Did you?"

"No."

"Then who—"

John jumped up and grabbed Maggie firmly by the arms. "Did you hear that?"

"Hear what?" She stumbled as she stood beside him. "I didn't hear anything."

"I must go!" he shouted before jumping down the steps two at a time.

"John?"

A thunderous roar filled the space, a near-deafening echo, like the growl of a giant tiger trapped in an endless cave.

"I must go!" he cried again, charging up the path as if a dog were biting at his heels. In a panic, Maggie moved to the porch and pressed her body as close to a wooden pillar as possible. No predator followed John, but Maggie's shaking knees told her that something hungry lay in wait nearby.

Soon, John disappeared into a speck, a tiny fish swallowed up by an infinite ocean of fog.

His voice suddenly leaped across the tops of the flowers. "Open the door! Hurry!"

From here?

"Do it!"

She couldn't see the door clearly but knew she could do as he asked just by concentrating. Within seconds, the sound of wood slamming against wood resonated up the path, and was soon replaced by other sounds which bounced against the gazebo's roof.

As the milkman's happy whistle seeped from one world into the next, as Maggie tried to force her eyes to stay shut against the morning sun, an angry cry followed right behind her, bellowing in her ears. Before she was able to decipher the cry, or understand to which world it belonged, her dreamscape vanished from sight, all sounds replaced by the earthly commotion of honking horns, glass bottles clanking against one another as they dropped into milk cans, and energetic school children as they headed to the bus stop on the corner.

Chapter Seventeen

"Stop worrying, Suze," Maggie told her best friend. "I'm fine. Really."

She wrapped the phone cord around a finger as she paced through her kitchen. She flinched at the distorted reflection staring back at her from the toaster, with its dark circles under the eyes and unkempt hair. She tightened the belt of her robe around her waist as she held onto the phone with her chin.

"What about the melancholy?" Susan asked.

"I'm better now."

Maggie opened the refrigerator and closed it again. She turned on the water from the tap, placed the tea kettle underneath the stream of water, and placed it on the stove to boil.

"I'm glad you're better," Susan said, "since it's easier to say what I have to say, and I've wanted to tell you for weeks, but with you having melancholy and all, and the news about Sam not being able to...well...you know..."

Maggie waited for Susan to spit it out.

"I'm going to be a mommy."

"Oh. That's wonderful, Suze."

But Maggie had barely heard Susan's words or her own as she sat hard on a kitchen chair. She could think of nothing but John.

Young beautiful John in his short white tunic, his perfectly sculpted body, his radiant eyes, his soft yellow curls, his unassuming—

"Maggie, you there?" Suze asked.

"What? Yes. Of course."

"The least you could do is show some excitement over what I just asked you."

"I'm sorry, what did you ask?"

"I want you two to be little Joe's or little Gwendolyn's Godparents. I've already talked it over with Charlie, and he agreed wholeheartedly; you know how much he respects Sam, being a doctor and all."

Sam.

Strange how Maggie hadn't thought about him once since he'd left.

"Of course," Maggie said. "I'll tell him the good news the moment—" Where was he? "Chicago. When he gets home from Chicago."

The tea kettle began to whistle. Maggie sat where she was, staring at the pattern of daisies on her tablecloth, picturing her dream-field of flowers.

"Is that the kettle?" Susan asked.

"Yes."

Maggie pushed herself from the chair, took the copper kettle off the burner, placed it on a trivet in the middle of the stove, and turned the burner off.

"You don't sound at all like yourself," Susan said. "You're sad with Sam away, aren't you?"

"Yes," Maggie lied.

"Oh, honey. Why don't you come over for dinner tonight? It won't take but a sec to add a little more to my beef stew."

"No, that's all right," Maggie said. "I'm fine, really. With Sam away, I have lots of time to get things done around here."

She glanced around at her spotless kitchen, wondering what on earth she meant by that.

"Well, if you're sure," Susan said.

"I am."

"Okay, then. You call me as soon as you find yourself with nothing to do. What on earth would I do with Charlie away? Go absolutely insane, I can tell you that. I wouldn't know where to begin not having someone to take care of. After all, it's a wife's job to take care of her home, and a mother's job—oh, holy mackerel! I'm going to be a mommy!"

Maggie waited through another minute of giggly chatter about the wonders of motherhood. When Susan finally ran out of air, Maggie interjected, "I should go. Have to get to all those things on my list."

"Oh, sure. I know what you mean. A woman's work is never done, as they say."

Maggie mumbled, "Congratulations" one more time before hanging up the phone.

She made a cup of tea and started to pull a loaf of bread from the bread box, then realized she had no appetite. She rooted through the refrigerator for a lemon, pulled one from the crisper, and cut it into wedges. She held a wedge to her nose and pressed her lips against the pulp. She could barely taste it. She sucked harder, hoping to intensify the flavor by squeezing the juice directly into her mouth. But it was no use. She may as well have been sucking on a piece of cardboard.

Didn't they get their lemons directly from Florida? For God's sake, how hard was it to produce a decent lemon?

She threw the wedges into the trash, dumped her un-steeped

tea down the drain, and left the kitchen with a longing for something much more gratifying than food.

***

Maggie made herself comfortable on the couch as Dr. Germaine took his place behind his desk.

"You look tired," he said, cocking his head a little as if to imprint in his memory the circles under her eyes, the droop of her mouth.

She placed her pocketbook beside her and fanned out her skirt as always. If she acted normally during the session, there was no reason for him to suspect that anything was other than normal.

"I'm just having a bit of an adjustment period with Sam away. It's a big bed without him."

"I thought you both had taken to sleeping in separate quarters," Dr. Germaine said.

"Oh. What I mean is, the *house* is so much bigger with him away. All those little squeaks and bumps in the night…"

"And the dream?"

She nestled into the corner of the couch and tucked a small pillow behind her lower back. "Yes," she said.

Dr. Germaine clicked on the recorder.

"The dream came right away last night." She had rehearsed her lines in front of the bathroom mirror that morning. "I was asleep less than an hour, I believe. I wandered through the fog for a while, not seeing much of anything—just wandering. Then I saw the door."

"Did it look the same?"

"Yes. Large and wooden. Only this time, I was able to open it."

"That's wonderful, Maggie. Go on."

"Well," Maggie said, "it had never occurred to me until last night that all I had to do was ask the person behind the door to open it."

"If I remember correctly, you had asked the man to open it, but he was unable to do so. I can pull the transcript just to be sure—"

"That's not necessary. What I mean is, I asked him to open it, and he said, 'I can't open it alone. We have to do it *together.*'"

Maggie waited for Dr. Germaine to respond to her latest revelation, but he did not.

She went on, the palms of her hands perspiring as she tried hard to keep her voice steady. "I told him that would be fine. That I wanted to see him."

For a moment Maggie saw John standing before her, his arms out at his sides, his baby blues lit up like a child's on Christmas morning. She forced the thought away.

"Are you all right?" Dr. Germaine asked.

"Yes. Fine. So, next thing I know my hand is on the latch, and it opens more easily than I could have imagined, of course because he helped me. And there he is, standing right in front of me. Even in my dream a little voice in the back of my head kept saying, 'Dr. Germaine was right.'"

"Your father?"

Maggie caught the flicker of satisfaction in her therapist's eyes.

"Yes," she went on. "He looked a lot like me, that's how I knew who it was. Then he spoke to me. He said, 'I'm your father,' just like that."

"How did you respond?"

"I hugged him. Then I told him that he shouldn't have

abandoned Mother and me and my little sister, and I couldn't believe what he said next."

Without a word, Dr. Germaine waited.

"He told me he was sorry for leaving, but he hadn't been happy. He never wanted children, never wanted a family to take care of. How about that? Seems we have a lot in common."

"What happened next?"

"I told him I forgave him, that I understood exactly how he felt, and that anybody could tell I was his daughter. Not only do we think the same way, but he has the same red hair as me. I think he's Irish. Anyway, that was pretty much it, at least what I can remember. He stepped back across the threshold and told me to visit anytime."

"How do you feel about that?"

"I feel like a weight has been lifted from my shoulders. I'm happier today than I've been in months. Maybe even years."

"That's wonderful, Maggie."

"Yes. I no longer feel threatened by what's behind the door. And you were right from the beginning. My fear of abandonment was the problem all along."

"And that's all?"

"You mean the dream? Yes, that's all."

"Not the dream. Your fears. Do you believe we've reached the crux of what has been causing your depression?"

How Maggie had begun to hate that word. She wasn't depressed about anything at the moment other than being taken away from her perfect world for the last few hours.

"I don't feel depressed at all. As a matter of fact, I feel quite chipper."

"Then we can stop the pills."

"What?   Why?"

"We only had you taking them to get to the reason for your dream, remember? Now that the mystery is solved, you don't need the tranquilizers anymore. This should make you happy."

Did he see through her lie? Was he toying with her, hoping to make her spill the truth?

"I don't understand," Maggie said.

"Having figured out that the man in your dream is your father, and knowing he welcomes you anytime, the burden of *how* you will get there is no longer an issue. Though I do suspect that your dream will stop completely now that you—"

"No. I mean, yes. I'd like to go back. I'd like to see what else my father has to say."

"Maggie, this man is not your real father. He's a manifestation of your own fears and emotions. You created him in order to—"

"I did not!"

Dr. Germaine's face remained placid.

"I'm sorry," Maggie whispered.

"Take a deep breath and listen to what I have to say." He waited a moment. "As your therapist, I recommend we wean you off the tranquilizers. I think it's best if we don't keep you on them any longer than necessary."

"But what if I stop taking the pills and I still feel the need to dream about my father?"

"Maggie, the pills are merely a catalyst. A little push. Now that you know how to open the door as well as what's behind it, getting there will be the easy part. It will be up to *you* to get there, if you still feel you need to. Not the pills. Trust me."

Maggie thought hard for a moment. Maybe she should have told him the truth. What would have been the harm in that? Or maybe she should have pretended she still couldn't open the door. Then he surely would have kept her on the tranquilizers.

But she had lied, and there was no going back. If she told Dr. Germaine she'd been untruthful, he'd never trust her again. He may even have her placed in an institution for pathological lying. Which, lately, had become her forte.

Damn it, she thought, *this is my dream. I designed a magnificent world; a perfect man.*

She had created John, hadn't she?

A tremor of doubt tried to reach her core, but she angrily squashed it.

"Please," she said, trying to hold steady, to keep her voice from begging. "Just one more week. Then you can do whatever you like. I promise."

Dr. Germaine's voice was stern. "You may stay on this dosage until our next session. Then we start weaning. Understood?"

Maggie nodded and pressed her lips together to prevent them from curving upward in a smile.

Chapter Eighteen

It was remarkable how the dream came to her so easily now. Maggie's head had barely touched the pillow when the fog, like a family quilt, surrounded her.

I'm filled with absolute joy, she thought as the door appeared before her.

John's voice floated through the air, making her stomach flutter. "Maggie?"

"I'm here."

"It feels like an eternity since I last heard your voice. Please. Open the door."

His request was followed by a loud sigh slipping through the narrow crack along the bottom.

The latch gave way under Maggie's thumb, and the door swung open as if the hinges had been oiled since her last visit. The wood itself even seemed less dense.

"Maggie," John whispered, striding toward her like Gene Kelly and kissing her on the cheek. "Come."

He shut the door behind him before Maggie had a chance to notice what lay beyond the threshold. He took her hand and led her up the familiar path, the field of flowers swaying in the light breeze, and beyond that the large oaks stretching their branches to the sunny skies. The rainbow stretched over their heads like a bridge to heaven, white puffy clouds in perfect symmetry on either side. Any fear that an invisible entity was nearby, watching, perhaps waiting, disappeared as they approached the gazebo.

Standing on the steps, John said, "Do you want to know more?"

"Of course."

"Then I will show you. But I cannot do it without your help." Pulling her by the hand, he trotted to the center of the gazebo. "What's your favorite animal?" he asked, excitedly hopping from one foot to the other.

"Horses," Maggie said without hesitation. "I always wanted to ride them as a young—"

"Look," John said, his cheeks glowing, a finger pointing to a place behind the gazebo.

Maggie spotted four horses grazing in a field of green clover. "They're beautiful," she said as she knelt on the curved bench and leaned over the white railing. "Did I do that?"

"Of course."

"How?"

"You can have anything you want in here. Well, most anything."

"What things can't I have?" Maggie asked.

"Oh, things that do not matter anyway. Let us just play with the things we can have."

John darted down the gazebo steps. Maggie watched as he rounded the other side, ran up to the tallest of the horses, and stroked the animal's neck. The stallion looked up from his grazing. His lips curved back.

"He's smiling!" Maggie said.

"He wants us to ride."

"How do you know?"

"Do you want to?" John asked.

"Yes."

"That is how I know. Whatever you want, you will have."

John stood scratching the horse between the ears until Maggie joined him behind the gazebo.

"He likes me," John said.

"Yes, he does," Maggie said, reaching up from the tall grass that tickled her legs, and rubbing one of the horses on the muzzle.

John's eyes traced Maggie's face, her hair, her shoulders, her body.

"Do you?" John asked.

"Do I what?"

"Do you like me?"

"Yes," Maggie whispered as she glanced nervously behind her. For just a moment she was sure that Sam would come barging through her dream, come running across the field and into her private world.

"I am so happy right now," John told her. "I am here in your world with you, and it feels like the most perfect place. You really have a knack."

He whispered something in the horse's ear. The steed lowered his body down, and John climbed up onto its back.

"Pick one," he told Maggie.

Maggie stepped toward a mare with eyes and hair the color of warmed chestnuts.

"What do I do?" she asked.

"Ask politely if she will take you for a ride."

Maggie whispered her request in the horse's ear. The horse bowed majestically and didn't stand upright again until Maggie was comfortable and secure on her back.

"Are you ready?" asked John.

"I'm afraid," Maggie said. "I haven't been on a horse since I paid a nickel once at a fair. And that was just a worn-out pony walking in circles."

John laughed. "Do not be afraid. This is your world. Nothing can happen here. You are as safe as you will ever be."

"But what about—" She didn't know how to describe what she couldn't see. "The thing that frightened you before."

"Do not speak of it."

"But—"

"Please. Let us be happy."

Maggie leaned forward and wrapped her arms around the horse's neck. "What if I fall off? What if I get hurt?"

"Do you want to get hurt?"

"Of course not."

"Then you will not," John told her. "It is as simple as that."

Without hesitation, the two horses lined up shank to shank and slowly worked their harmonized trot into a gallop. Maggie sat on top of her horse, letting the warm wind and smell of lemons wash over her. She laughed when John hooted like a cowboy. Soon, they left the large meadow and made their way over a small hill, then down the other side into a luscious valley.

"Where are we going?" John asked Maggie.

"I haven't the faintest."

"Take us somewhere magical!" he shouted through the wind.

Maggie had always wanted to ride on horseback along the edge of the sea. In an instant, the sound of waves slapping sand came to her, and the smell of salt filled the air.

"Maggie!" John said. "This is magnificent! I have not seen the ocean in a long time!"

How long was long? Maggie wondered. Was it weeks, months, years? Was it centuries? But what did it matter? John was only here because of her. She had made him up. Yet he seemed so independent for someone born of imagination.

Together the horses slowed their gait, and once they reached the water's edge, they halted and bowed down, allowing Maggie and John to slide onto the sand.

"Seashells!" Maggie exclaimed, bending over and picking up a sizeable conch, then placing it against her ear.

"You do not need that to hear the ocean," John told her.

Maggie looked out over the water toward the horizon. The sun shone overhead but didn't burn Maggie's sensitive skin like in her other world. It warmed and comforted her, the beams reaching out and draping over her head, her shoulders. She placed the conch shell back on the sand.

"What's beyond the ocean?" she asked. "Are there ships? Is there more land somewhere?"

"You are funny," John said, taking her hand in his. "It is refreshing to be with someone who is not angry like—"

He cut himself off and stared over the water. Maggie watched the glow from the sun encase him like a great halo.

"Like who?" she asked.

He didn't answer. Instead he faced her, his sandaled toes only inches from hers. He took her face in his hands, gently.

"You have brought this to me," he said. "And for that I am grateful."

John placed his soft full lips against hers. His kiss was tender and sweet, and Maggie wanted it to last forever. "Forever is a long time," John whispered. "Do not forget that."

For how long they stood in their embrace Maggie wasn't sure. She only knew that when he finally stepped back from her, the sun was setting behind the ocean, casting oranges and yellows across the water's surface, creating a reflection of fire in John's blue eyes.

"Who are you?" Maggie asked.

"Does the answer really matter?"

She watched the horses nearby, nibbling on a patch of sea grass, and thought about the question. Perhaps it did not. Perhaps it only mattered that she was here with this man now.

John sat on the sand and pulled her down with him.

"Why did you run off last time?" Maggie asked. She let her fingers explore the sand, discovered a small shell, observed the perfection in its delicate spiral, and set it down again.

"I had no choice," John said.

"I don't understand."

"Some things are beyond my control."

"Are there things beyond *my* control?"

"Of course."

"But how can that be?" Maggie asked. "This is my world. You told me so. Your exact words were, 'You call the shots.'"

"You have much to learn."

"Then teach me. Help me understand."

"This is your world," he said.

"Right."

"And you control it."

"Right."

"But you cannot control everything."

"That's a paradox," Maggie told him.

John shook his head. "You control what is in here. You do not control what is out there." He pointed toward an unseen place beyond the sea.

"I don't have control over what's beyond *this* world?" Maggie asked.

"Exactly."

"So, what's out there?"

"You know what is out there."

"I do?"

"Of course, Maggie. You live it every day."

"You mean *real* life?"

"Do not discount the fact that *this* is real life, too."

The sand tickled Maggie's fingers as it sifted through them. Sand that was soft and warm, like the flour she used for baking in her kitchen—a kitchen that seemed as far away as the edge of the solar system.

Without looking up, she said, "Tell me what frightened you."

"I cannot," he said, gazing out over the sea.

"Why not?"

"Maggie, the only things you need to know are this: You are happy here, I am happy here, and together, whenever we come here, we will be happy." With a soft hand he stroked her arm. "Let us enjoy each other in the moments we have. Let us not bring other worlds into this one. They can never mix."

John's words were enough for Maggie. After all, what did she care if there were details she didn't quite understand? She was here, now, in this world that she created, and no amount of uncertainty could shatter the way she felt. She was filled not only with a profound awareness of her own contentment, but an inner sense of peace she had never experienced before. There was no stress here. No domestic fires to extinguish. No husband whose moods dictated all that she did or said, whose sensitive disposition she had to be overly wary of in order to placate his ego. There were no worries about whether collars had enough starch or meatloaf had enough tomatoes. No stares from friends who were too afraid to mention the word "baby" in front of her. No fears about what would come tomorrow, the next day, or the next. This moment was all Maggie needed.

"All right, John."

"You are getting the hang of it," he said smiling.

He placed a gentle arm around her shoulders, and together they sat in silence as the sun dipped its feet into the sea at the edge of the horizon, causing their shadows to lie down on the sand behind them.

Chapter Nineteen

Time had disappeared. It was as though the sunset had always belonged there, as though she had always been sitting on the beach with John, as though she always would. The two horses still stood peacefully next to each other, eyes closed as if in deep meditation.

John gently pressed Maggie down onto the sand.

"John…"

"This is your world. This would not be happening if you did not want it to."

Part of her understood that to be true, but a deeper part of her felt the pangs of a guilty conscience.

"This is not wrong," he told her as he slowly undid her sash and slid it out from under her. "It cannot be wrong if you feel it is right."

"I'm being unfaith—"

"You are not of that other world right now. You are here. In all of its wonder. In all of its perfection."

He got up on his knees and undid his own belt. He pulled his tunic over his head. Underneath the dress he wore nothing.

Maggie realized then that she, too, was nude beneath her clothes.

John gracefully slid Maggie's tunic down over her shoulders, past her bare breasts, and along the rest of her body. Still kneeling, he looked up into the sky which had now turned to darkness.

"Where is the moon?" he asked. "Where are the stars?"

A full moon obediently appeared over their heads, its fullness casting a soft illumination directly upon them. White pinpricks of light dotted the dark canvas.

"How about some dolphins?" he asked.

A few seconds later, the chatter and splashing of dolphins could be heard less than a yard away.

"You show so much love by what you create," John said. "Show me the same love, Maggie."

He placed his warm body on top of hers, his smooth skin like a satin sheet. Her hands held onto his chiseled buttocks as he kissed her deeply. His tongue tasted like honey. She moved her lips away from his mouth and licked his neck, his body clean and washed, without the expected taste of salt.

John whispered, "You and I are here as one. We are—"

The ground beneath them started to rumble.

"John!" Maggie screamed.

John pressed a hand against Maggie's mouth.

The ground shook harder, the weight of his body nearly suffocating her. His fierce breath entered her ear.

He's afraid, Maggie thought, feeling their intimate power steadily being sucked away, like lights flickering during a storm only moments before a black-out.

John rolled onto his side and pulled her up, his eyes wide with alarm, a finger against his lips. They threw their tunics haphazardly over their bodies, retying their belts as they tried to keep their balance on the trembling earth. They watched as the waves grew from five to ten feet before crashing hard against the undertow. Like nimble fingers, they reached out, grabbing for Maggie's feet. John held onto her arm, stumbling as he dragged her backward and away from the pounding surf. They made it to where the horses stood, their frightened animal eyes darting from the trees to the ocean to the sky, their frenzied whinnies barely heard beneath the roar of the ocean.

The grumble below their feet intensified. Maggie was sure the ground would crack open and consume the two of them. Consume her perfect world.

"Make it stop!" Maggie cried.

"I cannot!" John told her. "Hurry! Put us somewhere else!"

Maggie wished for the gazebo with its smooth railing and ornate roof line, surrounded by waving flowers and artistically designed trees. She pictured the brilliant sunshine, the clouds which clustered overhead like rolls of fleece, the rainbow that floated without effort.

Within seconds they were sitting high on top of their horses, galloping back the way they had come. Back in the middle of the field among the other horses, they dismounted simultaneously. Maggie ran to the gazebo, the only shelter she knew. She expected John to follow, but when she reached out her hand behind her, no one took it. In a panic, Maggie scanned her surroundings and spotted him running up the foggy path that led toward the castle, his tunic crooked, his dangling leather belt trying to trip him.

"John!" Maggie shouted. "Come back! This is my world! We'll be safe here!"

Whether or not there was truth in her words didn't matter— she had to keep him from leaving. Every time he left her, the fear of being abandoned overwhelmed her. What if he didn't come back? What if she became stuck here, alone, forever?

Forever is a long time…

The shaking grew more violent as Maggie staggered across the porch. She crouched in a corner of the gazebo under one of the benches. Her eyes darted toward the castle, then to the left across the flowers to the forest beyond the meadow.

She closed her eyes.

Wake up wake up wake up…

When she opened her eyes again, she was still tucked beneath the bench.

"Maggie!" John called. "Open it! Hurry!"

John's voice was suddenly drowned out by the deafening pounding of footsteps, hastily approaching from somewhere beyond the oaks, like the angry thuds of a giant's shoes in a fairy tale.

Maggie pictured the door and willed it open. In her mind's eye, she watched as John stepped inside and the door slammed shut behind him.

The footsteps were unrelenting. One slow methodical step after another.

Thud! Thud! Thud! Thud!

She would be squashed like a bug! The giant would discover her hiding place, take one definitive step, and she'd be crushed under the mammoth hooves of the monster who wore them.

The dream had to end, but Maggie's head began to spin as she tried to recall the details of her real life. She tried to picture Sam, but his face dissolved the moment he entered her thoughts. She tried to coax Dr. Germaine's voice, heard it scolding her for lying to him—she would take the scolding over what was happening now—but it, too, drifted out of reach.

Please, she begged her subconscious. *Wake up…*

The footsteps turned to thunder, falling down from the heavens and rising up from the ground like two loud drummers vying for attention. The gazebo, her only shelter, threatened to shake apart at the seams.

Suddenly, a thought came to her that was as perplexing as it was clear: *This is my world! These sounds are coming from within me!*

Still confused but less afraid, she crawled out from beneath the bench and ran to the top of the gazebo steps. She scanned the forest beyond her sunny world for whatever evil was trying to invade but could see nothing.

A shrill bell rang from somewhere in the distance, stopped, and started again.

I know that sound!

The intruder's footfalls gained momentum.

Thud-thud-thud-thud-thud-thud!

A growl, buried deep within the ground, rolled beneath the crashing footsteps. The intermittent ringing grew louder. It was high-pitched and intrusive, causing Maggie's head to vibrate.

"You are not welcome here!" Maggie shouted into the thickening fog. "This is *my* world. You cannot come here!"

The footsteps ceased. Maggie waited for them to return, but they did not. She turned to the horses. They still grazed upon the clover, standing in a cluster under the sun. A warm wind caressed her body. There were no sounds now except for the ringing, which reached for her through the thickening fog.

In her bed, Maggie slowly opened her eyes, shielding them from the sun streaming through the thin crack in her curtains. She reached over, nearly knocking the telephone off the end table.

As she wiped drool from her mouth, she placed the phone to her face and panted, "Hello?"

"Maggie?"

"John?"

The voice offered a thick silence before responding, "It's me, Sam."

"Sam?"

She tried to remember who Sam was but could not.

"Oh, Maggie."

The man on the phone sounded disappointed. Had she done something wrong?

She looked across the room. On top of the dresser rested a group of framed photographs. She sat up and peered at them more closely. There she was, in every picture, hugging, kissing, holding hands with a man.

But, of course, the man was not John.

"Sam," she said as she remembered.

"Maggie," Sam said. "I don't understand."

"Nothing." The word came out flat. "Nothing's wrong. Everything's fine."

"Everything is wrong, Maggie. Everything."

She waited for him to elaborate, but he did not.

"I'm fine, Sam. I just got a little mixed up. I was dreaming—" She stopped herself. She could not—*would not*—share her secret world with him.

"You were dreaming about someone named John."

Hearing Sam say the name out loud sent an angry arrow through her core. She bit down on her lip to keep herself from saying something mean.

"Well," Sam said. "At least he's only a figment of your imagination."

Maggie sat on the edge of her bed and tucked her feet into her slippers. Her eyes still squinted in pain from the light. "Yes, Sam," she said. "Just a dream."

A long pause fell between them, turning their marital fracture into a bottomless gorge.

"The conference is going well," Sam finally said. "In case you were wondering."

"Good."

"Yes, it is good. I'm learning the latest on cancer and polio treatments. Things that could change the world."

His world.

"Hello?" he said. "Are you there?"

"I'm here."

"Maggie, are you…do you…miss me?"

She didn't answer.

"Oh, Maggie. I'm a good husband aren't I? Don't I make you happy? I know our limits have been tested, but we could adopt, couldn't we? There's a doctor here at the conference who manages a pregnancy clinic just outside of D.C. He meets women every day, young women out of wedlock, forced to make difficult decisions. Why can't we adopt? It doesn't take bearing children to be good parents, does it Maggie?"

"Whatever you want, Sam. You always know what's best."

"When I get home this weekend, we can discuss things."

"This weekend," she said. "Yes."

On her fingers, Maggie tried to count how many days that would be, how many more times she would have the opportunity to be with John. But she could not remember when Sam had left or even what day it was. How long had she been asleep?

"Maggie?"

"I'm here."

"We can work things out, don't you think? You and me? The way it used to be?"

The way it used to be wasn't clear to Maggie. The only

moments her memory could conjure up were recent ones of lying on the beach with John's breath meshing with hers, riding horses with the wind in her hair, watching the sun melt into spectacular colors over the horizon. Even the nightmarish part of her dream was overshadowed by the other more magnificent elements.

"Sure," she said by rote. "Work things out. Of course."

"Then I'll see you Saturday. You're still my little magpie."

Maggie cringed at the nickname. "Saturday," she said dryly and placed the phone back in the cradle.

Like a zombie, she slipped into her robe and made her way downstairs. She forced herself to eat some toast, downing the dried bread with a glass of orange juice. She glanced at the clock on the kitchen wall, but the large black numbers blurred before her. The calendar on the pantry tried to inform her of the date, but those numbers, too, were unclear. How much time had passed, she did not know. Did not *want* to know. She was angry at time and its intrusiveness. Angry that it was one element she could not control.

Well then, she would simply ignore it altogether.

She went back upstairs, shook a pill from the bottle, and swallowed it with some tap water. She unplugged the telephone, pressed in the little "off" button on her alarm clock, and stuffed it in the end table drawer. If time had anything left to offer, she would squeeze in as much of it as she could. With or without awareness of the exact date; with or without comprehending the clock's hands; with or without a monster lurking within the hidden furrows of her subconscious mind.

Chapter Twenty

She stood at the wooden door, though for how long she did not know. Her legs never tired, but the fog had crawled through her skin, dampening her core.

Where did John go when they weren't together? Was he sitting in a candlelit parlor reading a book? Gazing out a back window at a landscape she did not have privy to? Sipping hot tea? Fishing in a nearby stream?

A moat, more likely.

She placed a cool hand over her mouth as a nervous giggle bubbled up from her throat.

It occurred to her that she was afraid.

I shouldn't fear that what is only in my mind can hurt me. Why would I want to hurt myself?

Dr. Germaine's voice tried to rise within her, but she pushed it away. No. She didn't want to be psychoanalyzed right now. There was no room, no patience for her therapist, real or imagined. Things were perfect here.

Except for that sliver of fear that tagged along behind her like a hungry dog.

She placed her ear against the wood. At first there was only silence, then that odd sound of something, perhaps a sack of potatoes or a bail of hay, being dragged along the floor, seeped through the crack above the threshold. She knelt on the ground and peered through the crevice. Her eyes took in the first few inches of the stone floor, traveling into darkness. Beyond that, she could see nothing. No feet. No life of any kind. Only that sound somewhere beyond the castle walls.

She sat on her bottom and leaned her back against the door.

Maybe this world wasn't so perfect after all. If it were, she wouldn't be feeling such torment—

Something came to her: She had never swallowed two pills in the same day before. Is that why the door wouldn't open? She should have been patient and waited until bedtime to take the second one, or waited twenty-four hours like prescribed.

Sighing again, she stood up, placed her hand one more time against the castle wall, then walked away from the door and headed along the path in the direction of the gazebo. From the middle of the raised porch, the sun warmed the roof above her and the rainbow spread its colors across the field. The horses still grazed behind her, countless flowers bloomed cheerfully, and the oak trees in the distance moved in unison in the breeze. Like a painting hanging in a museum, everything was just as it had been a short time earlier. Everything was just right.

Or was it?

She suddenly felt like the baby bear coming home to discover that someone—or *something*—had tasted her warm porridge, sat in her cozy chair, slept in her comfy bed.

The path bridging her world and John's was the same stone path, still meandering between the two like a snake made of stone. But the trail appeared to be shorter than she recalled.

From the gazebo steps, her eyes traveled along the path. If she remembered correctly, the cobblestones had stretched about a quarter of a mile between the gazebo and the castle. Before, the tower appeared to be far away from the gazebo, like a distant view of the famous Neuschwanstein Castle. Now, she could see the entire structure more clearly, the intricacy of the stonework, the grain of the huge wooden door in its center. This clarity was because the building stood only a few hundred yards away.

She sat on the top step and tried to fathom how this was possible, giving in to her mind's explanation in psychological terms.

You're feeling guilty, Dr. Germaine's voice told her straight away.

Why should I feel guilty?

Sam.

I haven't done anything to Sam.

And your marriage.

What are you saying?

What do you think I'm saying?

I haven't any clue.

Maggie, you feel guilty because you've met another man. You are slowly replacing Sam with this figment of your imagination.

I told you he was my father.

But he's not, is he?

No.

So you feel guilty.

If John is imaginary, how can I be guilty of anything?

I never said you are *guilty. Only that you* feel *guilty.*

Even if I did feel guilty, and I'm not saying I do, what would that have to do with the path getting shorter? Or the castle moving closer?

The world you've created in your dream is without the frustration that comes with having to worry about someone else's emotional tribulations, least of all your own. It's as close to perfection as you can get. John's world beyond the castle door represents what you can't have. Or, what you know you shouldn't have. Now that your husband has found out about your new friend, even knows his name, you are deliberately sabotaging your perfect world as penance for what you are doing to Sam.

I'm not doing anything—

Let me re-phrase: what your subconscious believes *you are doing to Sam. By bringing the two worlds closer together, you allow yourself the opportunity to ruin this new relationship. John told you not to blend his world with yours. Yet here you are, mixing them anyway, knowing if you do, things will surely disintegrate.*

How do I know that for sure?

Because John told you so.

But I made him up. I can make him do anything I want.

Can you?

It's my world.

Is it? Dr. Germaine's imaginary voice asked.

Yes.

Pause.

Are you sure?

Maggie didn't want to hear any more.

Get the hell out of my head. There is nothing wrong with me, and there is nothing in this world I can't have by wishing it. You don't belong here, just like I don't belong on your couch!

Dr. Germaine and his two cents disappeared.

Maggie walked down the gazebo steps and onto the path.

My world. Mine.

She would call to John, and he would come, and they would ride horses back to the beach and continue what they had started, before her emotional side got the better of her, like so many of the pathetic protagonists in the novels she devoured.

The name rolled softly from her lips: "John."

Only the wind whispered back, caressing her face like a hand in a cotton glove.

She pushed some loose strands of hair from her forehead.

"John," she said a bit louder, staring toward the castle door as if mentally penetrating his name through the wood.

Dr. Germaine's imaginary voice managed to poke through one more time: *Are you sure?*

"Yes," she whispered.

She waited a moment.

"John!"

One of the horses whinnied from the field of clover. She looked toward the cry, but could not see the horses from this side of the gazebo. She turned back to the fortress, its high tower obstructing much of the sky behind it, the stones from top to bottom glistening like they had recently been dampened by rain.

Had the castle moved even closer in the few seconds her back was turned?

Disquiet entered her world like an entity. It was in the stones that made up the path; in the wet mud and moss between the stones; in the vibrant flowers; in the lush forest that bordered the field's edge; in the lemony air itself.

This is new, she thought, rubbing her damp palms on her tunic. *I've never perspired here before.*

She took a deep breath and held it. As she exhaled, she shouted as forcefully as she could, "Jooohhhnnn!"

The word flew through the air, slamming against the castle then bouncing back to the gazebo like a boomerang. Back and forth it vaulted, until Maggie dropped into a squatted position, covering her ears. For how long she remained in the middle of the path she wasn't sure. It could have been seconds, hours, days.

Time has no place in this world…

When the echo had completed its last rebound, Maggie removed her hands from her ears and stood up. The breeze had stopped. Her breathing ceased to make a sound. It was as though she were standing in the calm before a tornado.

She took a step forward. Once again, his name tried to creep out of her mouth.

"J—"

But that's where the name stopped. The path vibrated under Maggie's feet, and the mysterious world at the end of the path began to change. The castle grew, the tower stretching higher toward the sky, eclipsing the sun, its dead-eye windows elongating like comic strip pictures stretched out on Silly Putty. The tower cast a shadow over Maggie's gazebo, causing the temperature to plummet, turning her arms to gooseflesh. A creaking noise caught her attention. Her eyes darted toward the door: It had begun to swell, the wide planks growing thicker and wider and, she could only assume, heavier.

She ran back up the gazebo steps and looked over the back railing. The horses had scattered in different directions. Two ran through the woods, and the other two in a direction she had never noted before, a barren desert with bleak mountains beyond. Thick dark clouds, like those before a squall, tumbled over one another in the sky, sucking up the sun. Beyond the forest, a quick and violent lightning bolt zigzagged its way across the sky then zapped whatever target it had chosen, spewing a thin line of black smoke into the air. A mixture of rain and hail fell in sheets and with it a cold wind, like an invisible wave, rose and fell across Maggie's world. In her field of flowers, each bloom hung limp and exhausted, the life knocked out of them, one leaning against the other for support.

The path buckled more vehemently, its stones jutting up at all angles, grass sprouting from the cracks and oozing out with the mud. The stones became a gutted trail of small hills and valleys, every few feet dipping beneath the earth or rising up like an overpass, reminding Maggie of a roller coaster that during her childhood had made her scream with delight.

But there was no delight in what she was seeing now.

The fog had ebbed, exposing the castle walls as far as she could see. They expanded and moved along the earth like active cells under a microscope, the stones multiplying then continuing their journey outward and upward.

The castle was transforming into something evil, its windows turning into dead but glowing eyes. The crest of the tower became a large, cathedral-like hat. The wooden door suddenly swung open, wide and hungry like a vulture's expectant mouth. For the first time, Maggie gazed into its throat, but she only had a moment to catch a glimpse of a fiery glow before the mouth shut again. In front of the fortress, just below the wooden door, fresh earth was sucked into the ground and aggressively churned outward by invisible spades until a deep trench was formed. Water from some hidden place gushed into the channel. The narrow but fierce moat disappeared into the grayish fog now clinging to the sides of the building. A foot beneath the door, a massive piece of wood forced its way through the thick stone from somewhere beyond the castle walls. The wood took form, growing quickly and fiercely into a wide and lengthy plank. Like a huge lizard's tongue, it stretched across the top of the moat which was filling with water and landed within feet of the path with a reverberating thump, creating a drawbridge.

Then she heard the locks.

Bolts slammed into their pockets. She felt like Houdini, imprisoned in one of his magic boxes. Each time a bolt clicked in place, Maggie's heart stopped beating; each time a chain link clanked along its track, her lungs froze. She watched as heavy iron chains fell from the castle door frame and reached out for the end of the plank, then latched on as though the plank were a piece of metal and the chains magnetic. Stretched tightly, they heaved the drawbridge higher and higher, gaining momentum as the plank ascended into the air. Faster and faster it rose, until the top of the drawbridge slammed hard against the front of the castle, creating a new door nearly twice as big as the one it had swallowed; the door that had been the only gateway connecting Maggie and John.

She was jolted out of her shock by one final torment: John's anguished cry.

"No!" Maggie screamed.

As abruptly as the transformation had begun, so it ceased, and the world fell back into silence. The sun remained hidden behind the dark clouds. The hailstorm had ended but had left behind bone-chilling air. The horses were nowhere to be seen. The path had stopped crinkling. The water in the moat showed no ripples and made no sound. The tower loomed over what used to be a magnificent garden but was now a battlefield of lifeless plants. The castle, with its drawbridge in the center of its endless walls, stood shockingly close to the bottom step of the gazebo.

It was now a part of Maggie's world.

She inched her way along the rickety path, up one curve, then down another, tripping and falling into a slimy substance, a type of dream-mud, when she reached the edge of the moat. As she landed on all fours, her eyes fell upon the smooth water, so much like a mirror that the castle's reflection was meticulously copied on the surface.

She leaned over and caught her reflection. The face staring back at her was not her own—it was the face of another woman. A face much more stunning than hers could ever be. The face of an angel or a goddess. Her skin was clear and white, without the life-long collection of freckles. Her nose was straighter and more dignified. Her eyes larger and brighter. Her hair golden and curled. Like John's.

Curiously, Maggie touched her own face with her hand. The woman in the water did the same. They smiled at one another.

John's distressed "Please!" fell against the other side of the castle door with a muffled thud.

Maggie scrambled to get up, but the mud held her firm. She fought against its grip, finally plucking out her feet, as one of her sandals was sucked away by the soggy earth. She sat in the sludge on her bottom and dipped a muddy toe in the water. She yanked her foot back—the water was frigid—then collapsed onto the edge of the moat, mud seeping through her dress, one foot without its sandal.

With her arms wrapped around her body, she glanced back at her own world. Her perfect work of art had turned to ruins. Chipped paint flecks from the gazebo's railing floated through the air like volcanic ashes, and hundreds of deep furrows decorated the roofline. The fancy gingerbread from under the eaves lay in splintered pieces on the ground like piles of kindling.

Maggie shook with rage as she scooted back from the moat and forced herself to stand. She grabbed a firm hold of her sandal sticking up out of the mud and pulled it onto her foot. As she stood, enormous strength and concentration filled her.

"John!" she shouted toward the sealed drawbridge. "I'm going to save you! I promise!"

No answer.

"John!"

The water once again began rushing through the channel,

stopping her voice from reaching its destination.

She stood there a moment, trying to decide what to do next. Her mind wasn't as sharp as when she was awake, she realized. In this world, although she was brave and strong, thinking clearly was a challenge. She could only contemplate tasks which appeared before her. As hard as she tried, she could not speculate or make apt decisions.

She would wake up and devise a plan! Then she could—

Don't you see what is happening? Dr. Germaine's bodiless voice interrupted her thoughts. *You are bringing these two worlds together. You alone, Maggie—*

No. Someone or something locked him up. I'm going to save him.

What if you're the one who put him in there to begin with?

Why would I do that?

To prevent yourself from getting more deeply involved with an imaginary man who is keeping you from repairing your real-life relationship. To prevent yourself from falling in love with a man you can never have.

But I can have him.

How is that possible, Maggie?

She didn't know how it was possible. Not yet, anyway. But she would figure it out.

If you should discover there is truth to your theory, said the voice, *fill me in. I would love to publish in the medical journals regarding dream control. You and I could make medical history together…*

Maggie turned off Dr. Germaine's voice as swiftly as she clicked off the radio in her living room. She didn't want to make medical history; she only wanted to be with John. The man she had created. The man who believed in Maggie's longing for freedom because he, too, craved freedom.

But she'd have to find a way to save him first.

Chapter Twenty-one

Her head throbbed. Her skin felt dehydrated, her eyes sunken. She downed a pair of aspirin and slid into a skirt and blouse and a pair of ballet flats. To dress like any normal woman on any given day made her feel more lucid.

As she passed the full-length mirror, her reflection tried to catch her attention, but she didn't need or want to see. She knew the woman in the mirror, the one who was no longer a deity but an everyday woman living an everyday life, would try to talk her out of what she proposed to do.

Exhaustion followed her down the stairs as she held onto the railing, concentrating on placing one foot in front of the other. She had done nothing but sleep for—how long?—and yet she felt as though someone had taken an Electrolux and sucked the marrow from her bones, leaving nothing in its place but acrid hot air.

John was so close in her mind, she believed for a moment she would find him sitting in her kitchen, reading the newspaper and drinking a cup of Maxwell House. Black with just a touch of cream would be his style. He'd be wearing a pair of trousers, much like the ones Sam wore. And a business jacket. After all, what would the neighbors say if he stepped onto the front porch in a tunic and bent over to get the paper?

She laughed in spite of the sorrow that filled her heart, and held onto the kitchen table for support. Her uncombed hair fell into her face as she leaned over, shaking her head, fighting back tears.

It would be impossible for John to sit in her kitchen discussing politics or Robert Frost or the latest John Wayne movie. He would never step foot in her house, stride down Charles Street, shop at Anthony's Fish Market. He would never meet her friend, Susan. Or Dr. Germaine. Or Sam, for that matter. It wasn't as if John could simply jump on a train bound for her world like the typical Joe on holiday.

She had to be quick about deciding her next step. Not only because her concern for John was growing by the second, but because she only had a few tranquilizers left.

You do not need pills to get to your dream…

Although she wanted to, she couldn't afford to believe Dr. Germaine's theory; didn't have time to buy into others' notions with Sam coming home soon. In her other world, time meant nothing. But in this one, the clock breathed against the back of her neck as a constant reminder that seconds were ticking away.

Frightening ideas poured through her. What if she didn't make it back in time to save John? What if she returned to her dream, and he was nowhere to be found? What if the castle had taken over her world completely? Or, worse yet, disappeared altogether? She shouldn't have left so abruptly. She should have stayed and dealt with whatever was preventing her from getting to John. After all, it was her dream, so she had to assume some responsibility, didn't she?

Smothering her scolding inner voice, she pulled a pad of paper from the junk drawer next to the stove. She sat at the kitchen table and scribbled *Things to bring* at the top of the page. Below the heading, she wrote the numbers one through ten in a column on the left-hand side. The list started out simply enough:

1. *Pen.*

2. *Paper.*

Even though she couldn't imagine why she would need either of these first two items, she always felt more secure knowing they were handy.

3. *Rope.*

She scratched out the word and wrote next to it: *A long, thick rope.*

4. *Flashlight.*

Maggie suddenly felt like a member of the Boys Club of America. Weren't these the same items they brought along should they meet up with wild beasts in the woods?

The words *wild beasts* sent a shiver up her spine. Her hand shook as she continued:

5. *Rain boots.*

For that awful mud.

6. *Ladder.*

A ladder could be used for many things, like placing against a window, for instance.

7. *Weapon.*

A shotgun? A pistol? Just because she had worked in a weapons plant didn't mean she knew how to handle a gun. Perhaps she should bring a knife instead. A knife could come in handy. For cutting rope. Or sawing through chains.

Chains?

What made her think of that?

Stop asking stupid questions! You're wasting valuable time!

She crossed out *Weapon* and replaced it with *Knife.*

Then she wrote:

8. *Hacksaw.*

Just in case the knife didn't do the trick.

Ah! she thought, a weird smile pulling on her lips. *Something to store everything in*!

She wrote:

9. *A large canvas bag.*

Like Sam's military bag.

Sam. Why was it he had to creep into her thoughts just when she was feeling on top of things?

Forget Sam. Finish the list! *Time is ticking*!

But was time ticking away for John at this very moment while Maggie sat in her pretty Cape Cod? Was he actually waiting for her, somewhere in the deep confines of the cold castle walls while she wrote out a list in her modern post-war kitchen surrounded by Formica? Or was he nowhere? Nonexistent? Extinguished until she returned to her dream and recreated him?

She thought of the many fairy tales she had read as a child where characters spring to life as soon as the book is opened. But what happens to Rapunzel or Cinderella once the book is closed and put back on the shelf? Are fairy tale princesses suspended in time? Does Rapunzel remain forever with her golden hair hanging down from the tower window? Does Cinderella, one foot bare, become immobilized on the palace steps if the book is closed just before the chime strikes twelve?

Maggie believed her dream world was like a fairy tale, everything just as she had left it, patiently awaiting her return.

She wrote one last entry:

10. *Champagne.*

To celebrate John's escape, of course! She imagined the two of them, sitting side by side on the sandy beach, sipping bubbly, watching the endless sunset over the perfectly sculptured waves—

The telephone rang, startling her, causing the pen to scratch a long line along the bottom of the page. She stared at the intrusive telephone with contempt. On the fifth ring, she stood up to answer it, a flicker of anger igniting beneath her exhaustion.

"Yes?" she said with desperate impatience.

"You missed your session," Dr. Germaine said.

"Missed…?"

Hadn't she already had a session that day? Or was it the day before? It felt as though—

"Hello?" Dr. Germaine said.

"I—I lost track of time…"

The clock on the kitchen wall showed both hands pointing straight up. What did it mean when they pointed toward the ceiling at the same time?

"How late am I?" Maggie asked.

"You don't know?"

She shook her head as though he were sitting beside her.

"Maggie, your appointment was two days ago."

Two days?

Dr. Germaine went on. "I thought maybe you'd gone to Chicago to be with Sam and had forgotten to call. But I drove past your house last night on my way to play Bridge, and most of your lights were on. You've caused me some worry. Is everything all right?"

Maggie could tell him now. She could simply say, "No, Dr. Germaine, things are not all right. I've been sleeping since the last time we met. I haven't eaten in God knows how many days. I'm madly in love with a man who lives in a castle near my dream world. And, well, you won't believe what happened! I tried to visit him, but suddenly the castle turned into an ogre, and the door got eaten by a drawbridge. You know, like in a King Arthur tale? To make matters worse, there's a rather chilly moat that stops me from reaching him, and I believe he's in danger. You see, there's a monster hiding nearby, though I don't have a clue where it came from or why it's so angry. Oh, and I almost forgot! I look absolutely Fifth Avenue in my other-world tunic!"

Maggie realized just how insane it all sounded. She didn't suffer from melancholy—she was deranged. Dr. Germaine had misdiagnosed her. She was a prime candidate for Belleview; maybe even a contender for electroshock therapy.

She looked at her list again, trying to make sense of what she'd written, the phone drifting from her shoulder, her hand barely holding it against her chest.

A muffled voice floated up to her: "Maggie? Are you there?"

She shook her head, sure that her mind was slipping out of reach and would keep slipping until there was nothing left but dead air. She slowly placed the phone against her ear.

Papers ruffled on the other end of the line.

Dr. Germaine said, "You're not well, are you Maggie?"

"Oh, God, what is wrong with me?" Her sobs came hard and fast, attacking her diaphragm and throat, causing her to gag. "I'm—so—tired—"

"I'm coming over. I'll cancel my next patient."

"No. Okay. Yes, yes. Maybe we can…"

Can what? she wondered. *Put our heads together to save John from the evil that lurks within the castle walls?*

"I'll be there in twenty," her doctor told her. "Just relax. Take deep breaths until I get there. Pour yourself a cup of tea."

"Yes. Tea."

The simple task of boiling water and dipping the tea bag into the cup seemed both absurd and daunting.

"Yes," Maggie said again. She wiped her eyes with a flowered dish towel.

Dr. Germaine hung up, leaving the silence in Maggie's kitchen to wind itself around her shaking body, nearly squeezing the breath out of her.

Chapter Twenty-two

"Why don't we sit?" Dr. Germaine offered, taking off his hat as he stepped into the foyer. "Living room, perhaps?"

Without a word, Maggie closed the front door and led the doctor through an archway and into the formal living room. An RCA radio-phonograph that had belonged to her mother sat near the large doorway, and an outdated black and white television squatted in silence in a far corner—Sam planned to buy the new 630-TS as soon as it hit the market. Two stark-white couches faced one another from the long sides of the antique coffee table, and two stylish olive-green chairs sat across from each other on the shorter ends. In the center of one wall was a nearly spotless fireplace that hadn't been used but once that winter. A lovely pastoral oil painting hung over the mantel which was dotted with gold framed photos. The rest of the room was lined with bookshelves filled with everything from medical journals to stacks of *LIFE* to best-selling novels. A few magazines were neatly piled next to a small vase of plastic daisies on the coffee table's center.

Dr. Germaine draped his coat over the back of a sofa. He went first to one window and then the other, closing the heavy winter drapes Sam would expect Maggie to replace soon with more cheerful spring curtains.

"Please," Dr. Germaine said. "Sit wherever you feel most comfortable."

She chose the couch facing away from the windows and tucked herself against the arm.

"That's fine," he told her, sitting on the sofa opposite. He placed his hat on the small stack of *National Geographic* magazines on the coffee table, covering a close-up photo of an alligator. "Relax. Good. Keep breathing. Let all your fears and worries fall away. That's it. Just breathe now."

She did as told, working hard not to let tears of fatigue break her concentration.

In and out. In and out.

"Now then. Tell me what is distressing you." He pulled a small pad of paper from his shirt pocket and held his pen at the ready.

Maggie shifted her weight, crossed and uncrossed her legs. Her hands went to her hair which hadn't seen a rinse or a brush in over a week, and she pretended to fix a hairpin. She dropped her hands to her lap and twisted the tear-damp dish towel she still held onto, wringing it like she was trying to squeeze out the water. She bit down on her lower lip until it hurt.

"Yes," she finally said. "All right then."

Relief suddenly washed over her. It might be cathartic to disclose her secret; to share her guilt with another.

She recalled her first confession at the age of eight, kneeling in the dark booth with the thin trellis between her and Father Tom. At first, she was afraid to say anything, but once she began, a long list of wrongdoings streamed out of her like logs blocking a dam had been removed. She had blurted how she disrespected her mother every so often, even stuck her tongue out behind her back. That she had accidentally killed her sister's goldfish by overfeeding them, secretly dumping them in the stream by their house and blaming their disappearance on the cat. She admitted to kissing Toby Taylor on the playground outside the cafeteria, the other schoolchildren paying pennies to watch. The liberation she'd felt by purging these transgressions was like rinsing gritty sand from between her toes. Maggie had believed the man behind the screen, the one she knew not only from church, but from sharing her mother's Sunday lamb stew or cabbage soup, had a direct connection to God. It was as if Father Tom was magically able to flush the sins out of her system, so she would be duly forgiven and granted a seat in the house of the Lord.

"The dream is real."

There. She'd said it. She'd told the truth. What Dr. Germaine did with that information she did not have the energy to contemplate.

"I see." His pen made a quick journey across the notepad.

"No matter what you believe," Maggie said, "it's real. There's no other way to explain it." She closed her eyes. "The door, the castle, the moat, the—"

"Moat?"

She opened her eyes. This would be no different than confessing to Father Tom, only without the privacy screen between them. Dr. Germaine only nodded and wrote as she shared the details, including the fact that she had lied to him during their last session.

"Maggie," he said. "Our dreams are to help us escape, but also to bring us solutions—ones that we already have within us. Sometimes these solutions are easily recognized, other times they are more difficult to decipher."

"You're going to tell me that everything in my dream represents something else."

"All dreams are filled with symbols," her doctor explained. "Let's say you dream of a child. You are, in effect, that child. Filled with innocence, vulnerability. It can also represent your full potential, aspirations, dreams for the future."

"I'm not dreaming of a child. I'm dreaming about a man."

"A man you look up to."

Maggie nodded.

"This man could represent a type of guide," Dr. Germaine said. "Someone you admire. A part of yourself that can lead you in the right direction."

Maggie said, "I do admire him, but he's more than a guide. He's magnificent. He's magical. Strong and gentle at the same time."

"Perhaps he symbolizes both the male and female parts of who you are. We're all born with masculine and feminine traits."

"We are?"

"Certainly. It's just that few people recognize this for fear they'll go against society's expectations of what gender truly means."

"Are you saying that John is me? A masculine part of who I am?"

"It's your dream. What do *you* think?"

"I think he's real and in trouble. And I have to save him."

"Are you sure you aren't trying to save yourself?"

Maggie didn't answer.

"Fine," Dr. Germaine said. "You need to save *him*. Why is that?"

"Because if I don't, I'll never see him again."

"What will happen if you don't see him again? If this element within you disappears?"

"I'll...I'll be..."

She found it difficult to explain her feelings in mere words. They rolled around in her mind as blurry images rather than attainable vernacular.

After a moment, she said, "I think we're in love."

"But he's only a part of your dream. A manifestation of—"

"I used to tell myself the same thing," she said. "But it's more than that. It really is. You have to believe me." The tears began to fall again, but she spoke shamelessly through them, occasionally wiping her cheeks with the dish towel. "If you could only see what I see and experience what I experience when I go there, you would understand. If you could only meet him, then you would believe me. You would."

"I'm not here to believe or disbelieve what you're telling me. I'm here to analyze, theorize, and help you come up with solutions to make your life better."

"My life in that other world *is* better. It's beyond anything I've ever experienced here."

"How so?"

"I'm beautiful there."

"You're not beautiful here?"

"Please. It's no secret that red hair and freckles are what made Howdy Doody famous. And I've always been fine with it. This is who I am. But in my dream, I look like a goddess. I *am* a goddess."

"In real life," Dr. Germaine explained, holding the notepad up to his face, "we wear a mask to show the public. This mask displays to others what we believe they want to see. It alleviates having to explain ourselves, especially when we don't do what society dictates." He brought his hand down again. "In the dreamscape, this mask is removed to show the real person beneath. This is known as the *Persona*."

"I'm not only beautiful there, Dr. Germaine. I'm strong."

"You're not strong in this world?"

"I have no reason to be strong here," Maggie said. "Strength isn't necessary. There, in my other world, I have powers. I can do or be or have anything I wish."

"What is it you wish for?"

"A life filled with magic and wonder. A life where it doesn't matter if I bake or clean or iron. A life that hands me whatever makes me happy."

"This man you call John," Dr. Germaine said. "Tell me about him."

"He's sweet and beautiful. Smart, but not in a scholarly way. More like a philosopher; a wanderer who knows things without having been taught them. As though he came into being this way. He shows me a side of myself I never knew existed."

"What side is that?"

"The side that feels complete satisfaction."

"Maggie, why do you suppose you can't find satisfaction here? Why would you have to travel so far away to find it?"

"This is the first time in my life I've felt it. It's a new sensation. If it weren't for John, I never would have tasted it. Now I crave it all the time. Simple satisfaction. Simple pleasures. A simple life. With John."

"And now you aim to save him."

"Yes."

"You will be his savior. Like—say—a goddess. Or a heroine."

"Yes. I mean…"

Dr. Germaine placed the notepad on the coffee table. "Maggie, listen to me. John is not real."

"Oh. But he is."

"Everything that appears before us in the dreamscape is an

extension of ourselves. Our disappointments. Our fears. Questions we need answers to. You created him to solve—"

"Yes, I know. To solve a problem that lies deep within my subconscious mind." Maggie's words came out sardonically, but she didn't care. "Early on, you were convinced he represented my father."

"You led me to believe that he was your father."

"And I'm sorry for that," Maggie told her doctor. "But how can I convince you that my other world is real? It took me a long time to believe in its validity, so I understand your skepticism. But you have to trust me."

"I am taking you off the pills—"

"No!" Maggie stood up. "I need them to last me. I have to save him. I thought by letting you come over, by being honest with you, you would help me do that!"

"Please, sit down."

After a moment, Maggie did as he asked.

"Let's say we let you go back to your other world, and you get John out of the trouble he's in. What then? Have you devised a scheme which will somehow allow you to evaporate from this world and permanently relocate to the other? There is no science on this planet that would support that theory."

"I hadn't got that far," Maggie said. "My first step is to save him."

"So, then, you do as you plan. You save him. Are you willing to let him go once you get him out of his predicament? Are you willing to risk your mental stability in this world to save this figment—"

"He's not a figment—"

"And forsake all that you've accomplished in this world so far—"

"I've accomplished nothing! Don't you see that? Nothing! I do dishes with Palmolive. Scrub the sinks with Bon Ami. Make sure there's extra starch in Sam's dress shirts. I shop at the market every Monday so I can make tuna casserole on Tuesdays and meatloaf on Fridays. Here it is, I finally have the chance to do something amazing! To do something no other woman—"

Maggie stopped herself.

"Go on," Dr. Germaine prompted.

"To show the world…"

"Which world?"

Maggie stared at the plastic flowers on the coffee table as if the answers were written on the petals. "Oh, my God, I'm—I'm crazy," she whispered. "I'm insane. I'm not normal like other women. I'm nothing but a circus freak." She waved her arm through the air as her voice rose. "Step under the big top to see the crazy lady who lives in two worlds at once! Only a nickel to see the crazy lady save the man of her dreams!"

"Maggie—"

"Why can't I be like other women? Why does that other world keep pulling me? Why can't I let it go?"

She felt her face twist, felt her eyebrows gather together and her lips distort into a sneer, and knew she looked like a madwoman. Of course she did—she *was* a madwoman.

"Let's go there together," Dr. Germaine said.

"We—don't have—a lot of time—"

She gagged on the words as her head grew dizzy.

"I need you to breathe, Maggie. If you don't relax, you will hyperventilate."

She closed her eyes, concentrating on the measured beats of her heart. In less than a minute, she had slowed her breathing enough to make her head stop spinning.

"Good," said Dr. Germaine. "Now. I'll be with you the entire time. Right by your side."

"Yes. Yes. That would be wonderful. Then you can help me save—"

"Please. Let me finish. Keep your breathing in check." He waited a moment, taking deep breaths along with Maggie before speaking again. "We need to keep your heart rate steady and your breathing as smooth and consistent as possible. Then we'll take it one step at a time. Slowly, carefully."

"But I don't have a lot of time. Oh! I made a list!"

Maggie jumped up and ran to the kitchen. In a matter of seconds she was back. She handed the piece of paper to Dr. Germaine.

"What's this?" he asked, scanning the sheet.

"Those are the things I'll need in order to save him," Maggie said, resuming her position on the sofa. She rubbed the edge of her skirt between her sweaty fingers and licked her dry lips. "At least I think so. Maybe not all of them."

"How do you propose to get them there?"

"Well, I—I figured that if I wrote them down, they'd be imprinted in my memory, and then, once I got to the gazebo, they'd be waiting for me."

"Interesting."

"It's the only way."

Dr. Germaine placed the sheet of paper on the coffee table. "Maggie, before we get started, we have to discuss some things. First of all, there is always the chance that you can't save him."

"I know."

But I will.

"And," he went on, "even though you feel in control right now, dreams can change when we least expect it."

"Yes, I know they can."

But not if I can help it.

"So, even though you have your list and your intentions are very clear and specific, there is always the chance that your dream will take you where you've never gone before. Scenarios could change in ways that shock you. John could turn into a gorilla. Or not show up at all. The castle could turn into a department store. Maybe you'll see your reflection and it will be your own sweet face again. Whatever happens, you need to be prepared for things to change. As you've already experienced, within our dreams, change is inevitable."

"I know."

"Where you're sitting right now—across from me, on your couch, in your living room, in this town—this is real life. Sam being a doctor, you being his wife, me being your therapist, all those things are real."

"But real life can change, too," Maggie said.

"Absolutely," Dr. Germaine agreed. "Much of the time, we have some control over those changes. Conscious mind equals control. But subconscious mind equals little or no control."

"But I have control. You'll see when we get there."

"If you have so much control, then why was John taken from you without your say-so? Why did his world suddenly encroach on yours if they were meant to be separate?"

"I don't know."

"Then let's find out, shall we?"

As they stood, Maggie pulled the pill box from her pocket.

"No, Maggie."

Dr. Germaine held out his hand.

"But—"

"We will get there through hypnosis," he told her. "No pills. Trust me."

"Yes," she said, trying not to let her doctor see the twitch that was slowly settling in her right eye. "Fine." With nervous reluctance she handed over the tiny box.

He slid the container into his pants pocket. "We will do this wherever you feel most comfortable. Here, in your bedroom, wherever you think is best."

"Upstairs," Maggie said, scooping up her list from the coffee table. "I seem to thrash about when I dream, so it's probably the safest place. I have to apologize for the bed not being made."

"Apology accepted." Dr. Germaine tucked the pad of paper under his arm and put the pen in his breast pocket. "Lead the way."

Chapter Twenty-three

She sat nearly upright, leaning back against two pillows, a light blanket covering her legs, her shoes on the floor beside the bed, the folded list held tightly in one fist. Dr. Germaine sat on a vanity chair which he'd placed next to the bed. Whether it was because exhaustion consumed her, or because her therapist's voice was as hypnotic as his words, Maggie wasn't sure, but within seconds of closing her eyes, she had fallen into her other world. She stood in the middle of the path—the very short path that led between the castle and the gazebo.

"Can you hear me?" Dr. Germaine asked. His voice fell into her world loud and clear like Zeus speaking to her from beyond the clouds.

"Yes," Maggie told him.

"Tell me where you are…what you see."

"I'm on the path," Maggie whispered. "I can see everything. The oak trees. The castle. The drawbridge. Two tall narrow windows along the top of the tower. Water in the moat. There's fog, but it's not as thick as before."

She turned around and saw that the gazebo was no longer in shambles. Under the clean white bench lay a green bundle. "The duffle bag!" she shouted.

"Are you sure?" Dr. Germaine's voice asked.

She didn't respond to his doubting voice as she hopped over potholes along the warped path. As she started up the gazebo steps, she tripped and fell hard against the bottom one.

"Ouch!"

"Maggie?"

"The rain boots I ordered come all the way up to my knees!"

She laughed as she regained her balance, then hobbled up the rest of the steps and over to the bench. Kneeling down, she slid out the khaki green bag and loosened the drawstring. She knew how silly she must look, pulling items out of the bulging bag like a child dumping out the contents of her Christmas stocking. She briefly wondered if, in the other world, her hands were reacting in pantomime.

"Here's the flashlight…and the rope! My, it's very long and heavy. But thick, just like I wanted. Here's a pen…and a legal pad." She moved the items to the side and continued digging. "Goodness!"

"What is it?"

"I thought I knew what a hacksaw was, but now I'm not so sure. This thing looks like it's made of shark's teeth." She slid it to the farthest edge of the pile. She stuck her hand into the bag and pulled out a long leather casing. From the slit in the end, a pearl handle protruded. "I imagined a kitchen knife, the kind for chopping vegetables. But this one…" She gently pulled it out of its pocket. "It's a sword. A saber, I think it's called." She lightly rubbed a finger along the silvery surface, careful not to cut her hand on the sharp edges. "It's beautiful." Placing the sword at her side, she realized the bag was empty. She patted her hands against material, flattening it out. "Something's missing."

Maggie felt the list being gently pried from her fingers, an odd sensation, since her fingers in her dream world didn't move in response. It was like having two bodies; two minds.

"Champagne?" Dr. Germaine asked.

"To celebrate with," Maggie said. "After I rescue John. I don't see it. Maybe I'm not supposed to—"

"Yes?"

"Nothing."

"Hey," she said, taking a look around. "I asked for a ladder, too." She clomped in her rain boots to the back side of the porch. "There it is!" she shouted, peering over the railing. "It's leaning up against the gazebo! And my horses are back!"

She picked up the notepad and flashlight and tucked them under her fabric belt, then wound her hair into a thick bun and skewered the pen through the clump like a hat pin. Finally, she grabbed the looped rope, placed it around her neck like an oversized necklace, and wedged the guarded saber beneath the other side of her sash. Feeling a bit like a comic book hero and smiling at the thought, she plodded down the steps and around to the back of the gazebo. She made her way along the edge of the field, allowing her fingers to glide across the tips of the revitalized blossoms. On the other side of the gazebo, the four horses stood together, chomping on clover. The wooden ladder lay on its edge, leaning against the trellis that enclosed the bottom of the porch. She rubbed her hand along the side.

"This is exactly as it should be," she said.

"What is?"

"Everything."

She stared at the castle. It stood there blankly, facing her like a façade in a stageplay. If she went around to the other side she was sure she'd find wooden supports holding it in place and empty paint cans strewn about.

"I feel at peace," she told Dr. Germaine. "I'm happy here."

Happy though she was, it surprised her that the castle didn't evoke any fear at the moment. The windows seemed no more menacing than a pair of puppy eyes. The high tower didn't cast a threatening shadow. Even the water running along the bottom edge of the castle wall gave the impression of a gentle stream rather than a foreboding obstruction.

She placed her hands on her hips and eyed the ditch only a few yards away. Although the channel appeared only a bit aggressive, it seemed to have an intelligence of sorts, as though patiently waiting for Maggie to make a decision. She bent over and picked up one end of the ladder.

"Why are you grunting?" Dr. Germaine asked.

"This ladder is heavier than it looks."

"What do you intend to do with it?"

"I'm going to drag it to the moat and lay it across like a bridge."

Maggie dragged the ladder toward the moat, unaware if Dr. Germaine responded or not. It was a strenuous task, but she finally managed to haul it over the buckles and dips and jagged stones in the path. Her primary focus was on positioning the ladder next to the trench without it slipping from her grasp. She peered over the edge into the water to see if she was still a goddess, but ripples distorted the other woman's face. She placed the ladder on its side along the rim of the moat and leaned it against her legs.

Maggie unclasped a hook on each side of the ladder's center and worked to lengthen it from seven feet to fifteen. "There," she said, staring across the moat.

She waited for Dr. Germaine to give her some advice, but if he offered any, she did not hear it.

"I can't do it," Maggie said after a moment. "I have no leverage to get it across."

"Perhaps you aren't supposed to save him at this time—"

"Don't say that!"

"Relax, Maggie. Stay in control."

"Without the ladder," she explained, "I could drown."

"Maggie, you are moving about in your subconscious mind. You cannot die there."

"What should I do?" she asked her doctor, a small part of her finding it amusing he was helping her with this task.

"Is there some type of dock or wooden ledge on your side?"

"Only an embankment about a foot above the water"

"Is there any place for the ladder to land on the other side?"

Maggie examined the face of the castle. "There's a stone ledge just above the water. I think it goes all the way around the building, but I'm not sure. It looks wide enough to stand on."

"Perhaps you could try to position the ladder upright on your side, and then let it fall to the other."

"Yes, that could—" She sucked in her breath.

"Maggie?"

She strained to listen. A clapping sound bounced along the top of the water from somewhere upstream.

Clap-clap-clap-clap—

"There's someone else here," she whispered.

"Who?"

"I can't see them. I can only hear."

"What do you hear?"

Maggie didn't answer. As she cautiously leaned over the moat to take a closer look, she caught a glimpse of a shadow moving beneath the surface. Before she made the choice to take a step back, an enormous mouth emerged from the darkness, spewing a fountain of water as it breached. Massive jaws snapped open and closed, like a giant pair of forceps, exposing hundreds of sharp teeth behind green veined lips.

Maggie was staring directly into the face of a gigantic reptile. The top of its head was round and scaly like a turtle, but its muzzle was similar to an alligator's. Penetrating black eyes seemed too small for its large head. Large scales like misaligned roof shingles rose along the back. Its skin was a dark brownish green, the color of muck from a swamp. The constant movement of the mouth opening and closing, spitting out some kind of smelly froth, seemed to be more of a reflexive action than a conscious decision to make Maggie its dinner.

This thought did not make her any less terrified.

"It's a monster," she said. "In the water. It's guarding the castle. I think…"

Mud sucked on Maggie's boots, so she bent down and yanked them out of the sludge with her hands. As she stumbled away from the edge, her flashlight loosened from her sash and tumbled into the moat. The monster gobbled it up, its sharp teeth hacking it to pieces, bits of debris spraying into the air. Its head bobbed like a buoy on the water's surface, taking in gallons of water as it made that horrific snapping-clapping-chomping sound with its mouth.

"Everything you encounter is a part of you," Dr. Germaine said. "You created it. Tell it to leave."

"Get out!" Maggie shouted toward the water. Her words bounced against the castle wall and back again.

The monster, its mouth locked in an open position, something moldy and gooey dripping from its lips, stared up at Maggie, its head cocked to the side, its eyes a glistening dark in contrast to its Pepsodent-white teeth.

Was the creature smiling?

"Go away!" Maggie yelled. She stomped her feet on the soft ground. Mud spattered against her legs and along the hem of her tunic. She grabbed onto the sheath, the sword still tucked inside. "Get out of my world!"

Maggie watched as the creature started gasping, its large black tongue dangling out of its alligator mouth, its eyes rolling back in its turtle head. It took a final puff before disappearing back under the water.

"It's gone," she said after a moment. "I don't think it can breathe out here."

She listened for the monster's return but heard nothing as she rubbed her hand along the sword's leather cover. She took a tentative step toward the moat, and then another. Near the edge, she gazed into the silent shadows of the water.

"I'm sure it's gone," she said again, more to reassure herself than to share the information with her doctor.

Dr. Germaine responded, but his words were buried under another's:

"Maggie!" John's voice was barely audible behind the thick plank that blocked the castle's entrance.

Maggie took a firm hold of the ladder and shimmied it to the best starting point. Carefully, she lifted it upwards. It towered over her as she managed a foothold. She eased the ladder straight up, her muscles contracting from the strain, smiling to herself, thrilled to be so strong and even more excited to show it. The ladder feet sank a few inches into the wet earth. The mud gathered around the bottom and held it in place. She slid her fingers up the sides, raising her arms as high as they could go, stretching and pushing at the same time. The ladder began to rock forward and back, and for a moment she was sure it would fall in the wrong direction, splitting in two and crushing her in the process. But with one last push, the ladder gained momentum, careening forward as she released it and the top catapulted through the air. It crashed hard on the other side, taking a perfect position at the base of the drawbridge.

"I did it! I'm going to climb across."

"Remember," Dr. Germaine said, his words slipping in and out of the clouds, "nothing within your subconscious can hurt you."

She sat on the edge of the embankment, cool mud seeping through the back of her tunic. After counting to ten, she scooted herself forward, then on all fours crawled onto the ladder. If she'd been wearing loafers, or a pair of Keds, she may have had the courage to walk across. But in her cumbersome boots, with a heavy rope around her neck, and a sword beneath her sash, crawling across was the surest way, albeit the slowest. She clutched the ladder's sides as the boots' rubber soles found their own grip against the rung behind her. She held her position a moment and slowly, one hand in front of the other, each foot following carefully behind, inched along the bridge, her destiny waiting for her on the other side.

Chapter Twenty-four

Dr. Germaine's voice sounded far away now as his statement fell into her dream: "You've been under for quite some time."

"Time doesn't matter here," Maggie explained.

He said something else, but she didn't pay attention. She continued to crawl along the ladder, alternating her right hand, right foot, left hand, left foot. As she reached the center, the bridge began to sink under her weight. Maggie froze, her boots held firmly against the rungs, her right hand removing itself from the sagging ladder in favor of gripping the sword.

She heard the monster's cry in the distance.

"It's back," she whispered.

"The monster? Do not worry. You are in control…"

Maggie's eyes moved along the seemingly endless moat, first to the right and then to the left. She could make out nothing past the thick gray fog swirling in the distance.

The strange beast's howl floated to her from somewhere upstream. Or was it downstream? Maybe it was coming from the other side of the castle—if there was another side.

The ladder sagged more, dunking Maggie's knees in the water.

She was a mere eight feet from the castle. If she was so

inclined, she could spit and hit the wall. She moved more quickly now, hightailing it past the center, relieved when the ladder straightened out. Her knees no longer touched the water. She found a smooth rhythm in her forward motion.

"I've made it," she told Dr. Germaine, stretching out an arm and placing a hand against the wet stones.

"I knew you would."

Hoisting herself onto the ledge and sitting for a moment to rest, Maggie glanced back across the moat. On the other side, the end of the ladder still sat snugly on the ridge, connecting her world to this one. She craned her neck and peered up at the tower, the thick stones stacked one on top of the other, disappearing into the high clouds above. The two rectangular windows sat near the very top at least fifty feet above her head.

"The windows are too high," Maggie said.

"What about the door?" Dr. Germaine's faraway voice asked.

"It's behind the drawbridge."

Just to the right of the drawbridge, Maggie positioned herself with her toes pointed toward the wall, her arms outstretched, her palms against the stones to help keep her steady. She couldn't be too careful. Who knew how many other monsters lurked somewhere below, waiting for her to take one tiny step back, lose her balance—

"Maggie?" John's sweet voice fell into her ears easily even though inches of wood and stone stood between them.

Maggie placed her cheek against the wood. "John!"

"Do you see him?" Dr. Germaine asked.

"Get rid of the doctor," John ordered.

"Why?"

"Why what?" Dr. Germaine asked.

"Because he is not here to help you," John said. "He is only here for himself."

"That can't be true."

"What can't be true?" Dr. Germaine asked.

"You do not need him," John said. "You only *think* you do."

Wasn't it because of Dr. Germaine that she was here at all? She didn't believe she could have made it this far without him. Still, she wanted to keep her conversation with John private. How could that be possible with her therapist sitting right next to her?

"Oh," Maggie told her doctor. "I thought I heard him, but I was wrong."

"Good," John told Maggie. "Find a way to get rid of him. We must hurry."

"What if I can't get in?" she asked, her voice trembling.

"I have faith in you," Dr. Germaine told her.

"He is a smart man," John said. "And you are a strong woman. You can do anything you wish. *Anything.*"

After a moment, Maggie said, "Dr. Germaine, I need to do the rest alone."

From the clouds, Dr. Germaine's voice rained down. "I'm afraid that's impossible. You cannot do this without my help."

John's voice seeped through the wall. "Maggie, he is wrong. You do not need him. You are strong enough to do this alone."

Maggie said, "Dr. Germaine, I promise I don't need your help anymore."

"Three hours ago, you begged me to help you."

Three hours?

"I will not leave you," Dr. Germaine said. "I am responsible for your welfare."

Maggie thought a moment. She not only felt strong, but suddenly wise as well.

"You're right," she told her therapist, sighing loudly for

effect. "You should be here with me. I just didn't want to be a burden."

"A patient is never a burden."

John said, "Maggie, he can't—"

"Do you trust me?" Maggie asked.

In unison, Dr. Germaine and John said, "Yes."

"Any advice on how to get inside?" she asked.

Dr. Germaine spoke first: "Windows and doors often appear when needed most. Perhaps you will find one on the other side of the building."

"You may be right," Maggie said. "Give me a moment while I try that."

But Maggie did not move from her spot on the ledge.

"Excellent, Maggie," John said through the wall. "Here is what you must do: Get as close to the center of the drawbridge door as you can. Directly underneath is a stone that is darker than the others. That will be your way in."

Maggie moved a few inches along the ledge until she stood directly in front of the sealed drawbridge.

"Look underneath the ledge."

Maggie carefully slid her body down the wall and lay on her right side along the ledge. She tried to lean over far enough to see the rock under the shelf, but could not do so without falling.

"These rocks sure do look the same," she said.

"Do they?" Dr. Germaine responded.

"You will have to get into the moat to see the darker stone," John told her. "Once you find it, you can climb back onto the ledge."

"I'm afraid to go in the water," she blurted.

"Why would you have to go in the water?" Dr. Germaine asked.

"What I mean is," she said, catching herself, "I hope I won't have to."

"Nothing can hurt you," he reminded her gently.

Maggie repositioned the rope more securely around her neck and took three deep breaths to prepare for the cold shock.

"You're breathing has become erratic," Dr. Germaine said. She felt a gentle touch against her wrist.

"I'm fine," Maggie said. "It just seems like this castle wall goes on forever."

"You will find an entrance, if that's what is needed to discover your resolution."

"Of course," she replied, placing her hands on the ledge and slowly sinking into the frigid water, but as soon as she did so, she lost her grip on the wet stones. The weight of the rope and the awkwardness of her boots caused her to sink rapidly into the moat. She flailed her arms in a futile attempt to swim. Her boots slammed against the muddy bottom. She pushed herself upward, then realized with exhilaration that she was standing—the water only came up to her shoulders!

She scanned the wall beneath the ledge and located the stone. It was much darker than the others, just as John had said, and much more dull like it had been painted years before. "I see it!" She pressed her lips together as soon as she shouted the words.

"See what?" Dr. Germaine asked.

"Maggie," John warned, "you must be more careful."

"The sun," Maggie said, amazed by how clear her critical thinking skills had become.

"In the dreamscape," Dr. Germaine told her, "the sun often represents what we believe will be a brighter future…"

"Turn the stone to the left," John instructed. "But be careful.

If you do not move quickly, the drawbridge may come down on your head."

Maggie grew uncertain as questions zipped through her mind: If the castle didn't belong to John, and it wasn't hers even though this was her dream, then who did it belong to? Who had locked him inside, and why?

"Please," John said. "Hurry."

The desperation in his voice got her moving. She placed a palm on the face of the round stone and gripped it. It fit perfectly in her hand, like one was made for the other, but when she tried to move it, it refused to budge.

"Maggie," John said, "you must be quick about it."

Still, the stone remained fixed.

"Try harder," he told her. "This is the only way. Please. Now is the time."

Now is the time.

The words rolled around in her head as she gripped the stone with both hands, employing every muscle. Her biceps tensed the same way they had the first time she used a drill press. Her back muscles grew as solid as the rock she grasped. Miraculously, it began to turn.

"That is it!" came John's joyful words. "I knew you could do it."

The stone moved slowly like a tightly sealed jelly jar lid, then unscrewed itself from the wall. It leaped with a loud plop before sinking beneath the surface.

As Maggie watched it disappear, she heard the distinct racket of chains being released and sliding through pulleys. She looked up to see the heavy drawbridge gaining speed. She didn't have time to move to the side. Instead, she ducked her head below the water's surface just as the giant wooden plank came crashing down. It slammed into the ladder, smashing it to bits, large wooden splinters torpedoing through the water. She lay against the bottom of the moat until the avalanche of wood and sound diminished.

Dr. Germaine's voice floated down to her. "Maggie…"

She scurried along the bottom looking for a place to surface. A large shadow loomed over her, cast by the drawbridge. As she swam through the chilly moat, it came to her: She had unlocked the drawbridge. It would only be moments before she reached John. She would finally be able to save him!

Save him from what?

She shook the thought away as her hands groped the mud to maneuver more deftly along the bottom. Once out of the drawbridge's shadow, she stood up a few feet from where the ladder used to be. Her eyes followed the elaborate chains that began at the outer end of the bridge and ran diagonally to the top corners of the stone archway. Now stretched across the moat, the drawbridge had become the new link between the end of the path and the castle. She placed her palms on the heavy wood, hiked a leg up, and pulled herself onto the platform. She clomped with excitement in her boots along the solid bridge, thrilled that she had only one more task before rescuing John: opening the door.

"Maggie!" John's voice sounded so close. "We must hurry. The whistle will soon blow!"

Whistle?

"Maggie," Dr. Germaine said, "do you see anything yet?"

"Not yet. But I think I'm getting close."

When she reached the door, she immediately placed a palm against the wood and knew that on the other side, John's hand mirrored hers.

I will save you.

Maggie closed her eyes and concentrated as she placed her hands on the door handle.

"Good, Maggie," John encouraged. "Hurry."

She yanked hard on the latch. The heavy door opened one inch, then two, and she felt an indescribable power flow though her arms and hands. She took a step back as the door swung open. There stood John, arms limply hanging down in front of him, rusty iron shackles tightly binding his wrists together.

As she placed one boot against the threshold, a shrill whistle echoed from deep within the fortress, reaching for her head and beating against her skull. She covered her ears to keep out the pain, but the screeching was merciless. She doubled over in agony and fell to her knees.

Dr. Germaine's voice barely broke through the noise. "What is the matter?"

And then John's voice underneath the other, barely perceptible, though she could have read his lips even if his words had been inaudible: "…too late."

Still holding her ears and refusing to accept what John had just told her, Maggie forced herself into a standing position. She finished her short journey through the entranceway.

"Who did this to you?" she shouted.

"Maggie!" Dr. Germaine called.

The whistle's scream was abruptly cut off, leaving behind an almost tangible trace that kept Maggie's skull vibrating. She removed her hands from her ears and took a final step toward John, her arms outstretched. She wasn't too late after all. She would save him now, and they—

A familiar voice came crashing into her secret world, ripping a hole through its center. A voice that was as angry as it was intrusive.

"Who the hell are *you?*" the man's voice demanded.

"I'm Dr. Germaine. You and I met on New Year's Eve—"

His words were interrupted by the unmistakable explosion of a fist against a jaw.

"You son-of-a-bitch! What are you doing with my wife?"

Then the shaking began. The world around Maggie began to lose focus. John's face blurred, his blond curls melting against his forehead and cheeks. The stone walls wobbled, and for a moment she was sure the earthquake would bring the castle down, crushing them both. The floor tilted, spilling her against the hard stones, sending daggers through her knees. Maggie crawled to the doorway, her arms extended outward, grabbing onto the frame, trying with desperation to maintain her balance.

"Maggie!" the man's angry voice shouted. "Wake up!"

The slap of a hand landed hard against her cheek.

"She's my patient!"

John fell to his knees, eyes cast downward, linked fists beating the floor. "Maggie," he cried. "You are too late…"

Maggie stretched an arm toward him, her fingers scratching the air in front of her, trying to grab onto the fuzzy image he had become. But the hands that shook her were more powerful than her own.

"John!" she screamed.

Her hands lost their grip on the shaking doorframe and she fell backward onto the bridge. She felt the rush of air pressing against her damp clothing as the heavy door slammed shut. The castle grew into a blurry painting, the gray hues swirling together like a painter's dirty palette.

"I'm sorry, John!" Maggie screamed. "I'll come back! John!"

As Maggie was torn from that other world and thrown back into the one she now hated, she heard another voice calling

John's name—an unfamiliar and frightening voice that did not belong to Dr. Germaine or Sam. The voice seemed to come from both worlds, the volume pummeling Maggie over the head like a giant hammer and echoing in her mind long after she opened her eyes. It was the voice of a woman.

A very angry woman.

Chapter Twenty-five

Her peripheral vision was barely able to discern her husband's face. As if he wanted to make himself known to her, he leaned over her, a cave man with his five o'clock shadow and sunken eyes. Behind Sam, Dr. Germaine stood next to the dresser, rubbing his chin and gazing through stunned eyes.

"Maggie," Sam pleaded. He stared at her like she had just burned down their house. "Help me to understand."

"Sam," she said.

Her voice would have sounded apologetic a few weeks or even days earlier, but not now. Now she was angry.

As angry as the woman who had screamed John's name?

"You had no right to wake me up," she told him.

Sam shot a seething look in Dr. Germaine's direction.

"You were supposed to be gone until Saturday," she added.

"I came home early. As a surprise."

Maggie held onto Sam's neck as she swung her legs over the bed, placed her feet on the floor, pushed her tousled hair back from her damp face, and took in a deep breath. She tried to ignore the spinning sensation in her head and stomach.

"I only wanted to save him," she whispered, mostly to herself.

"Save who?" Sam asked. "*Him?*" He pointed a thumb at Dr.

Germaine, whose hand was no longer rubbing his chin but was jotting notes down on his pad.

"Stop it, Sam," Maggie said. "You have no idea what you're talking about."

"Then why don't you enlighten me?"

Maggie stood up. The nausea and dizziness tried to overtake her, but she closed her eyes a moment and concentrated once more on her breathing.

"What did you do to her?" Sam sputtered at Dr. Germaine.

Maggie pushed passed Sam and went into the bathroom, slamming the door behind her.

"Come back here!" Sam exploded from the bedroom. "You at least owe me the courtesy of an explanation!"

She splashed cold water on her face and patted it dry. She pushed her hair behind her ears and stared at her sullen face in the mirror, suddenly detesting her freckles, her thick waxy lips, her red hair, her untamed curls.

Dr. Germaine's voice seeped under the bathroom door.

"Your wife is delusional, Dr. Lerner. I placed her under hypnosis, hoping to get to the crux of her issues. Something plagues your wife's mental faculties. Professional guidance is her only—"

"My wife does not need the uninvited help of a stranger. She needs a stable home with children, and a husband who can give her both."

"Your wife is torn between two worlds. The tangible one in which we live, and the imaginary one that haunts her subconscious. She is convinced that the man in her dream is real. That the world she has created is—"

Maggie stormed into the bedroom.

"Stop talking about me like I'm a lunatic!" She turned on Dr.

Germaine. "You were there with me! How can you say it isn't real? You witnessed the moat, the ladder, the monster—"

She was stopped by Dr. Germaine's look of pity. He hadn't heard or seen anything. He had only sat beside her, watching the expressions on her face. Observing her arm and leg twitches. Listening to fragments of her one-sided conversations.

"Monster?" Sam asked, his eyes darting back and forth from his wife to her therapist.

"In Maggie's other world she's strong," Dr. Germaine explained, his voice low and steady. "The ultimate heroine."

"Give me my pills," Maggie told Dr. Germaine.

"I cannot do that."

"Give them to me!"

"Your other world is not real."

Sam said, "I don't understand—"

But Maggie didn't have time to make Sam understand, even if she could. Time was running out. Perhaps it already had…

"I'm sorry, Sam," she mumbled as she picked up her flats from the floor and hurried through the bedroom doorway.

"Where are you going?"

Maggie didn't answer. She nearly tripped down the stairs and grabbed onto the railing as she slid on one shoe, then the other. In the center of the kitchen table sat a blue vase filled with a bouquet of daisies and mums. The small envelope displayed in pretty script, "For My Little Magpie." She stopped, but only for a moment, before grabbing her coat from the back of a chair. Sam's keys lay on the table. She grabbed those too. A minute later, she was backing down the driveway, the Silver Streak's tires squealing against the icy pavement.

As she drove out of the neighborhood, she was positive she could hear Sam's voice calling after her. And from somewhere beyond the town's borders, beyond the horizon, beyond the Biblical heavens in which she had been raised to believe, she could hear John's voice calling, too.

Chapter Twenty-six

In the back corner of Peterson's Drug Store behind aisles of magazines and hats and scarves, Maggie stood in the phone booth. The smell of grilled cheese and fresh coffee wafted under the door from the nearby soda fountain. Her hand shook as it held the telephone.

"Yes, I'll hold."

She nearly cried with relief when the line clicked.

"Maggie?" Jocelyn said. "Maggie Lerner? Well, how the hell are ya, hon? I haven't heard from you in ages."

"Joss. I need something."

"Oh…"

"Look. I'm sort of over a barrel here. Do you still…you know…"

"No problem. Where and when?"

"Meet me at—" Maggie spotted the happy families lined up along the lunch counter, eating burgers and fries, stirring their chocolate milkshakes and root beer floats. "No," she said. "Not here…"

"Let's meet over at Eastern," Jocelyn said.

"Won't someone see us?"

"What someone? That place is as quiet as a turkey farm the day after Thanksgiving."

"What are you talking about?"

"Didn't you hear?" Joss asked. "Eastern went belly up."

Eastern had closed? How could Maggie not have known? Where had she been these last few weeks?

Not in the real world, her mind told her.

"I can meet you in twenty," Joss said. "Maggie? You there?"

"Yes. Fine. I'll see you there."

***

Breath in, breath out, slowly now…

She drove through the empty parking lot and around the east side of the building, then pulled the car alongside the long brick wall and parked. A faded blue Buick surrounded by pigeons inanely pecking at the asphalt was parked by the back door. The birds fluttered away when Maggie stepped out of the car and slammed the door. Except for the Buick's engine clicking in response to the cold air, the place was silent. Standing in the slush, she looked around the empty parking lot. The factory seemed as though it had never been a factory at all, only an abandoned brick building, comparable to so many others on this seedy side of Baltimore.

She walked up the slick cement steps, the same steps where she and her coworkers had shared lunches and gossip. A million years ago, it seemed. The metal door felt heavy in her hand as she pulled it back and entered the building. As the door swung shut behind her, she was immediately pummeled by the feeling of claustrophobia, the total blackness stealing the air out of her lungs.

When the plant was up and running, the employees had worked between four windowless walls under long rows of lights dangling high overhead. But the power had obviously been shut off, and the gloomy day only allowed scraps of light to enter through the dormers which ran the length of the tall building's roof line. The darkness that flooded the remainder of the space had turned the factory into a giant tomb.

But Maggie didn't need light to help her find her way around. She knew from memory the plant's simple layout. The time clock hung to the right of the door. If she turned in that direction and walked all the way to the wall running perpendicular to the frontage road, she would find the steel staircase. The stairs led up to a closed-in loft with a huge glass window looking out over the factory—Sander's office. Next to his office was a bathroom, next to that an elevator that had never worked the entire time Maggie was employed at Eastern. Just below the mezzanine, another bathroom sat directly underneath the one upstairs, only this one was located inside a men's locker room that had been split in two by a dividing wall to accommodate the women. The break room sat next to that, with its temperamental Coca-Cola machine, flickering bulbs, tattered chairs, and overflowing ashtrays. If she walked in the other direction, following the wall on her left, bypassing the work stations that monopolized the center, she would eventually reach the massive roll-up door where the dock loaders prepared the assembled parts for pick-up, packing and stacking crates the size of baby elephants. Next to the roll-up door, another small bathroom and a supply closet stood side by side.

A whirring noise caused Maggie's eyes to dart up to the ceiling. Morning doves had often roosted up in the eaves, but this sound was not the cooing of doves. With her head tilted, she listened to the uneven hum of the two large fans, one on each side of the dormers. Maggie had never been able to hear the fans over the sounds of drills and smelters, but now she listened as the winter wind dragged itself across the roof and forced the blades to rotate. As they whirred in their cages, they created a show of distorted shadows. They seemed lonely and isolated way up there above her head.

Something scuttling across the floor took her attention away from the ceiling, and her eyes scanned the darkness before her. Probably a rat. Or a mouse. Long whiskers and pink nose and beady eyes she could not see but could easily imagine.

Her breath drew in and out in sporadic puffs. Underneath the lingering odor of burned oil and grease, the room smelled stale and moldy, as if no clean air had entered or escaped the building in years. Perhaps it had always been this way, and she had never noticed until now, her other senses compensating for her temporary lack of vision.

Had this really been her place of employment along with three hundred others? Where had everyone gone? How much time had passed since the war had ended? Since the plant had closed?

How could it be that she did not know?

She forced herself to exhale while whispering into the dark, "Jocelyn?"

She took a few steps forward and ran her shin into a crate. She clenched her jaw to keep from yelling out, rubbed her hand against her leg, and stepped around the crate. As she moved forward, her arms extended, her eyes began to adjust to the feeble streams of light trickling down from the dormers. She could barely make out the drills and smelters and riveters, no longer operational, turned over on their sides and taken apart, the debris in odd piles along the long steel counters. Beneath her feet, metal shards lay like carpet across the wide expanse of cement floor. Empty boxes and crates that at one time had stood in evenly stacked towers were strewn across the floor in every direction. Sand castings had been randomly tossed about like a tornado had ripped through the room.

Or a bomb, Maggie thought numbly.

A cough came from somewhere in the shadows, from the place where the nuts-and-bolts girls used to perform their tedious jobs, first cleaning the hardware, then screwing one piece into another, and finally placing them in neat little rows on a speedy conveyor belt.

"Joss?" Maggie whispered, hopeful, her voice echoing through the cave and bouncing off of the steel beams overhead.

A flicker of light shocked Maggie's eyes, then vanished, leaving behind trails of green and yellow.

"Back here."

Maggie stepped around a ladder on its side and continued toward the back left corner of the building. Pieces of broken glass felt like gravel against the soles of her shoes as she sidestepped overturned bins of machine parts and tried not to knock her head into the heavy chain hoists suspended from the ceiling.

Jocelyn sat on a stool with her legs crossed in front of the lifeless conveyor belt. She wore a black coat, a plaid scarf, and a pair of galoshes below her skirt. A lit flashlight lay across her lap, the beam reaching randomly into the dark.

"Welcome back to old times," Jocelyn said.

"What happened to this place?" Maggie asked.

"I can't believe you didn't hear. It was Sanders."

"Sanders closed the plant?"

"He didn't close it. The Feds did."

"Why?"

"Apparently Sanders is as stupid as he is ugly. Get a load of this. He had a little business on the side selling illegal weapons.

Guns mostly. Rumor has it that someone from Eastern ratted on him."

"Who was he selling them to?"

"Black market," Joss said. "A lot of Americans are afraid of every little thing. Commies, Japs, Nazis who don't want to admit the damned war is over. Sanders had quite a market to tap into."

"What did they do to him?"

"Trial's in a few weeks. I'll bet his bald head was as red as a Russian flag when they arrested him on that Cuban beach."

"What about the guys?"

Jocelyn shrugged. "On to find work in other places, I suppose. Lots of jobs out there, or so the government keeps saying. I got a placement at Macy's perfume counter. It's pretty slow this time of year, what with Christmas only six weeks past. But it's right next to the men's suit department, so that's a gas. Come in sometime. I'll spritz you with Chanel."

They remained silent for a moment.

"Well, let's get on with it," Jocelyn said, sliding off the stool. She tucked the flashlight under her arm and straightened out her skirt. "How many?"

You don't need the pills to get there.

"Maybe a dozen?" Maggie suggested. "No. Two."

Jocelyn started to walk away, shining the light in front of her and leaving Maggie in the dark.

"Where are you going?" Maggie asked.

"To get what you came here for."

"You don't have them with you?"

"Just stay here, Mags. I'll be back in a jiff."

Maggie asked no more questions as Jocelyn disappeared into the shadows. To ask questions would only delay things further.

As she waited, she rubbed her hand along the edge of a rusty scaffold and thought about what Joss had told her: Sanders. Illegal guns. Black market. The whole lot sounded like a Depression gangster story.

She peered into the dark, hoping to see Jocelyn's beam of light, but none came. After waiting nearly ten minutes, Maggie grew agitated. She whispered, "Joss?" but the only answer was the sound of an unknown critter as it scurried across the floor nearby. She put her hands out in front of her and found the stool, then sat on it with her feet on the rung.

What was taking Jocelyn so long?

Maggie hopped back off the stool and took a tentative step forward, landing directly on a piece of metal sheeting, creating a sound like a violin bow across a saw. The sour tune transmitted a long flat note from one end of the building to the other as the metal flexed under her shoe. But beneath the sound of the flimsy material, Maggie heard hushed voices. She stepped off the sheet and tiptoed around it with her hands still extended, touching an occasional steel support pole as she inched forward. She bumped into abandoned boxes, some full, some empty—she could tell which was which by how easily each box moved when she ran into it. She continued on, the whispers growing louder, though still unintelligible.

She could tell she had reached the back of the factory by the smell of the latrine, used by the crew that had spent their days sorting through thousands of rivets and other hardware, determining which was passable, which was a dud; greasing and cleaning parts so they could be safely and economically used. Beneath the latrine smell was the scent of Ajax.

Next to the bathroom, the supply closet stood with the door partly open. A dim yellow glow escaped from within. Hiding behind a steel girder, Maggie strained to see the silhouette standing in the middle of the tiny room. She could barely make out Jocelyn's profile, her European nose poking out from all that thick black hair. In her hand, she held onto a small glass bottle that rattled as she spoke.

Murmurs rose into the still air, the unintelligible words gaining strength and flying out of the tiny room.

From behind the door, a woman's accusing voice whisper-screamed: "You've brought her *here?*"

"What's the big deal?" Joss asked. "It's not like she's going to tell anyone."

"Give them back to me."

"What—" Jocelyn was suddenly jerked behind the door, disappearing from Maggie's view.

"How could you be so stupid? You got rocks in your head or something?"

"It's only one person," Joss said.

"I don't care!"

"She doesn't know."

"I said, I don't care!"

Maggie unknowingly left her shelter behind the steel post and drifted to a spot ten feet from the doorway.

"Get out," the woman said. "Now."

Jocelyn came into view again. She threw her hands up in the air in exasperation, opened her mouth to say something else, but snapped it shut again. She stormed out of the closet and slammed the door behind her. The flutter of wings sounded from somewhere above.

"Come on," Jocelyn said, grabbing Maggie by the wrist. "The party's over."

"What about—"

"No deal."

"But I need—"

"Look," Joss said, stopping and turning to Maggie, her flashlight positioned inches beneath her chin, turning her into a gargoyle. "I said 'no deal.' Sorry."

Maggie, in a panic, tried to keep up with Jocelyn, whose gait was like an angry alley cat's, stepping with confidence over or around the toppled machines and dismantled parts and empty crates.

"But I need them," Maggie said, shocked by the desperation in her own voice as she followed the ray of light that was quickly disappearing into the darkness ahead.

"Yeah?" Jocelyn answered. "My heart bleeds for you."

Maggie stumbled over a cement block and landed hard on a knee.

Jocelyn looked back, briefly scanned Maggie with the light, then continued moving forward, her boots drumming the cement. As Maggie worked to stand up, the drumming vanished behind a slamming door.

"Jocelyn?" Maggie called, wincing as she straightened out her knees. "Joss?"

She felt the rip in her stockings, felt the blood with her finger tips as it seeped through. Tears rolled in thin streams down her cheeks. Her lips trembled uncontrollably.

An engine revved outside, then disappeared.

Her only connection to John had just slipped away.

Maggie stood in the middle of the factory, hugging herself to keep the shaking from taking over. She turned around, again facing the direction of the loading dock.

She could ask for the pills herself, Maggie reasoned. What dealer wouldn't be thrilled to get rid of the middle man? There was more money to be made that way, wasn't there?

Maggie tried to see something, anything, through the black. She didn't only feel alone, she was alone. Except for the person selling the pills.

The factory was ice cold, the winter wind forcing its way through each and every crevice. Maggie wrapped her scarf more tightly around her neck and headed again in the direction of the closet. She felt her way past the crates and boxes, past the steel beams and the conveyor belt. Up ahead, the thin slice of horizontal light she had seen earlier was no longer visible. Standing a few feet from the door, Maggie heard a muffled voice. Without uttering a breath, she stood still and listened. One voice. The quiet whisper of a woman.

"Joss?"

But Joss was probably on the highway by now.

The slow and even rhythm of the voice snaked its way around the cavernous factory, reminding Maggie of all those years in Sunday school, counting *Hail Marys* or *Our Fathers* on a rosary. The voice in the dark thinned until it disappeared altogether, like the person had drifted off to sleep.

Thankful for the last hint of twilight drifting down through the dormers, Maggie inched closer to the door until she stood right in front of it. She couldn't be guaranteed that the person behind the door would be cordial; she certainly hadn't been with Jocelyn.

But it didn't matter. Maggie wasn't here for a social hour. Before she had a chance to change her mind, she tapped one light knuckle against the door.

No answer.

Maggie put her ear to the door, but no sound came from within.

She turned the knob slowly, cracked the door a few inches, and finally opened it all the way.

The room was pitch-dark. Maggie stood like a block of ice as she waited for a breath, a rustle of any kind. The room was unoccupied, she could tell even without seeing. The other person must have left the room while Maggie was walking toward the other side of the building with Jocelyn. She was probably in the bathroom, reciting her prayers, chanting, sleep talking, or whatever it was Maggie had heard. Maybe she had already left the building through another exit.

Maybe she's watching me from the corners, Maggie thought, glancing behind her, the sudden urge to run causing her calves to twitch.

While staring into the dark closet, she absently placed a hand against her nose. Smells of unwashed hair and soiled clothes swirled around her. She reached along the wall and located the switch. Dim lamplight lit the space. Maggie gasped. The room had turned into a bird's nest, or the den of a wild animal. What was once a closet for brooms and buckets and cleaning agents was now filled with mounds of refuse. The stench seemed to carry weight, like a thick cloud from one of those Midwest dust storm photographs that had made Dorthea Lange famous. The windowless space was only five feet by five feet square. In the center lay a stained twin mattress haphazardly covered by an old wool blanket, moth holes as big as quarters. The wall to the right was lined with stacks of magazines and newspapers two feet high. In one corner sat a rusty stool next to a small utility table. On the table was a glass of dirty water next to the lit lamp which had no shade. Precariously balanced next to the lamp sat another mountain of magazines. Under the table sat a large glass jar filled with a yellow oily liquid, the worn label telling her it was "Citron Cleaning Fluid" which promised to "Clean just about anything!" but warned the user to "HANDLE WITH CARE!" Amid the clutter, empty pill bottles were strewn about, some on the table but most on the floor, their lids missing, most likely buried somewhere in the mess. With her foot, Maggie tentatively grazed a pile of soiled shirts and coveralls.

Trying not to step directly on the rubbish, she went to the low lit table and stared at the magazines, which weren't really magazines at all but comic books, damp and reeking of mold, most likely salvaged from the break room. A faded *Superman* stared up at her. She slid it out of the way and sifted through the pile, uncovering the commonly known faces of *Captain America*, *The Phantom*, *The Green Hornet*, *Zorro*, *Aqua Man*. She saw covers of comics she had heard of but had never seen, like *The Cat* and *The Phantom Lady*.

Out of habit, she pushed the splayed-out comics into a tidy pile. She cocked her head to the side and listened. All was quiet except for the rattle of the dormer windows each time a truck zoomed across the overpass, or the B&O screamed against its tracks in the distance.

She looked around the tiny space again. Rusty water stains spread out like giant squashed spiders on the ceiling. Mouse droppings decorated the corners. The walls shed paint in thick mushroom-colored ribbons.

Who would choose to live like this?

Someone addicted to drugs, her mind told her.

Fatigue and paranoia pelted Maggie. Fear of being discovered, or something even more unimaginable, crept up behind her, breathing hotly on her neck. She had seen enough gangster movies to know how these scenarios sometimes play out. What woman in her right mind would walk into a dark deserted building on a winter evening on this side of town?

She stepped backward across the threshold, pulling the door

closed, mindful of the trash behind her heels. With her hand still on the brass plated knob, short bursts of whispers floated around her, yet came from nowhere specific. She froze, gripping the knob like a weapon. As she held her breath, the voices slowly faded. Within moments, she could hear nothing other than her own heartbeat which had vacated her chest and pulsated in her throat.

I am losing what is left of my mind.

She pulled the closet door until the latch clicked in place and turned around. The factory was even darker now, sinister nighttime shadows consuming everything. As Maggie moved away from the closet, the sound of her footsteps were accompanied by the two fans above as the wind cranked the large rusty blades around and around. She hiked faster now, her steps creating their own uneasy rhythm. Without stumbling, she made her way back to the door on the other side of the building. Soon, she was turning the ignition, pressing her foot against the accelerator, and speeding out of the parking lot. She raced onto the side street that would lead her to the highway.

"I'm coming, John," she breathed as she drove, vapor from her words hitting the windshield and creating a hazy circle.

But how? How could she do it without the pills? Without her therapist?

Maggie had no choice—she would have to find a way.

Chapter Twenty-seven

"Six dollars." The motel clerk's face was as expressionless as his voice.

Maggie pulled a wad of bills out of her wallet.

I will happily give up my next few manicures. I will happily give them up for the rest of my life.

The motel room was nearly as tiny as the closet back at the plant and smelled almost as bad: old sweat hidden beneath a hint of bleach. Next to the full-size bed sat an end table with an ugly green lamp on top. Maggie opened the drawer and placed her hand against the Bible's black leather cover for a moment. She closed the drawer again, slipped out of her coat and tossed it across the worn chair, then turned the lock on the door. She pulled the drapes so not one sliver of the setting sun could sneak through, then glanced toward the radiator, silently begging it not to clang or whistle.

Whistle.

She slipped off her shoes, stretched out on the musty bed, rearranged the uneven pillow beneath her head, and straightened out her skirt. She closed her eyes. In and out she breathed until her face relaxed and her lungs moved in and out like a slow-motion accordion. In and out, just as she'd been taught. In and out, until her hands and feet felt invisible and her body floated up and away.

Germaine was right, she realized with wonder as she effortlessly sank into her other world: no pills necessary. But she didn't need Dr. Germaine's help either; she didn't need anyone's help. This was getting easier all the time. Like perfectly performing a magic trick after a few rehearsals.

There she stood on the drawbridge in front of the castle, just a few moments earlier than when she had left it. Her wet tunic clung to her skin. The air was thick with the scent of lemons.

"Everything is as I left it," she said out loud, caressing the sword beneath her sash.

"Maggie!" John's voice came from beyond the castle walls.

Now she could speak to him. She could shout and laugh and cry, say or do anything she wanted without intruders. It was amazing—unbelievable even—to have such freedom!

"John!"

In her clunky boots, she took large strides up the drawbridge toward the door and willed it to open while pressing on the latch. The door swung open and there, just as she had left him, stood John, his hands still trapped in chains.

"Come with me!" she shouted, stepping over the threshold.

But as she reached out her arms, the whistle screamed, and even though she thought she was ready for it, the searing pain forced her to cover her ears. As she waited out the sound, she felt the intense whoosh of air. John had fallen to his knees and was shaking uncontrollably. She removed her hands from her ears, the shrillness stabbing knives into her eardrums, and dug her fingertips into John's shoulders.

"Get up!" Maggie demanded as she yanked on his arms. She would not let John's momentary paralysis prevent her from saving him.

He barely managed a squatting position.

The door moved another foot closer to its frame.

She stood behind him and firmly grabbed him by the elbows, forced him into a standing position, and pushed him toward the doorway.

But it was too late. John moved too slowly. The door slammed into its frame. At the same time, the whistle stopped.

Heavy silence and absence of sunlight filled the entryway.

"Oh, Maggie," John whispered, his surrendering words trickling through the buzzing in her ears.

The foyer was damp and cool, like a root cellar after days of rain. The walls appeared to be limestone, glistening like the wet stones outside. Orange and yellow light came from flickering candles skewered on vertical spikes along the wall twenty feet in front of them, and a few more rested in iron wall brackets on either side of the door. The only exit leading out of the foyer was a hallway just ahead to the left. And, of course, the door that had just slammed shut behind them.

"It is too late," John told her. He fell back onto the floor, landing hard on his bottom. He leaned his back against the wall with his legs straight out and hung his head down, his blond curls falling in front of his eyes.

Maggie wanted to tell him it was his fault; to scold him for not moving more quickly. Instead, she went to the door and reached out to grab the handle. There was none. She let her fingers crawl all over the wood, even the frame and the wall along the door's sides. Her hands found nothing.

"Is there a back entrance?" she whispered, squatting next to John and taking his chin in her hand. She pushed his hair from his eyes.

John glanced toward the narrow hallway. Darkness swallowed

up the corridor like a hungry cave. "I do not know," he said.

"But you live here."

He paused. "No."

"Yes. You said—"

"That this is not your world. I never said it was mine."

"Then where is yours?" Maggie asked.

"It does not matter," he told her. "It is too late."

"We should at least try to find a way. Do you think there's another door?"

"I do not know."

"Is there any chance we can get out that way?" Maggie nodded toward the passageway.

"Maybe…"

"What about windows? Are there any besides the ones in the tower?"

"I have never seen any."

"How can you be trapped in here, yet know nothing about where you are?"

"This is not the time for idle conversation. If you believe you can get me out of here, then do so. My wrists are screaming."

Maggie rubbed her fingers gently along his wrists made raw by the heavy iron handcuffs that bound them.

She whispered in his ear: "Let me save you."

Their eyes locked, and Maggie knew John would do whatever she asked.

With a bit of effort, she helped him stand. Then she drew the sword from its jacket. "First, we need to get you out of those chains."

"That sword will never work."

"How do you know?"

John said nothing as he raised his hooked wrists.

Maggie took the sword and placed it against the center of the chain then carefully slid the blade back and forth. All she managed to do was sand off some of the rust that lived between the links.

She ran the blade with more rigor, tiny beads of perspiration breaking out along her upper lip. "I thought for sure…"

Again she looked toward the dark passageway. She put the sword back in its leather pouch, slid the rope from her shoulder, and placed it around John's neck. She stood on her toes and took hold of the least melted candle from one of the brackets beside the door. Hot wax dripped down her wrist as she handed it to John.

"Are you ready?" she asked, grabbing another candle for herself.

Without waiting for a response, she held the small flame out in front of her. Together they walked into the darkness, Maggie leading the way, the flickering light of their candles bouncing off the stone ceiling and walls, creating a menagerie of shadowy figures that danced on either side of them as they entered the narrow throat of the castle.

Chapter Twenty-eight

Like a devoted pet, John moved wordlessly beside her as Maggie's left hip slid against the wall, following the curve.

She wasn't sure how far or how long they'd travelled when they came upon a door. Simpler than the castle's front door, it stretched about six feet high and three feet wide. The wrought iron handle looked identical to the other though slightly smaller.

Maggie gripped her sword uncomfortably in the same hand that held the candle, and placed her other hand on the bolt. The latch easily moved under her fingers and clicked open with barely a sound. She pushed the door with her foot and walked through the doorway. The first thing that came to her was the sweet smell of lemons, now so overpowering it reached an almost toxic level. She could taste it in her mouth. It caused her eyes to water. She put the crook of her elbow to her nose as she and John stepped into the room.

The spherical cavern was an example of perfect contrast, as deficient in décor as it was immense. It was some kind of great hall, easily a hundred feet across and fifty feet high. With its magnitude and impersonal quality, the room could have been mistaken for a mountain cave.

"What is this place?" Maggie whispered, her words echoing

through the giant round room like a tiny ball bouncing across an empty gymnasium. The smell of lemons withered away, the lingering scent like an empty glass that had once been filled with Kool-Aid.

John said nothing as Maggie walked to the room's center. Six timber pillars at various points in the room extended from the dirt floor to the wooden crossbeams high above. Clusters of cobwebs stretched out like fishing line from one beam to the next.

She walked toward the wall on the far side of the room, curiously staring at long strips of black crepe paper hanging vertically against the stones. But as she approached the wall, her eyes adjusted to what she was really seeing: at least a dozen chains suspended from the ceiling, bolted to a thick beam along the top. Her eyes followed the chains from the ceiling down to where they ended, six feet above the floor. At the end of each chain was an iron cuff, heavier and more intimidating than the ones that kept John's wrists bound together.

"What in heaven's name—"

The rusty shackles could just as easily have been found dangling in medieval dungeons beneath English castles, in the hulls of slave ships, or in the northeast prisons where Salem witches had awaited their fate. She reached out her hand to touch one but jerked it away when John spoke.

"Another door."

She followed him around a large pillar. "This must be the way," she said, walking toward him. She gripped the door handle.

"Maggie," John said, placing a bound hand on her wrist. "Why are you doing this?"

"Because I have to."

"But why?"

Maggie glanced back at the empty chains, hanging there like they were waiting for a gang of criminals to occupy them.

"Because," she told John. "Everyone deserves to have their freedom."

***

John remained by her side, his breath emerging in warm puffs against her cheek. They did not speak as their steps fell in sync and their pupils adapted to the candlelit surroundings.

This hallway was much like the other, only the curve of the stone wall was more evident. Maggie suspected they were winding up and around the great hall. Her thigh muscles strained with each step, and the front of her boots pressed hard against the top of her feet.

A cool breeze suddenly entered the tunnel. It swirled around them, ruffling Maggie's hair, then moving down her arms and along the edge of her tunic. The draft blew out her candle, then John's. The blackout engulfed them.

Startled, Maggie dropped the useless candle to the floor and put a hand out in front of her. Her palm smacked against a wall directly ahead.

"It's a dead end."

Claustrophobic panic filled her throat as her arms flailed about with the sword's handle still locked in her fist. She reached for John, but he was no longer by her side.

"John?"

"Over here," he whispered. "Be careful with that sword. I would hate to lose my head for no reason."

She dropped the sword to her side. "Did you find something?"

"The wall is recessed," he said.

"Where?"

"Here. On my right."

Her fingers followed John's as he guided them along the wall until they located the square corners and the straight sides of the alcove. Maggie's hands became her eyes as she slid her palms toward the center and felt the wood. A few inches down she stroked the iron handle and then the thumb latch.

"Hold this," she whispered, cupping John's hands around her sword.

She placed one hand on top of the other and pressed down on the latch until it clicked. They stepped back in unison, allowing enough room for the door to swing past them and tap against the wall. The hinges creaked as splinters of light crept into the hallway, revealing a second door beneath the first.

"Oh," John said with a tired sigh.

Dr. Germaine's words slipped into her foggy memory: *Windows and doors often appear when needed most…*

Maggie placed her hands on the cross bars that created a window on the top half and pulled on them. The bars were made of an iron-like material. Rows of welded rivets attached a large hinge to the top and bottom left corners. This one had no simple thumb latch like the other doors. Instead, there was a flat square box, a large skeleton key protruding from a slender hole in the center.

"Shall we?" she asked, placing her hand on the key.

"I do not know…"

"What if this is the only way out?"

"What if it is not?"

"We've come too far to stop now," Maggie said.

She turned the key counter-clockwise. The click was loud and strong, the bolt sighing at having been set free. "See how easy that was?"

"Too easy."

Maggie pulled the door open. John followed close behind as they stepped through the doorway. He handed back her sword as they made their way down the wide curved steps to the bottom and into the center of the spherical room. Maggie followed John's gaze, observing the unfathomably high cathedral ceiling, its sides gathering together in a point at the very top, two cross beams intersecting just below the pinnacle, about a hundred feet above them. She moved her eyes downward and counted the open tapered windows: six of them, evenly spaced around the circular room, each one with a stone sill a few feet above the floor.

"We do not want to be here," John said. He walked to one of the narrow windows and stared out. "What have we done?"

Maggie strode from one side of the room to the other, carefully leaning her torso out each window. Two she believed to be facing the front, the other four overlooking places she had never seen before and could not see now, for fog blocked the view from any angle.

John's voice was filled with defeat. "We are doomed."

As if in response, a door slam suddenly plummeted down the steps. The bend in the staircase obscured her view, but Maggie didn't need to see to understand. The echo of a lock turning in place left its mark in the empty chamber; a second door slam completed the task.

She ran up the steps two at a time to find the iron door sealed in place, the second door behind it sealed just as tightly. She reached through the bars and forced her hand in the narrow space between the two doors, feeling for the key which was no longer there. She hiked back down the steps and stood in the tower's center, eyeing each and every nook while turning in slow circles.

"I can get us out of here," Maggie said.

"How?"

"I'll figure something out." She touched the pen still tucked in her hair and rubbed her hand along the sword casing.

"Let us say we are able to escape," John said. "Then what?"

"What do you mean?"

"You still do not understand, do you? This world in here is not yours to tinker with. Your world is out there," John said, nodding his head toward the window, "with your gazebo and horses and flowers. I warned you not to bring them together."

"If it weren't for me, you'd be stuck in here forever," Maggie told him.

"If it were not for you, my wrists would still be free, and I would not be locked away in a tower. You never should have knocked on the door."

"*You* called to *me*," Maggie reminded him. "*You* invited *me*."

"I never asked you to mix worlds. I only wanted you to open the door."

"Well, I did open the door. You chose to step through. I didn't control you."

"Yes, Maggie, you did."

She thought back to that first time. Back to the moment John placed a leather sandal across the threshold.

"I did?" she asked.

"Yes."

"I'm in control?"

"Out there, yes," John said. "But not in here."

"What about you? Do you have control…anywhere?"

"Of course not."

"How can that be?"

"Because that is how it works."

Maggie, confused, sat on the floor and covered her face with her hands. She fought hard to fight back tears. If she started crying, she would lose whatever confidence she'd convinced herself she had.

"I have tried to explain to you," John said gently, crouching down next to her. The dangling chain between his shackles clinked against the floor. "That world out there, with your sunshine and your ocean, is yours. This world, inside these castle walls, is not. Nor is it mine."

"Then where is yours?"

John stood up and leaned against the inside of the window sill, staring out into the mist like a romantic poet gathering words for his next sonnet.

"John?" she whispered. "Where is your world?"

He let out a heavy sigh. "I do not have one."

Chapter Twenty-nine

They sat beneath one of the windows. As darkness fell upon them, John's gloomy voice floated through the shadowy chamber. "You should go, Maggie. Stop worrying about me."

"Go where?"

"Back to your real world. Wake up."

"I don't want to wake up," Maggie said. "I want to stay here. With you."

"You would rather stay locked in a tower with me than go back to your real life?"

"I was locked in a tower there, too."

Maggie's eyes regarded the rope still looped around John's neck. Something, an idea, was coming. For a moment she churned it over, and after deciding it was the only way, she leaned toward John.

"It will not work," John said.

"Of course it will," Maggie told him as she removed the rope.

"What if it is not long enough?"

"It is."

"How do you know?"

"Because I dreamed it up. It's very long." She placed the pile of rope on the floor between them. "Here," she instructed. "Grab onto this end."

He did as she asked, tightening his grip as she walked backward. By the time she had unwound it, the rope was twice as long as the room was wide. She glanced around the dusky space from the bare floor to the lofty ceiling, now in complete obscurity as night advanced.

"Oh," she said, her shoulders slumping. "There isn't anything to tie it to."

She marched around the circular room, still holding her end of the rope, then looked up the winding staircase. "That's it!" she shouted, running up the dim stairs, stumbling once, then regaining her balance as she made her way around the curve.

Once at the top, she held the rope between her knees and gripped the bars of the door, thankful they'd been built for permanence. Taking the rope in her hands, she wrapped it around one of the center bars and tied it off in a knot. She pulled. It slipped a little. She undid the rope and this time weaved it through three of the bars, looping it around each rod twice, and finally tying it off in another knot. She doubled the knot. Then tripled it.

As she headed back down the stairs, she put all her weight on the rope, lying down against the steps and holding onto the end to make sure it was secure enough. It was.

"This rope will be our way out," she told John as she leaned out a window, squinting her eyes in a futile attempt to see through the fog.

"It is much too far," John said. "You could fall."

"I can't die here," she told him with confidence as she pulled her body back inside. From his hands she took his end of the rope and lifted it to the window. "Here goes nothing." The rope fell from her fingers over the ledge and was quickly swallowed up by the churning fog. "We'll go down like this," she said, holding her hands up and demonstrating with a quick pantomime, moving one hand below the other in perfect succession. "Keep your feet against the wall and inch your way down."

"I am not an acrobat," John said. "Even if I could somehow slide down the rope with them together, my hands would be shredded." He jiggled the chain linking his wrists.

"Let me think."

Darkness was ravenously eating up the remaining light.

"Maybe I should wake up," Maggie said, "only for a little while, then I could—"

"Wait," John said. Through the fading light, he fidgeted with his leather belt.

"What are you doing?" she asked.

"Help me."

Maggie unhooked his belt, slipped it from around his waist, and held it out.

"I can buckle this in a horse-shoe around the rope," he said. "I will hold onto the leather strap, which will slide along the rope instead of my hands. You go down first. Once you reach the bottom, hold the rope—"

"You should go first, so I can help you through the window."

"No, Maggie. You need to hold the rope taut at the bottom for me."

Maggie picked up the heavy rope and held it between her fingers. She was comforted by its weight as well as its thickness.

Again they gazed out the window. Fog floated into the room, erasing the walls that surrounded them. Maggie hoisted herself onto the ledge and straddled it, then rolled onto her stomach with the rope underneath her body. Her legs dangled into the mist as her elbows hooked her to the window frame.

John leaned toward her and guided the rope in between her

hands. "Thank you," he said, then pressed his lips against hers.

"See you at the bottom." She said the words lightly, like they were planning to meet for a drink or a cup of coffee.

"Hurry," John said, his linked hands pushing her hair from her eyes. "And remember, once you land, hold onto the rope until I come down."

Maggie nodded as her head disappeared past the window ledge and the fog gobbled her up just like the darkness had devoured daylight.

Chapter Thirty

The fog pressed against her, thick and cold. Maggie could see nothing but her hands and the point of contact they made with the rope. At first, John's whispering words of encouragement followed her down. But soon, she only heard her own heavy breathing and the slap of boots against the stones. The rubber soles were unprepared for the slippery moss and she kept losing traction. She had to stop to catch her breath every so often, the energy she'd possessed earlier whittled down to a toothpick. Her arms and legs were nearly spent, and the rope was getting soggy, causing her hands to slip. She envisioned falling the last fifty feet into the shallow moat below.

You cannot die in your dream…

Trying to keep her mind on topics other than death, such as what to do when she reached the bottom, or how much strength it would take to hold the rope for John once she landed, her boots suddenly gave way, and her hands screamed in agony as they skidded down the rope. She slammed her legs together and managed to lock the rope between her knees. Her feet finally planted against the wall again, but her hands stung and her shoulders throbbed in anguish.

Grinding her teeth together and wishing away the pain, she

continued downward, concentrating on the sound of her boots as they struck the mortared stones. She counted steps under her breath to keep her mind on track, recalling the rhyme she had shared with her mother while walking along the shore, collecting shells.

"One. Two. Buckle my shoe…"

She saw herself placing her tiny feet in her mother's footprints in the sand as they walked together, mother and daughter, out for a seaside stroll on a sunny day.

"Three. Four. Shut the door…"

Her heels hit the wall each time she said a number.

"Five. Six. Pick up sticks…"

She inched a little farther.

"Seven. Eight. Lay them straight…"

And a little farther.

"Nine. Ten. A big fat hen…"

Just a little girl, counting steps.

"Eleven. Twelve. Dig and delve…"

Slap. Slap.

"Thirteen. Fourteen. Maids a courting…"

That's it…keep counting.

"Fifteen. Sixteen…"

She stopped in her tracks.

What came next? Maids a teaching? No. Maids a milking? No, *milking* was from the "Twelve Days of Christmas." Frustrated, she closed her eyes to help her remember.

"Fifteen. Sixteen. Maids in the…"

Hiding just under her tongue.

Closer.

Closer still.

"Kitchen!" a woman's laughing voice shouted through the fog.

Maggie's eyes flew open, even though the world was still dark and she could see nothing.

Who are you? Maggie's mind asked.

When no one answered, she was tempted to ask the question out loud, but she didn't want to draw extra attention to the intruder scaling a wall that didn't belong to her. Without uttering another sound, she picked up the pace, placing one tired hand under the other, her feet working hard to keep from slipping, wondering with uneasy curiosity if the mysterious voice would have anything else to say.

Thankfully, for the rest of her journey downward, as she painstakingly placed one hand under the other, it did not.

***

The thumping of her soles against the tower rocks was all that could be heard for a time. But now, as she rested against the wall, sweat dripping down her temples, her boots planted a foot apart, her hands still as they kept their worn-out grip on the rope, she heard the distant slapping of small waves.

The pattern of hand movements as much by rote as the rhyme she had chanted earlier, she hastened her descent. The smell of mud and mildew rose up to greet her. The sound of water in motion grew louder.

"Yes," she whispered into the fog. "Yes."

Her bottom hit the chilly moat before her mind realized she'd made it. With her legs immersed, she opened her tender hands and cooled them in the water. She planted her feet against the muddy floor, no concept of where the channel's borders were, or where the castle wall started or ended. The foggy darkness had swallowed up everything within reach, adhering to the top of the moat and sealing it in like a coffin lid.

Standing up, Maggie held a firm grip on the rope dangling in front of her—she couldn't lose it now—and yanked as hard as she could, signaling to John up in the tower that she had made it; she had survived; and now it was his turn to do the same.

Chapter Thirty-one

She wished for light. Soon, the sun from somewhere high above burned its rays through the dark. She wished for the fog to disappear, but it refused to budge. Her blisters and sore muscles were miraculously fading, but her teeth chattered relentlessly. The water licked the side of the castle. The fog draped across her vision. Tilting her head back, she peered into the infinite cloud above.

Did John know she had made it to safety? Had she yanked on the rope hard enough to signal him? She thought about tugging again, but he had instructed her to hold the rope taut so he could descend more easily. Was he on his way?

She pressed her lips together, fearful that her chattering teeth could be heard through layers of stone.

Beneath her hands, the rope jerked abruptly. Then again. She wanted to shout words of encouragement as John had done for her. But she forced herself to remain silent as she wound a portion of the rope around her hands. Her back and shoulder muscles strained, but they were handling it. She would save him. They would soon be free!

What about happily ever after? What would they do after he had made it down?

Before she had a chance to respond to her own interrogation, Maggie lost her footing as the ground released a massive hiccup. Unprepared for the jolt, she was thrown backward into the water. Still hanging onto her end of the rope, she was able to pull herself up again but could barely maintain her balance as the castle walls trembled, like a giant pepper shaker jiggled by an invisible hand. As the world rocked around her, something fell into the water beside her and slapped against the water's surface. She reached out, her hands feeling their way through the water, grabbing onto something. Like a dead water moccasin, the escape rope floated before her. One end was frayed.

"No!" Maggie screamed, coiling up the rope and pulling it to her chest.

Had John been hanging from it when it fell? Was it possible he hadn't yet begun his descent, that he was still standing in the window?

Something else floated next to the rope. She reached out and captured John's leather belt, but as she held it up in front of her, something else hit the water, something much heavier than a rope or a belt, creating a wave that cascaded over her. A loud "Agh!" sounded across the moat's surface.

"John!" she screamed, her words bouncing against the stone. "Oh, God, John, answer me!"

The water around her began to churn, like cake batter in an electric mixer set on low. As its velocity increased, a whirlpool formed, generating an expansive ring of white froth. Maggie was pulled by the current toward the bubbles. She released the rope and belt to free her hands as she struggled backward. The vortex drew the rope and belt into its middle and sucked them under. A muffled animal cry rose from its center.

The monster's head popped up, those sharp white alligator

daggers behind an unmistakable grin. Maggie screamed. She turned around in the fog and smacked her forehead against the side of the drawbridge. She placed her hands on the platform and raised herself onto her elbows as the monster moved beneath her. Maggie froze, her legs dangling like giant lures in the cold water, her arms straining to keep her still. If she didn't move, maybe it wouldn't see her.

"Yes, yes. That's it. Go away," she whispered through her chattering teeth. "You aren't wanted here—"

The creature slammed into the bridge's underside nearly knocking Maggie from her grip. She wanted to reach for her sword, but that would mean letting go of the edge and possibly—

"Maggie?" John's voice called from somewhere nearby.

"Get out of the water!" Maggie screamed. "Hurry!"

The reptilian hybrid rammed into the drawbridge again, causing Maggie's fingers to dig into the wood, splinters piercing her fingertips.

Barely holding on, she kicked her booted feet for momentum. Just as she pulled her torso onto the plank, expelled air from the beast's mouth sent warm puffs across the back of Maggie's legs. She swung one leg up and onto the bridge, then brought up the other, stretching her body across the wood and gripping the sides.

The creature relentlessly banged the underside.

Bam! Bam! Bam!

Maggie's hands were raw. Her knees and shins were bashed and bruised. She wasn't sure how much longer she could—

The creature suddenly appeared on her left as it jumped high into the air, its alligator-turtle body twisting like a desperate fish trying to free itself from a hook. Its thick pointy tail cracked through the air like an enormous whip. Its body angled like it was preparing for a high-jump stunt over the bridge. But the monster had something else in mind: High into the air it rose, crashing down on the topside of the bridge, its gaping mouth only a foot from Maggie's face. It flopped up and down, its mouth of blades opening and closing like a giant shark left to die on the floor of a boat. Side pieces split apart and fell into the moat. Maggie tried to hold on, but it was no use. She lost her grip and plummeted into the channel.

Underwater, she kicked her legs and flailed her arms in a futile attempt to swim, trying to make headway across the moat. Whether or not she was headed in the right direction, she didn't know. Her rubbery boots, filled with water and suctioned to her feet, dragged her down. They may as well have been filled with cement. Exhausted, she finally gave in to the sinking, her air spent. The pain in her chest was replaced by another more pleasant feeling, her body becoming one with water, then as light as air.

You cannot die in your dream.

Oh, but I can. Look how easy it is.

Her bottom settled against the muddy floor. Her arms floated like they were no longer attached to her body. Her hair moved in slow motion around her head. She felt like a giant piece of seaweed.

Dr. Germaine's bodiless voice floated to her from somewhere far away: *Maggie…*

And then another, more urgent voice: "Maggie!"

Her eyes started to close.

"Maggie! Help me!"

John's tormented words became a shot of adrenalin.

With the last of her strength, Maggie peeled the boots from her feet. Cold clay greeted her soles. As she stood, she threw up the water that had pooled in her stomach. Her lungs screamed in pain as a rush of lemon-scented air entered her. She choked, her ribs aching, her throat burning.

Slowly her senses returned. The tightness in her chest and the mucky taste in her mouth started to fade. The monster prowled nearby, she could hear its mouth clapping open and shut, like someone had left it stuck in the "on" position. Her hands clutched the patchy fragments of what was left of the bridge as she inched her way through the water toward the bank—

Wham!

The monster slammed against the side of her leg, knocking her over. She regained her balance and stood up again. Again she returned her hands to the splintered drawbridge, knowing she would need to protect herself if she was going to make it; if she was going to save John. Her flashlight and pad of paper were long gone, and the rope was probably in the monster's belly. She needed a weapon. She would have to draw her sword, but that would mean letting go of the drawbridge again.

Wham!

Her knees were struck. She screamed as she fell onto her back. She spat out water as she floated next to the bridge. If she was forced to tread until she reached the embankment, she would never make it.

As she stood upright again, the creature's head popped up directly in front of her. Its eyes peeked over the water's surface as it treaded, its body twisting back and forth. If it'd had arms, Maggie was sure they'd be crossed in defiance.

"Why?" the slimy green creature suddenly asked, its head bobbing up and down like a crab pot.

It was fascinating but not at all surprising that the monster would speak to her.

"I need to save him."

The creature shook its snout, exhaled two streams of green slime from its wide nostrils, and cocked its head to the side. With one eye, dark and bottomless, like a snake hole in the middle of a bog, the monster regarded Maggie. "He ith not to be thaved."

It has a lisp, Maggie thought with strange pleasure. Beneath the water, electricity channeled through her as she slid the sword from its sheath. "You cannot stop me." Maggie held the sword out in front of her like a tribal matriarch protecting her village.

"I could thwallow that thord whole. I could do the thame to you."

"This is *my* dream."

The creature laughed then dipped his head under water. Air bubbles rose to the surface. Just as quickly it was up again. "Dreamth change," it told her.

"Why do you want to stop me?"

"Those are my orderth."

"Whose orders?"

"Athk only what I am allowed to anther."

Dr. Germaine's voice rose within her: *That creature is only a figment of your subconscious—a compilation of things that frighten you.*

"Do you believe your doctor'th wordth, Maggie?" The question dripped out of its mouth like poisoned honey. "Do you believe I am a thliver of your feral imagination?"

Maggie did not answer.

The creature looked directly into Maggie's eyes. "Your sthrength is much more beautiful than the other."

"What other?"

"It ith unfortunate that a creature ath beautiful ath you mutht meet with thuch a wretched ending."

The mouth opened wide and snapped down hard, so close to Maggie's face she could count its teeth if she had the desire. She took a wide step back and raised the sword high into the air. The creature laughed heinously as the saber sliced the space between them. It eluded her like a professional boxer, dipping beneath the water, sneaking up behind her, slipping below again, then appearing in front. Its mouth snapped open and shut like a marionette with its jaws attached to strings, controlled by hands from somewhere above. Maggie was tempted to look up, to catch this malevolent choreographer in action, but to look away even for a second could mean—

"Maggie!" John's voice traveled along the water's surface.

"Argh!" Maggie grunted, back-swinging the sword like a tennis racquet in preparation.

The creature popped its head up and spoke between breaths. "You have no chanth."

Its mouth and tail stopped moving. It backed up, tucked its head down, and lunged forward like a bull, slamming hard into Maggie's chest. Her feet flew out from under her. The sword fell from her grasp and disappeared beneath the surface.

"Maggie!" John called.

The moat was shallow, but there was no question now that she could drown. Losing her battle with equilibrium, she sank below the surface. Air. If she could only get some air…

"You must kill it!"

John's words had grown faint.

A peaceful darkness surrounded her as she absently ran her fingers along her cloth belt, landing on the empty leather case.

There is something else…

Her fingers searched her body frantically, not knowing what they were looking for. Her hands moved to her face and her head, then fell upon a tiny twig-like object sticking out of her hair.

She yanked on the pen and released it from her tangles. With the last of her conscious mind, if that's really what she was using, she pushed herself into a squatted position beneath the water, planted her feet firmly on the ground, and thrust herself toward the sky. Breaking the surface like a miniature whale, she flew upward, the bottom of her feet nearly tasting the air. She coughed and choked as she rose, whipping the pen about like a crazed killer.

The creature floated a few feet away like a tourist relaxing in a hotel swimming pool. It gave her a hungry reptile's smile. Before she could think of what to do next, it charged again. On impulse, she grabbed onto one of its scales. The sharp skin sliced her hand open, and she screamed in agony.

She pressed a bloody palm against her mouth. She knew the blood would make the creature happy, perhaps give it a tasty sample of what was to come.

Maggie was spent. The only thing to protect her from the creature was a pen. She couldn't protect herself from a rat with a weapon like this. How could she possibly defend herself from a creature twice her size?

"I told you," Maggie said to the monster. "I have to save him."

"We will discuth thith no further," it answered with its disgusting speech impediment, peering at Maggie like she was nothing more than an annoying fly. "I have been given my orderth."

It sped toward her, its jagged scales breaching the surface, leaving small waves to follow behind.

John's voice rained down around her: "Maggie…hurry…"

Maggie faced the oncoming monster as a sense of calm took over. She felt brave. Eager. Strong.

The creature came fast, but Maggie was faster. As it threatened to knock her down again, she stepped to the side. The large reptile didn't possess the agility that Maggie did; her smaller size made it easy to play dodge. Each time the monster torpedoed toward her, she dipped out of its way. The monster rose up in front of her and bared its assortment of teeth in a grin. She could smell its breath, a mixture of dead animals and soil and moss-covered wood.

The hungry smile told her the game was over.

It hurtled toward her, opening its mouth wider than Maggie would have believed possible. But when the creature tilted its head back to show off its rows of jagged teeth, Maggie leaned to the right, raised the pen high in the air, and brought it down so fast her arm was nothing but a blur. The instrument aimed for the target and entered it fully. Black blood, like aged oil, spewed from the creature's left eye.

A howl rose into the air, but it was filled with hopelessness, not pain. The creature flayed about, its tail missing Maggie by inches as it writhed. She slipped behind its blind side, pulled her arm back again, and slammed the pen down. Pungent smoke poured out of the other eye in a thick stream, causing Maggie to gag.

Like a jammed windup toy, the blind creature mechanically opened and closed its jaws. Its body jerked in crazy spasms. The border of the moat now lay flat against Maggie's spine as the monster rotated its head toward the sky, its agonizing wail filling her world. It slowly dematerialized, first turning to mist then ceasing to exist altogether. The only reminder that it had been there at all was the fading sound of its cry. Soon, that was gone, too.

Maggie scrambled up the side of the embankment, her bare feet slipping in the sludge. Once on the bank, she fell onto her knees and pushed her wet hair from her face, then ripped part of her hem from her dress. She wrapped the make-shift bandage around her wounded hand and tied it off with the assistance of her teeth.

"Maggie?"

"John!" She looked into the thinning fog to see him swimming clumsily toward her.

"The rope—cut from above. I couldn't hold on—we must hurry. She will soon know of my absence." At the edge of the moat, he held up his chained hands. "I found this—"

"My sword!" Maggie said, grabbing the weapon and sliding it back in its cover before helping John onto the muddy embankment.

"What if we're followed?" Maggie asked as they worked to pull their feet from the thick mud.

"We—do not have—any choice."

The terrifying voice exploded from everywhere at once, entering Maggie's lungs with its breath, her veins with its blood: "Geeeet baaaack heeeere!" It sounded the way Maggie imagined the *Old Woman who Lived in a Shoe* might sound. Only much larger, and much angrier. "Yoooou will be punished if you leeeeave!"

"Your world!" he told Maggie. "Now!"

The angry voice grew closer, as if the air itself were made up of only those screaming words. "Yoooou caaaan noooot haaaave hiiiim!"

Maggie said, "How do you know we'll be safe there?"

"I—do not." He leaned over and placed his hands on his knees. His curls hung down in wet ringlets as he still labored to catch his breath. "If she brings me back—this time—you will never—see me again."

"Come," Maggie said, grabbing John by the elbow and nearly dragging him along the short path that led away from the castle. They fell repeatedly, their bare feet tripping over the wide gaps in the stone as they made their way to the gazebo steps. The sun on her side of the dream had burned through much of the fog, and her flowers leaned into the warmth. The horses whinnied happily on the other side of the porch.

John collapsed against the top step as Maggie ran across the porch to the duffle bag, still tucked away under the bench. She reached inside, slid an item out, and ran back to John.

"Hold up your hands."

He did as she asked.

Maggie placed the hacksaw against the tight metal chain that joined the medieval cufflinks. She ran it back and forth until the metal snapped.

"You did it," he said, rubbing his wrists. He pulled Maggie to him and kissed her hard on the mouth.

They looked back at the castle. Sunlight from Maggie's world found its way along the top of the tower, pushing rays through the mist.

"You are the stronger one," John told her, unwrapping her bandage from her hand. The blood was gone, the wound nothing more than a tiny scar.

"Even if that's true," Maggie told him, "I can't go back there."

"You do not have to. She will come here."

"I don't want her here."

"She will follow us. There is no question."

Maggie again glanced at the castle. Had the walls inched closer still?

"Fight her, Maggie. You will win."

"How?"

"Look at all you have done so far. You will think of a way. I have faith in you." He took her chin in his hand and stared into her eyes. Wisdom and innocence swirled together in his dark blue irises. "I always have."

Chapter Thirty-two

They rode on horseback until the castle was far behind. Fresh salt air filled Maggie's lungs. On their left, a thriving forest took up most of the horizon parallel to the ocean on their right. In the shade of locusts and oaks and evergreens, they let the horses take a rest.

"This is the best way," John said, helping her down from the mare. He took her hand as they walked toward the ocean. "She will be much weaker in your world."

Maggie wasn't so sure. She remembered clearly the way the ground had trembled like a leviathan waking beneath them as they lay together that first time.

"And when she comes?" Maggie asked, looking out over the ocean, the calm waves lapping against the white sand. "What then?"

"You will know what to do."

They sat side by side in the soft sand. Maggie let her bare feet sink into its warmth.

"Why do I feel like this is the only world for me?" Maggie asked.

"Because you created it."

"But I created a life on the outside, too."

"Did you?"

"Of course."

"It was because of your husband," John said. "Without Sam you would not have created anything."

"That's not true."

"How is it possible to have created something in *his* world?"

"Because that's my world, too."

"No, it is not. It is *his* world. *Sam's* world."

"It's everyone's world," Maggie said. "Together. That's how it works on the outside."

"Is it?"

"What you are trying to say?"

"Your world belongs to a man," John said.

"In some ways that's true. But not in every way."

"Name a way in which your world does not."

Maggie said nothing, realizing that even if she did give him an answer, she would be defending a world she resented.

"Who paid for your house?" John went on. "Who bought you the clothes you wear out there? Or your hairdo? Or your pretty pink nails? Who do you think takes care of you?"

"How do you know what I wear? Or what I do from day to day?"

"I know that women are taken care of by their husbands and expected to appreciate their dependence."

"I don't need taking care of. I can be as independent as I wish."

"Can you?"

"Can't I?" she asked, suddenly feeling very sad.

"If that life of yours on the outside really made you happy, you would not be here now."

"What about you, John? Why are you here?"

"I have no choice in the matter. This is where I am supposed to be."

"Where? In that castle?" She touched the broken link still dangling from his freed wrist. "In these chains?"

John grabbed Maggie's thin wrist and held it up between them. "Just because you cannot see the chains, does not mean they are not there.

Maggie pulled her hand away as John rose.

"It is time," he said simply. He turned his back to the ocean, then placed his hands on his hips and faced the woods. He cocked his head to the side. "She has sent the others to look for us."

Maggie stood next to him. "*Others*?"

The thunderous sound of feet pounding against earth made the ground shake. The horses jerked their heads in the direction of the woods and took off galloping down the beach.

"The horses," Maggie said. "How will we…"

The footsteps grew louder. The waves swelled to twice their size as they crashed against the sand. The tiny white slivers of clouds that floated tranquilly above the sea turned black and tumbled over one another.

Maggie pulled the sword from her case.

"Promise me you will not wake up," John said. "If you do, it will all end."

"Yes. I promise," Maggie said, holding the sword with both hands in front of her like she was preparing to slay a dragon. She took a wide step forward and shouted through the rumble, unaware of whether or not she could be heard. "This is my world! You are not allowed here!"

The stampede grew closer. Its force shook the trees, the powerful energy pushing through the branches like a Nor'easter.

A collection of murmuring voices rolled out of the forest and onto the beach. Deep voices. Chanting voices.

Then the stampede came into view: nearly a dozen men, dressed in tunics and sandals, running toward them, their muted whispers carried on the howling wind, their feet moving at incredible speed but still synchronized. All had milky white skin like John, the same sturdy jaw line, the same blond curls, the same incredible blue eyes.

Each man waved a pistol-like weapon through the air as they stormed the beach. Maggie suddenly felt small enough to fit in the palm of someone's hand, like Alice after drinking the mysterious elixir.

"John!" she screamed. "I can't fight them! They will kill us!"

You cannot die in your—

Maggie hoped John would tell her what to do; show her that although he was fearful, the two of them could work together to fight this army. Look how much they had accomplished together so far. But when Maggie turned to him for support and saw his face, her legs grew weak and nearly collapsed beneath her.

John, hands on hips and head tilted toward the sky, with all the sturdiness of a Greek effigy and the confidence and pride of a man who has already won a war, greeted the army with a smile.

Chapter Thirty-three

The men held their weapons high as they encircled Maggie and John, moving around them like school children in a silly game of ring around the rosy.

Their words were decipherable now, though Maggie wished they had remained silent; for silence, although ambiguous, would not have expressed why these men had come. They chanted as one: "We have found you. We have found you. We have found you." Like a train gaining speed on a downhill track. "We have found you. We have found you…"

"Yes," John said.

The men stopped chanting and fell to their knees. In unison, they bent over until their foreheads touched the sand, then laid their weapons before them and splayed their hands palms down.

"What are they doing?" Maggie asked. She turned in a tight circle, her sword at the ready between her shaking fists.

"Thanking you," John said. He stepped back and became part of the loop.

Maggie's sword dropped to her side. One by one the men stood up. They revered her, standing alone in the circle's center as though she were Katharine Hepburn or Judy Garland in the flesh.

John held his arms out. "You have saved us."

"I don't understand."

The man on John's right whispered, "Tell her." The whole group joined in: "Tell her, tell her, tell her."

Maggie's fear radiated from her body and penetrated the world around her. She could see it in the way the sun was trapped behind the clouds. In the way the waves rocked nervously. In the way the air became thick, the smell of lemons erased by the sharp stench of panic.

"She is so different from the other one, is she not?" John asked the men, grinning like a circus ringleader.

"What other one?" Maggie asked.

"You are here to release us," John said. "For good. Forever."

"Release you from what?"

"Prison."

"You are all prisoners?"

"Oh, Maggie," John said. "I thought you understood."

"Well, I don't. I don't understand anything." She jerked forward, again thrusting her sword out in front of her. She stepped toward one of the men. The man backed up, as did his cohorts.

"ANYTHING!" she suddenly screamed at John. "You haven't told me anything!"

"Maggie—"

"Tell me now! Or I swear...I will..."

"What?"

"I'll wake up!"

The quick glint of fear in John's eye filled Maggie with a brief moment of satisfaction.

John said quietly, "Lower your sword and I will explain."

Maggie did as he asked, but kept her fists tightly wrapped around the handle.

"You are the *one*," he told her.

"The one?"

"To save us."

"To save us," the men said in unison.

She whispered to John, "I only wanted to save *you*."

"And you will. But you will be saving all of them as well."

"From what?"

"From *her*," he said, stretching his arm out in a wide arch toward the forest and beyond.

"Her?"

"We are here *because* of her."

"How did you get here?"

"The same way you did."

Maggie froze.

"The pills," he explained.

All liquid evaporated from her mouth.

"They are the doorway," John said.

"I only took the pills to help me—"

"Sleep. Escape. Yes. In the beginning. But they helped you do much more than that, did they not?"

"I dreamed about you before I ever took the pills."

"Not in the beginning. You dreamed of Sam. Your fear of him being dead. But he is home safe, yes?"

"How do you know these things?" Maggie asked, barely recalling the blurry silhouette that represented her husband.

"I do not know how we know these things, only that we do. You stopped dreaming of Sam. Then you found me. That is why you are the one. You do not need your doctor or the pills to get here."

"Then how—"

"If you want something badly enough, a way to reach it will always be discovered."

Maggie observed the clouds as they moved overhead, heard the oak leaves as they fluttered on the wind, tasted the salt air as it settled on her tongue. The warm breeze caressed her skin. The sand moved between her toes. Strands of loose hair tickled her neck. Everything in this world felt so incredibly real.

She looked at the men in the circle, letting her eyes fall upon each one's face. They breathed in unison, even seemed to sigh as one. If not for the seriousness of the situation, they would appear almost comical in their uniformity.

She squelched the desire to pinch herself. Of course this wasn't real. Real life didn't create beings like this, each one an exact replica of the other. Real life offered diversity and choices. Didn't it?

"How can this be anything other than a dream?" she asked John.

"To you it is a dream. To us it is life."

The men in the circle nodded in agreement.

"Why would I choose to dream up that angry woman? Why would I want her here, especially if she can harm you?"

"Oh, Maggie," John said, stepping toward her and touching her cheek. "You are so confused." He shared his look of pity with the others. "You did not create the other one. She was already here."

"How can that be?"

"That other world," John said. "The castle, where we have been held captive, is a dream, too."

"Whose dream?"

He pointed to a place beyond the forest. "*Hers.*"

Maggie looked around the circle. "None of you are a part of *my* dream?"

One by one the men shook their heads.

"But I created you," Maggie told John.

"No, Maggie. You only created this world."

"How could my dream mix with another?"

"We do not know how. All that matters is that you have come. And for that we are grateful."

"Why didn't you stay where you were?" Maggie asked.

"You saw where I was held captive." He held up the broken cuffs still dangling from his wrists. "How could I live my eternity there?"

"You trapped me into saving you." Maggie gripped her sword more tightly in her fist. "You tricked me. You pretended you were—"

"I am not pretending," John said. "I am in love with you."

"No, you're not." She looked around the circle at the dozen or so expectant faces. "You're all using me. To save yourselves. That isn't love, John. That's desperation. That's hope."

"You have had nothing but hope from the beginning."

As she stared at the men, she could feel her last bit of self-control sliding through her fingers into the cool steel of the sword, then dripping out the tip and into the sand. Anger crawled through the veins in her neck. Without thinking, she placed a hand on John's chest and pushed. He crashed into a man on either side, who flung their arms out to block his fall.

"You're not real!" Maggie shouted. "You've only convinced yourself that you exist!"

John said, "I am real, as long as someone makes me so. I can love, as long as someone needs my love. And I can live, as long as someone wants me to. That is what makes love and life real."

Maggie's sword carved a jagged line in the sand as she fell to her knees. She put her hands to her face and began to sob. "I can't do this. I can't pretend there's a perfect life for me out there, or in here, because there isn't. There isn't a perfect world anywhere."

John knelt on the ground before her. "Yes, there is." He gently took her hands away from her face. "Just stay here. With me. In *this* perfect world."

"I can't stay in here forever. My body out there will perish. It will need to eat. Drink. Move. What you're asking me to do is impossible."

"You can come back anytime you wish, as long as you want to. Without pills. Without a doctor's care."

"And how am I supposed to get rid of *her?*" Maggie asked. "Wish her away?"

John said nothing, only looked toward the ground, causing the circle of men to do the same.

"You want me to kill her," Maggie said.

He nodded.

"I can't do that."

"It is the only way."

The men's identical eyes remained fixed upon her as she contemplated John's request. Would she have the courage to do as he asked? And would it matter if she did? This was, after all, only a dream. She didn't have to abide by the morals and guidelines of the real world, did she? And what if she didn't do what John proposed? What would happen to him and all the others?

Then a thought came to her that caused the deepest fear of all: What if Maggie lost the fight?

"Maggie," John whispered, "she sent these men to kill you."

"But why? Why can't she have her world and I have mine?"

"It is not your world she wants. She does not care about the things you have created. She can have all those things and more. She is very powerful."

"Then what does she want?" Maggie asked. "What do I have that she doesn't have?"

John touched Maggie's arm and said simply, "My heart."

Chapter Thirty-four

"The men will be severely punished when they tell her we couldn't be found," John remarked as the small army marched across the beach and disappeared into the woods. "But they know lying is necessary. They must make her believe they are still her devotees. That they trust her as their leader. Though I do not know if that will be enough."

As Maggie and John trekked through the woods, the last bit of sunlight slipped away. The moon remained hidden behind clusters of nighttime clouds. A light mist ebbed and flowed along the undergrowth of the forest, making it difficult to see roots jutting up out of the earth, or the occasional log lying across their path.

At the forest's edge, Maggie rested on a tree stump. In front of them lay the expansive meadow, the flowers closed and sleeping. Beyond that, the outline of the gazebo could barely be seen in the distance. For a time they sat in silence, watching the starless sky and listening to the emptiness of her dark world. She tried to make a moon appear, but found that she could not. Without moonlight, the gazebo could as easily have been Poe's *House of Usher*.

"I feel weak," Maggie told John. "Maybe I've been asleep too long. Maybe I need to eat something. Or drink some juice." She suddenly craved her nightly mug of Ovaltine.

"No," he told her firmly. "Do not awaken. You need to stay until the task is done. If you leave now, she may alter things so that when you return, you will not be able to find your way back to me."

She forced herself off the stump and placed her hand in John's. Barefoot, drained, and with John in the lead, they headed across the meadow. From the top step of the gazebo they stared across the short distance to the castle. The path looked like a row of mines had exploded, bits and pieces of broken rock strewn everywhere, gaping holes every few feet. She imagined that Europe must look the same.

"What do you think she did to your friends?" Maggie asked.

"She is unpredictable. She may have flogged them, whipped them; perhaps she made them disappear altogether—"

"Disappear?"

"Yes. She has done so before."

"Has she ever—hurt *you*?"

"I am her favorite. Her desire for me is much more than her desire for the others. But in contrast, my independence has always made her angry. She wants to control me."

"What does she have you do?"

"Tend to her needs. Feed her when she is hungry. Fan her when she is hot. Rub her feet when they are tired. Other times she just wants me to sit with her. She tells me she enjoys watching me while I sleep."

"Is she…beautiful?"

"In here, anyone can be as beautiful as one wishes. Or as ugly. She created her world just as you created yours."

"What if I lose?" Maggie asked. "What if she is more powerful?"

"You cannot lose."

"How can you be so sure?"

"Because your strength comes from your heart. Her strength comes from the desire to control others."

"What should I do to prepare?" Maggie asked.

"This." John turned his body to face hers and wrapped his arms around her. He placed his mouth against her neck and nibbled his way along her throat and up to her lips.

"I don't see how this will—"

"Sh. We have these moments together. Let us make use of them. Before the sun rises."

He gently guided Maggie to the floor of the gazebo. It should have felt hard beneath her spine, but it did not. His hands were curious and kind, the smell of his skin like fresh air after a spring rain.

As he entered her, she opened her eyes and gazed upward, and as she reached her climax almost immediately, myriad stars peeked through the dark cloak that canopied the outer edges of the porch roof. The stillness of the night was suddenly broken by the singing of crickets and the croaking of frogs in a mixture of melodies sweeter than any choir. A large full moon inched its way out from beneath the clouds, spilling light onto John and Maggie as they rocked together and held tightly to one another. Soon, all memory of world wars, domestic discontent, and life in Maggie's other world rose away from her body and through her moans, drifting up to the endless sky and floating out of reach.

Chapter Thirty-five

The sun's rays crawled across her face. When she opened her eyes, John was sitting on a gazebo bench, staring in the direction of the castle. The last of the thinning fog still clung to the stone walls like a piece of wet muslin. The drawbridge that had been smashed to bits had become new again and solidly held onto the castle wall like it hadn't been lowered in centuries; the moat appeared calm. At John's feet lay the uncovered sword and the hacksaw.

Maggie pulled her tunic over her head, covering her naked body. She had never slept within a dream before. Did she dream in her dream? She wasn't sure, but she did feel refreshed, as though someone had fed her a hearty breakfast after eight hours of uninterrupted sleep.

"Good morning," John said, smiling.

She stood up, tied her sash, and peered out over the railing. Her horses were nowhere to be seen, and the oaks in the distance seemed more like an enemy's border than a meadow's boundary.

She sat on the bench beside John. "Are you sure we have to do this?"

He took her hand and kissed it. "If you want to be with me again."

"It's all I want," she told him. "It's all I will ever want."

"Then it must be done." He stood up. "Call to her. That is all you need to do."

"What shall I call her?"

"Queen." He said the name with contempt.

"Queen what?"

"Just *Queen*."

"All queens have a name. Queen Elizabeth, Queen Mary…"

"She prefers this."

"Very well," Maggie said. "I will kindly invite this queen into my world. I will sit her down and explain to her—"

John's laughter made Maggie flinch.

"That may work in the outside world within your political realm or the confines of a marriage, but it will never work in here."

"Why not?"

"Because she does not believe in negotiation. Her desperation has turned her into something vile. She was relatively kind, in the beginning. But she has changed."

"What made her change?"

"You know all you need to know for this task. Once you call to her, she will come. Do not beckon her until you are ready."

"What about you, John? Where will you go?"

"I will be right here."

"Here?"

"I have no other place to go."

Maggie looked at the odd assortment of tools at her feet. Her toe poked the edge of the hacksaw. "If she knows," she reasoned, "then she will come prepared."

"But she will be weaker out here."

Maggie chose the sword and held it tightly in her fist. She

stood before John to show him her preparedness. "I'm not afraid."

"I know," he said. He stood and cupped Maggie's face in his hands and gently, almost paternally, kissed her on the forehead. "I will be indebted to you forever," he whispered.

Forever is a long time rang in her ears.

She walked to the edge of the gazebo and let her eyes follow along the path. In her bare feet, she stood holding the sword and took in a long deep breath. The lemon smell, as strong as if she had basked in lemon verbena, drifted along the path and up the gazebo steps. When Maggie exhaled, the word "Queen" gently drifted through her lips.

The sound of thudding feet vibrated through her world. Maggie turned to John for support, but he was again sitting on the bench, his arm slung across the railing, watching as though the first inning of an Oriole's game was about to commence.

Maggie's eyes traveled along the path. She tried not to flinch each time a footstep fell; they became almost unbearable in their heaviness, their momentum, their certainty. Loose chunks of stone piled high in the path avalanched to the ground, tumbling over one another, disappearing between the fissures. The heavens seemed to rip apart along an invisible dividing line between her world and the castle's. Disengaging locks echoed from the other side of the moat as they slipped out of their iron pockets, and chains creaked with each pull like ancient anchors ascending from the depths of the sea. Maggie watched the restored drawbridge as it fell from the face of the castle and across the moat, the top slamming against the muddy embankment. A solid bridge now led from one side to the other, exposing the door that was the magical conduit responsible for bringing Maggie and John together, as well as a sinister doorway allowing evil to seep into her world.

The footsteps landed with permanence like they had always belonged in this world and always would.

But not if Maggie could help it.

The large door crept open. A large shadow filled the candlelit doorway, a silhouette of something Maggie could imagine but could not yet see. The shadow stood motionless like it was contemplating its next move—surely this hesitancy was a sign of prudence, perhaps even apprehension—then stepped through the doorway. A cloud of fog rushed to the opening, wrapping itself around the visitor like a cloak being draped across the shoulders of royalty. Into the mist the shadow stepped, features obscured, feet clomping one step at a time along the wooden planks. As it made its way across, the footsteps became softer, like the swish of a child's slippers against plush carpet. The fog seemed to stick to the entity as it stepped onto the earth, which would soon turn to the stone path. It—

No, Maggie thought. *An "it" would have no recognizable form, no human qualities. This "it" is indeed a "she"—*

"Queen," Maggie called. "You are now in *my* world. Out here there is nothing but beauty and you cannot—"

"Silence!"

The voice was clear and loud, a simple voice. Not weak, but not especially commanding either. The figure stepped out of the retreating fog, leaving the mist behind, revealing herself. She stood no taller than Maggie and certainly did not suggest the presence of a matriarch. Except for a small jewel-studded crown nestled on top of her blond curls, her clothes were no different than Maggie's, her lean arms and legs and average stride no more threatening.

"You may not speak to me as though we were school chums," the Queen stated as she entered the footpath leading to the gazebo, touching it first with the toe of her sandal as if to be sure of its authenticity. "You may not say anything to me."

The Queen moved gracefully along the path now, somehow sidestepping or hopping over each crevice without a worrisome demeanor, never taking her eyes from Maggie's.

"You are nothing more than a common insect," she continued. "Destined to be squashed beneath my shoe. That is, if I want to ruin a perfectly good pair of sandals. Which I certainly do not." The woman stopped to examine her sandals as though she were trying on a new pair of slingbacks.

Peripherally, Maggie saw John still sitting on the bench, watching the scene in silence. By the time Maggie brought her focus back, the Queen had already gained another few feet and stood within arm's length of the gazebo's bottom step.

From the top of the stairs, Maggie took in the woman's face.

Blond wide-ribbon curls, like John's, only longer, dangled from her head like a cherub in an Italian oil painting. She had perfectly rosy cheeks requiring no blush; clear skin which needed no powder; eyes that looked like cobalt blue glass. Maggie noted the willowy arms, falling gracefully from the sleeves of the familiar tunic, the white teeth behind perfectly shaped lips which were naturally pink. Her whole being was beautiful. *She looks like the woman from the moat*, Maggie thought with wonder. *She looks like* me.

"This man you have named 'John' belongs to me," the Queen said, offering a dramatic flip of her curls.

"He does not belong to anyone," Maggie said.

The Queen's laughter was deep and heinous, an ironic sound erupting from such a sweet-looking thing. "You are an idiot," she said. "You say things as if you know what you are talking about."

"You have no right to keep anyone."

"And you, apparently, do not know who I am." Then the Queen spoke directly to John. "You did not tell her who I am?"

"Yes," John responded, his voice as noncommittal as his face.

The woman squinted her eyes. "How clever you are, John, telling half-truths." To Maggie, she said, "There is no room for you here. You will leave now."

"You have no right to tell me what to do," Maggie said. She fanned out her arms, the sword still held in one hand, the sun reflecting its rays in the silver blade. "This end of the path does not belong to you."

"Of course it does. You must leave. Go somewhere that will have you." The woman flitted her hand in the air like a gnat was pestering her. "Back to that pathetically dreary world in which you reside. It suits you so much better, don't you think?"

"How do you know where I—"

"I know everything!" the Queen screamed. "Everything!" She paused and straightened out her tiara, then lowered her voice again. "I told you, you are common. You are not worth the material from which your dress is made, or the dime store sword you have there in your hand."

Maggie gripped the sword between her fists, even though she somehow knew it would do her no good.

"This really is quite simple," the Queen said. "You will give John back to me, or you will die."

"I cannot die," Maggie said.

"Hogwash! Anyone can die here. The men who found you, yet released you? Poof! Just like that! Gone forever. Never to be seen or heard from again. Of course, there are plenty more where they came from."

"This is *my* dream," Maggie said. "I can do or say or have whatever I want."

"Dear, dear John. You really must learn to tell the whole story."

Maggie glanced at John, but his face held no emotion.

"You fool," the Queen told Maggie. "None of this is within your control."

John was suddenly at Maggie's side. "Do not listen to her," he said.

"Maggie?" a third voice suddenly rang out, falling down from the sky like hail and landing on her shoulders. Maggie glanced around her. She had to think a moment. Whose voice was that? It sounded vaguely familiar...

The words came through fragmented, like a bad connection bouncing along a party line. "Can—hear me? Are—all right?"

"Yes, Maggie," the Queen said mockingly. "Are you all right?"

He's only in my head, Maggie told herself.

"You are wrong," the Queen said. "Perhaps you can use your doctor's visit to your advantage. Perhaps he can save you. Bring you back down to earth, as it were." The woman giggled.

"I don't need him to save me," Maggie said.

"Well, you certainly need someone. After all, this is not your dream. This is *my* dream. Every inch. All mine! I giveth, and I can taketh away! Tell her, John. Tell her about the other women. The ones who came before her. The ones who were just like her."

"Other women?" Maggie asked.

"Of course," the Queen said. "You think you are special?"

"She is special," John muttered.

"Yes, yes, yes, John. So you've said before. This one is special. This one is *the one*. When will you ever learn, John? There is no one more special than your Queen."

"She does not need help getting here," John told the Queen. "She can do it on her own."

The Queen paused. "You lie to me. For this you will be punished."

"It is true," John said. "She is nothing like the others. She does not need help."

"Of course she does. Everyone needs help. No one can do it alone. Even you should know that."

"Maggie is different."

"You are lying to yourself, John. It is not possible. This is *my* dream. This creature is an intruder."

"How can I be an intruder?" Maggie shouted. "I'm the one who—"

"I told you," John said. "Do not listen to her. She is trying to weaken you with fear. You must destroy her."

"Yes, Maggie," the Queen taunted. "Since I am only a figment of your overzealous imagination, why not destroy me right now? Let's see what brilliance your mind's eye is made of."

"I *can* destroy you," Maggie told her, believing her own words. "Just like I destroyed that monster—"

"Ha! You only maimed him. I am the one who gave him his ultimate punishment for being such a cowardly sentry."

"Maggie?" Dr. Germaine called, his voice in her ear like he was standing beside her on the gazebo.

"Get out of my head!" Maggie screamed.

"You must wake up…"

Gentle fingers touched her eyelids; touched her wrist.

"No!" Maggie screamed.

A hand tugged on her arm.

"Not now!"

Then a pinch.

"GET OUT!!!!"

Dr. Germaine's voice, intermingled with other stern but

unfamiliar voices, cascaded around her, little snippets drifting in and out of her secret world like ghosts, floating down from the sky and over the top of the gazebo. They fell off the roof, then sank into the ground and disappeared.

"And you," Maggie, suddenly filled with strength, told the Queen. "You, who does not even have a name. You do not belong here. You are trespassing. Leave now and I will let you live."

The Queen exploded, her voice filled with napalm. "NO ONE SPEAKS TO ME LIKE THAT!"

The ground rolled, shaking the gazebo until some of the shingles toppled from the roof and crashed to the ground.

"NO ONE!"

Maggie held onto a pillar as John scrambled to the far side of the porch and crawled under a bench.

The rumbling stopped.

"Is this a man or a mouse?" the Queen asked, sneering at John from the base of the steps. "Do you not see how weak he is?"

"He is only weak because you keep him that way!" Maggie took one step down, her sword slicing back and forth through the air. "This is *my* world! You are nothing but a monster! You represent everything that is awful in my life! You are trash!"

John said, "Yes, Maggie…"

For a split second she turned toward his voice, but when she spun around again, her eyes darted from the empty steps to the dying field.

The Queen had vanished.

Maggie ran down the steps, her sword at her side.

"She's gone."

John crawled out from under the bench and followed her down the steps. A corner of his mouth twitched. His rosy cheeks turned ashen. "No, Maggie, she is not."

"What do you—"

But the remainder of the question lay unspoken as the center of the path rose into a pointed mountain, demonstrating the birth of a small volcano. Black muck, the same liquid that had oozed from the giant reptile's eye, spewed from the pinnacle.

The smell of lemons was replaced by the smell of bile.

Gray shadows fell upon Maggie and John as an angry sky sucked away the sun. The flowers turned mildew green, then gray, then black before sinking into the earth. Lightning hit somewhere deep in the forest, catching the large oaks on fire. The wind howled, feeding the flames, sending spirals of thick smoke high into the air. Hail, nearly impossible to see through, fell like a rash of bullets against Maggie's skin.

The Queen's voice rained down on Maggie's disintegrating world, scores of puddles filling with a black oily substance where the flowers once swayed. "I will do what is necessary to get rid of you! In a way you will understand! The party is ooovvveeerrr—"

Like a needle plucked from a phonograph, the voice broke off, leaving behind a cold and silent drizzle in its place.

"When she leaves," John said, "it is never for very long."

"Where did she go?" Maggie asked.

"She must prepare." The slanted rain fell against them like cold tears. "She will be back soon. And with more power. When she comes, she must see your strength glowing in your eyes. She must feel it emanating from your being. You must show her you are the one. For me."

"Yes."

"For us."

"Yes."

"Because I have never doubted your strength. I have never

doubted what you are capable of. Without her anger to get in the way, all that you could not have out there, you can have in here."

"Yes," Maggie said, crying through the rain. "Yes, yes, yes."

Chapter Thirty-six

"What if there's a part of me that's evil?" Maggie asked John. "What if the Queen is an extension of me?"

"Your doctor offers these theories because he knows no other way to explain what he does not understand."

"Do you understand everything?"

"I understand enough," John said, placing the tip of his perfectly sloped nose against hers. "There is only one question you should be asking yourself."

Maggie waited.

"In which world do you want to be?"

"This one."

"Then that is all you need to know. Keep that thought when she comes back. You will need to stay focused. As she will be."

***

The Queen's voice was heard before she became visible, before any footsteps shook the earth. With each syllable, the tops of the burning oaks trembled as fiery tentacles reached toward the clouds above.

"You have one last chance to leave!" the voice proclaimed.

"I will not," Maggie replied to the dry and echoing air.

There hovered a slight pause, and then: "Very well. Let it be done."

An earthquake attacked Maggie's world. She lost her balance and fell forward, tumbling down the steps, landing hard on her palms and knees. The path beneath her cracked, tiny fissures coming together and then spreading to form one large gap. She jumped to one side of the fracture, grabbing onto the gazebo railing. It, too, split apart under her fingers, chunks of wood falling to the ground. The beautiful pine beams that suspended the gazebo roof broke in half. The floor sagged in the middle before caving in. The crash sent a gray mushroom cloud of dust up from its center, a miniature version of the explosion on Hiroshima.

"John!" Maggie screamed, tripping over a jagged rise in the path.

"Now let us see who is in control," the Queen said with measured calmness, without guilt or shame or conscience.

Maggie could see nothing through the swirling dust. As she placed her bare foot on the first step of the disintegrating gazebo, it split apart and her leg fell through. Grabbing onto some weeds still anchored in the dirt, she pulled her bloody leg free and crawled onto what remained of the dying grass.

"John! Where are you?"

She limped her way to the back of the gazebo where her beautiful horses once grazed and her flowers once bloomed.

"Maggie—there?"

She looked around. "John?"

"—me—Germaine—can—"

"Go away!"

"Very ill." An invisible tap against her cheek. "We—to help—"

"Get out of here!"

"Maggie—need—wake—"

"No! I have to save him!"

The Queen's voice collided with the sounds of roaring thunder and moving earth and splitting wood. "Yes, Maggie, save him! Be a hero! Show 'em who's behind the eight ball!"

The same pinch Maggie had experienced earlier pricked her other arm. Pushing away the searing pain that shot all the way up to her collar bone, she grabbed onto the unstable railing that encircled the gazebo, hiked her leg onto the porch, and heaved her body up. The deck had split right down the middle, each half of the gazebo leaning outward and away from the crack, the vertical support beams hunched over from the burden, barely keeping the remainder of the roof from collapsing. The ceiling hung so low she could reach up and touch it. Shingles showered down, some onto the ground, others slamming on top of Maggie's head. Covering her head with her arms, she looked under the bench where John had been hiding, but the spot was empty.

"John," she called, "I will save you!"

Dr. Germaine's voice broke through again. "Need—save—self—everything—dreamscape—extension—who we are—disappointments—innermost fears."

"Go away!"

"John is you," Dr. Germaine went on, his slow and steady voice sliding through with more clarity now. "The other woman is you."

"Go away! You don't know what is happening here!"

"I've been with you for three days…"

Three days?

She refused to believe him.

"Everything in your dream represents a part of—"

"No!"

"The female rival—anger you feel toward society's desire— keep you from finding your true—"

"No!"

"—latent masculine part of you; the side repressed by society's expectations—what being a woman really means. To free him is to—"

"John!" Maggie called, ignoring the unsolicited psychoanalysis.

"You no longer need to save him, Maggie. You have already proved how strong you are. You are already a hero."

John's voice overrode Dr. Germaine's: "Maggie! I'm down here!"

Maggie jumped down from the wavering porch and crouched next to the gazebo. John lay underneath, perspiration dripping down his reddened face, his dirty hair stuck to the sweat.

"I came here to hide," he told her.

"The gazebo is falling," Maggie warned. "It'll crush you!"

"My leg is pinned." A large four by four support beam stretched across John's calf. "The hacksaw," he told her, grunting through locked teeth.

She tore around the side, climbed onto the porch, dug through the rubble until she found the hacksaw, and brought it back to John.

"Don't move," she ordered.

He closed his eyes as Maggie fell to her belly and used her elbows to crawl under the porch. The earth smelled of wet moss. She took the saw and placed it against the wood. Within minutes she had cut the heavy piece of lumber in two. Together they pushed it from his leg.

"You're hurt," she told him, sliding like a snake backward and dragging him by the wrists, then depositing him a few yards away from the collapsing gazebo. They held onto one another as the building fell inward, sinking into an unseen vortex.

"Give him to me!" the Queen's voice rolled over them.

"Kill her, Maggie," John said, choking on his words, his face dripping with sweat. The purplish welt traveled from below his knee to beneath the hem of his tunic. "You are strong enough."

A world of total annihilation lay before her. The gazebo was nothing but a pile of white powder; the path like the aftermath of Tokyo's 1923 earthquake. Her enchanted forest of wild oaks lurched in the distance like tall black skeletons, their leaves burned to nothing, scorched branches reaching to the sky in surrender. The grass, no longer a patchwork of greens and browns, had been eradicated; the remaining plants poking through the surface were black, charred things, growing in wild directions, like a chaotic map of electrical wires.

"Maggie," John said, his fingers digging into the bones in her arms, his body quivering. He placed his lips against her ear, the faint words barely penetrating her eardrum. "She knows."

Maggie's face remained close to his. She could smell his sweetness coming through his sweat. But she could also smell his dread.

"Knows what?" she whispered.

"Who you are…"

Lying here on the ground should have felt like it had the first time they lay together on the beach. But now, with John's leg distended and his body shaking, and her heart beating erratically, Maggie didn't experience any of those earlier feelings. She only felt fear as it crawled through her tiny pores and buried itself beneath her skin.

Maggie moved her lips, slowly, delicately, worried that if she asked the question too loudly, something else in her world—

something within a part of herself she had yet to understand—would break.

"What do you mean?"

"Her jealousy," John said. "She can no longer manage it. It has taken over what she used to be."

"What did she used to be?"

"Weak."

"It doesn't matter how she was before," Maggie said. She touched the side of his face; his smooth jaw that by now should have sported a five o'clock shadow but did not. "She is strong *now*. Stronger than I will ever be." Her blond curls fell downward, sliding against John's cheek. A tear fell onto his neck.

"No," he said. "Do not allow yourself to believe that. She will only exploit that feeling."

Maggie's head was spinning. For a moment, she thought she would faint, here in her dream. What would become of her if she did?

"I'm not feeling quite right," she told John. His face spun out of focus, then became clear again. "Something is happening to me." She made it to her knees, pushed herself onto wobbly legs, and tried to reclaim her balance. She glanced across the decaying meadow.

As she fought off dizziness, the now familiar silhouette appeared in the distance, stepped confidently across the forest's threshold, and once again entered Maggie's world. Her silent footsteps moved her forward.

"You must go back," the Queen ordered.

"Go back?" Maggie asked.

"Yes," Dr. Germaine said. "It's time to come back. Easy now."

Back to where? Was she still dreaming? Or was this real life?

The two seemed intricately melded together as though it were impossible one could exist without the other.

"This is *my* dream," the Queen said, advancing closer. "*My* world. Not yours."

"Not mine?" Maggie heard herself ask.

She wasn't sure if what she saw was only in her imagination: The Queen appeared smaller, paler, weaker; the shimmering tiara slid from her messy curls and fell to the ground, only to be sucked away by what was left of the hungry vines.

"Do you not feel yourself drifting away?" the Queen asked.

Maggie could feel it. She wanted desperately to give in to the feeling.

"But I have to save…"

John winced as he leaned up on one elbow. He was lying on the ground at her feet, yet he seemed so far away.

"Kill her, Maggie," he begged.

"Something is happening to me…"

"Yes, John," the Queen said, now a few yards away, dragging her feet through the black vines that were hastily devouring the rest of the meadow. "Something is happening to your sweet little Maggie."

The Queen's face was changing. The soft roundness became more angular, the lines more strict. The tunic hung limply against her skin, as though it were two sizes too big. Her yellow-white hair was darkening, first the roots, then spreading all the way to the ends, turning into the nondescript color of a robin's nest. The shiny glow in her cheeks dimmed, the sallow color matching the sickly sky.

She's becoming one of those vines, Maggie thought sleepily.

But how could she be sleepy? This was her dream…

"No, Maggie," the Queen said, her voice calm, almost forgiving.

"It is not. It is *my* dream. You just happened to stumble in."

"John called to me…"

"He forgets each time. At this moment, he truly believes you have the power to save him. There have been others before you who have tried—"

"Who?"

"Though no one quite as obstinate. And no one who believed this was real. Their visits were fleeting, especially once they realized they had no power here."

"Do not listen to her," John told Maggie.

The Queen stepped closer, stopping just feet away from Maggie and John. In her hand, something shiny flickered for a moment, then was gone. Her voice grew muffled, like a child speaking into a tin can.

"John's tragic downfall is that he does not know he is real," she told Maggie.

"Real?" Maggie asked.

"Real. Like you. Or me."

"But you're *not* real," Maggie said, the words barely making their way through her lips.

"I told you, Margaret Lerner. This is *my* world. John has a difficult time remembering things. Mixes things up. He even forgets *who* he is. So I have stopped reminding him. It seems to work better this way."

Maggie looked down at her perfect John, those soft flaxen curls, his smooth shiny skin without blemish or scar, almost mannequin-like in the way it rested across his bones; blue eyes so angelic and innocent, peering into the very essence of who Maggie was and why she existed.

"Why are you really here, John?" Maggie asked.

But the Queen answered for him. "I brought him here."

"Why?"

"To make him what I want him to be."

"What do you want him to be?"

"Maggie," John begged. "Do not listen to her."

But Maggie chose to listen, as she was suddenly overwhelmed by a keen awareness she would finally have the answers she'd so desperately been searching for. That this Queen with no name—this woman—with her dull green eyes and even duller brown hair, her skinny wrists attached to even scrawnier arms, held the key to all that Maggie needed to know.

Chapter Thirty-seven

Black vines danced around the woman's ankles, caressing her feet, teasing her calves. She spoke to Maggie, no different than her friend Susan, sitting across from her sipping tea, and just as close. The smell of lemons became brutally strong, making Maggie wince.

"I am not a part of you," the woman said. "Though I am sure your doctor would love for you to believe that."

"How did you get here?"

"That does not matter. What matters is that there is only room for one of us."

"Please," Maggie begged. "I want to stay…"

"I'm sorry," Dr. Germaine's said in his hypnotic voice. "You must come back."

"Listen to your therapist," the woman said.

"But why can't I stay?"

"Because this is not your world!" the woman suddenly screamed, falling to her knees on the perishing ground and throwing her arms up toward the sky. The object waved about in one of her hands, but it was moving so quickly it was nothing more than an ambiguous shape. "This is my world! Everyone must do as I say! You are no different! Why can't you understand that?"

Adrenaline coursed through Maggie's brain as thoughts entered her mind with amazing clarity, once again pushing Dr. Germaine and her miserable real-life world far away.

"You cannot control *him*!" Maggie seethed. "You cannot control *me*!"

"Now is the time," John whispered.

Maggie spun around, jumped onto the rickety path, and sliced the sword through the air, the tip reaching out for the woman, finding its mark, and slicing her chin. At first there was no blood, but then, as if gravity and air were suddenly allies, a thin red trail filled the slice, dripping down the lowly woman's chin and onto the path between her feet.

She absently wiped it away with the back of a bony hand and laughed. "You think that will show your strength? You have no strength here."

"Yes, I do," Maggie said as she lowered the sword to her side. "I have strength for John's sake."

"This man is hardly worth your time! Why do you stay where you are not welcome, just for this man?"

"I'm in love with him!"

"Ha! He is an idiot. Each time I bring him here, he forgets where he came from! He has no brain here. No thoughts of his own. He would be nothing without me."

"Then why did he call to *me*?" Maggie asked. "Why is he here with *me*, instead of there with *you*?"

The woman said nothing, only swayed a little on the broken path.

"I'll tell you why," Maggie said calmly. "Because he doesn't love you. He only obeys you."

The words spilled across the blackening meadow, causing what remained of the trees to shake.

The woman gave a brief turn toward the forest.

"You see," Maggie continued, "the one who recognizes the difference between devotion and submission is the one who has the most control."

"You are not in love with him," the woman said as she tried to take a step forward but stumbled in the black weeds. With one arm behind her back, she struggled to stand. "You are in love with a world you think you have created. How can you be so blind? Married to a doctor. Living the life of Riley. This is what makes you pitiful: that you cannot see how lucky you are! Go back to your other world."

"If you aren't a part of me, then how do you—"

"I know everything! I know about your ridiculous desire to be independent in a world where you cannot be this way. About your husband leaving you in favor of the war, your factory job, the way you cooed over collecting soup cans, your dream come true when handed a drill press, your need to feel accepted by the men, donning your dirty nails and soiled uniform like a medal of honor!"

"You have no right—"

"This is *my* world. It is a mere accident that you have come here. A wretched coincidence. You have no *right* to be here! Only I decide who is welcome and who is not! How dare you speak to me about rights!"

The woman was evil, Maggie was sure, but she could also sense the hopelessness that hovered over the woman like a rain cloud. The lost and desperate way in which she stood there, trembling, vulnerable, pathetic; an abandoned dog who repeatedly gets shooed away because no one dares to touch such a mangy animal. This paradox made Maggie want to spit at her, yet at the same time offer comfort.

"You can keep your world," Maggie told the woman.

"Good, Maggie," Dr. Germaine said, his voice soothing, his words draping over his patient, causing her mind to relax.

"I do not want this after all," she said. "I only want him."

She squatted behind John and wrapped her hands around his neck.

The woman said, "You cannot have one without the other."

"I found a way in," Maggie reasoned, "so I will find a way to bring John out."

"Then you leave me with few options."

She stepped onto the ruined path and brought her concealed hand into the open. In her shaking fist she produced a small black gun. A Colt M1911. Everyone who helped with the war efforts had seen or at least heard of the most commonly manufactured weapons. Magazines bragged about them. Billboards advertised them. Nearly two million distributed during WWII. Famous for carrying .45 bullets, large enough to bore a clean hole through nearly anything at close range.

"You can't win 'em all," the woman said, bringing the weapon up. With both hands gripping the handle, she placed a bony finger on the trigger and a thumb on the hammer. The thick ivy wrapped more tightly around her legs as she stood there, pointing the gun in Maggie's direction.

"I'm not afraid," Maggie said. "I cannot die here."

The woman's lips twisted into a sneer. A loud click echoed through the desolate world as the bullet escaped its chamber and sped through the air, whizzing past Maggie's ear. It disappeared somewhere into the fuzzy dreamscape behind her, but she did not turn to witness its final destination.

"I cannot die here," she stated again.

The woman shifted the weight of her vine-covered feet. Again she raised her arm. Another bullet tore through the air, this time hitting the ground next to Maggie's foot.

"You fool," the woman said. "You should have gone back when you had the chance. The others paid dearly, and you will, too."

Another bullet grazed Maggie's right thigh. She cried out in pain as she fell to her knees.

Dr. Germaine called out, his voice directly in Maggie's ear. "That's it," he said. "Open your eyes now. There is nothing to be afraid of…"

"No!" Maggie screamed, the word filled with equal amounts of pain and anger. She lifted the edge of her tunic a few inches, exposing her thigh. The blood that had started to ooze through the white material had already clotted. The graze on her leg healed before her eyes, the skin smoothing over like candle wax in a table crack.

Maggie smiled as she stood. "You did not believe me."

A flicker of doubt in the woman's eye was clear.

Maggie took a daring step forward.

"You do not belong here!" shouted the woman. Another bullet tore through the air.

Maggie let out a loud, "Oof!" as she collapsed to the ground, clutching her stomach. She curled up in a ball, counting breaths until she reached thirty. She looked down at her midsection. Her tunic was stained red but she only felt sticky dried blood. The deep puncture, as well as the pain, was quickly receding. Within seconds, all that was left of the bullet hole was a small tear in her dress.

Again she rose to her feet. Her head buzzed with dizziness, but the realization that she was all-powerful overrode her vertigo.

I am indestructible.

The crazy woman's disintegration was complete. She had turned into a frumpy washwoman with frizzy hair that stuck to her forehead like a pile of loose twine and traveled down her cheeks, covering most of her dirty face. The oversized tunic was replaced by a scruffy smock that fell below her knees, and her bare feet had completely disappeared beneath the hungry black vines.

"Maggie," her doctor called, "you know the truth. Come back now…"

"Yes," Maggie told the woman. "You are only a part of me. The part I hate. Things were perfect until I started to question my place in the world, believing my life was nothing, that it could somehow be better than it already was. Perfect until this dream—until you—took over my life. Why did you coax me into coming here? Why couldn't you have stayed where you belonged, in the deep corners of my mind where I didn't know you were hiding?"

"You are wrong," the woman said, her shoulders slumped, the arm holding the gun falling limply to her side. A thin line of drool crawled to the edge of her lower lip and dangled there. "All I ever wanted was a world that would make me happy; that I could call my own. I didn't coax you. I had nothing to do with your coming here. Please go. You are ruining everything. You are defiling my perfect world."

The woman's gaze followed Maggie's to where the looming castle used to stand. Small clouds of dust swirled in mini tornadoes above the vast pile of sandy rubble. The fortress could easily have been nothing more than a giant sand castle, destroyed by a bully's feet. The once violent moat had nearly dried up, leaving in its place a thin muddy stream trickling through its center. All signs of a heavy door or iron chains or castle drawbridge were obliterated. The fog had completely cleared. For the first time, Maggie viewed the sky beyond the castle, the place where darkness met the land along the horizon, neither frightful nor happy, elusive regarding what that distant part of her mind was trying—or, perhaps, *not* trying—to convey.

Maggie surveyed her dream world, one that in the beginning was her interpretation of the Garden of Eden but was now a wasteland of decaying earth and pallid sky. "There is no such thing as a perfect world," Maggie told the woman, realizing the truth in her own words. "No matter how much you yearn for it, your search will be futile."

"Maggie?" John called from behind her. He writhed on the ground, his leg bent in an odd way, his hands gripping his thigh. "If you leave, she will kill me."

"Oh, John, she can't kill you," Maggie told him, smiling sadly. "I created her. I created *you*. The gazebo…the horses…the flowers…even the castle. And now I'm destroying it, bit by bit. I suppose I don't need this world anymore."

"No, Maggie," John said. "She has great power."

"But only if I let her. Look at her. See how weak she is. The dejected way in which she stands there. The look of resignation on her face. She's the part of me that is restless, confused, dissatisfied. A part I need to relinquish. Finally."

"That's wonderful, Maggie," Dr. Germaine said.

"No," John told her, grimacing as he pushed himself up on all fours in an effort to stand. "She will kill me."

"If I can't die in my dream," Maggie assured him, "then I can prevent you from dying too."

He fell back onto his side, panting. "Then why am I still in pain? Why are you not helping me? Why has my leg not healed?"

"Maybe I feel that you need to have pain because—"

"Because I am real!" John suddenly cried out. "You are only *dreaming* that you are here. I *am* here! She brought me here!" He pointed an accusing finger toward the woman as he once again he tried to stand, but failed. He grabbed a hold of his twisted leg and cried out in agony. "I am *real*!"

The woman's nervous twitter bounced along the tips of the dead grass.

"I'm sorry, John," Maggie said gently, leaning down and running her hands through his curls. She smiled as she took his face in her hands. "My therapist was right all along. This is only a dream. A place I needed to see in order to realize how wonderful my life really is. This is simply a place to escape to from time to time. But not forever. Forever is a long time."

"No."

The dread on John's face caused Maggie to hesitate.

"Yes," she said, fixing her posture and flattening out her tunic. "I created you. I am the one in control after all. I can have all the blue skies and silvery moons I want, whenever I want them."

"It is coming back to me," John said, glancing toward the forest. "I…I am beginning to re—"

"He remembers nothing," the woman interrupted, her wet twitchy eyes moving back and forth between John and Maggie.

"You aren't real," Maggie told John. "You have no future without my giving you one. You have no past. There is nothing to remember. I'm sorry. I convinced myself you were real. That I was in love with—"

"Bing Crosby," John said.

"What?"

"The crooner."

"You've got rocks in your head," the woman whispered.

"The music," John said.

"What music?" Maggie asked.

Heavy intakes of breath separated the words as he sang, "*By the light…of the silvery moon…*"

Maggie stood over him.

His voice cracked as the song spilled into the air. "*I want to spoon…to my honey I'll croon love's tune…*"

"What are you doing?" she asked.

"The news reports," he said, closing his eyes. "The whistle…"

Whistle…

"The incessant drilling. Lunch meetings. Dragging all those bags for Sanders, filled with leftover parts…"

Sanders…

"Andrew Sisters. War bonds. Pearl Harbor. Hitler. Hiroshima." He opened his eyes and looked up at Maggie. "Your mother's death."

"Enough of your two-cents worth," the woman said, wiping her eyes and attempting but failing to push the wild hair from her face with the barrel of the gun. "It is time to start over. Back to square one, as they say on the line."

The line…

"You only know these things because you're a part of me," Maggie told John with forced conviction. "Just like her."

"No, Maggie," John said. "I know—who I am."

Their eyes met. For a fleeting moment, his irises flickered from sky blue to muddy brown.

"You are a pair of fools!" the woman laughed. "You should team up with Laurel and Hardy!"

Once again, the gun was extended, but this time the weapon was not pointed at Maggie.

"I know who I am," John pleaded. "Maggie, you *know*—"

"If you can't beat 'em," the woman said, "you may as well join 'em."

The gun clicked.

"No!" Maggie screamed as she jumped into the air with her hands out in front of her like a mad woman deliberately throwing herself before an oncoming train. As the bullet tore through the air, Maggie landed hard on top of John, her body experiencing the loud snap as his ribs cracked under her weight. Hot air exploded from his lungs against her face.

The woman's crazed laughter shook what was left of Maggie's world.

Maggie straddled John, her weight on his chest, causing a loud groan to escape his throat. "Tell me who you are!"

"Come back to us, Maggie," Dr. Germaine said.

John's arms rose up and gathered weakly around Maggie's neck, pulling her to him. He whispered in her ear. "My love is real. It will last forever."

"Forever is a rather long time," the woman stated.

"Tell me," Maggie said through her tears. "Please…John…"

"Look what you made me do!" the woman screamed at Maggie, taking a final step forward. "You had everything! A name. A place. You have no right to take things that belong to others! Why couldn't you leave well enough alone?"

"Maggie," Germaine coaxed, "open your eyes…"

"The party's over," the woman added. "Over."

"No," Maggie pleaded. "No…"

"Open your eyes," Dr. Germaine said again.

"Yes, Margaret Diana Lerner," the woman said, sinking to her thighs in the creeping vines. "For the first time in your life, open your goddamned eyes."

"John?" Maggie said, cradling his head in her hands. The

blood seeping through the middle of his tunic was quickly spreading outward. His face grew ashen, the shine in his hair muddied like a polluted river. Her fuzzy vision intensified. Salty tears streamed down her face and into her mouth.

"Please, John…"

His eyes fluttered blue, then brown, then blue again.

"Maggie, wake up," Dr. Germaine called gently, like words from a lullaby.

Her wrists were suddenly aching, the veins in her arms pulled tight like over-stretched violin strings.

"Are you with us now?"

"No!" Maggie screamed. "Not yet! John, tell me!"

Her lips felt cold, her teeth clamped tightly together. Could John hear what she was saying? Were her words coming out at all?

"You must leave now," John told her, his voice floating away like a kite that has found its place high in the wind.

"But what about you?"

"Nice guys always finish last," he said. "Didn't you know?"

Maggie forced her blurry vision to focus. Under her fingers, John's blond curls transformed from flaxen to dusty brown. Flawless skin became ruddy with years of sun and wind and cold, the obvious result of alternating seasons. Tiny crow's feet branched out from the corners of his eyes. Thick stubble covered his chin and cheeks. A faded tattoo of a parrot appeared on the outside of his bicep.

The only thing that did not change was the dark blood pooling on the ground around his body.

"Perhaps you will find your perfect world elsewhere," he whispered.

Maggie's own body was turning against her. Her arms grew

longer, taking on their real-life lankiness, their bony wrists. The hair on her head felt like there were little bugs crawling through it, and the curls that fell past her shoulders and upon John's upturned face became Orphan Annie red. Dark freckles once again dotted the backs of her hands. Her wedding ring, which had never before followed her into her dream, materialized on her finger, the sizeable diamond in the center sparkling like a chandelier prism.

No, no, no…

John's brown eyes stared up at her with resignation and sorrow, those soft familiar eyes that had silently supported her through the long years of war, scores of intelligent conversations, moments of uncertainty, days of feeling forsaken. He offered her a reassuring smile.

"I didn't know," Maggie said crying, her tears raining onto his fading face and sliding between his chapped lips. "I only wanted a chance to be strong."

"You are strong," he whispered.

"Only in here."

"No. You can have anything you want in that other world as well."

"But how?"

"You will find a way. You are the strongest woman I have ever known."

She held onto John's shaking body as she felt herself falling between two worlds, a wingless dove tossed out of heaven, hands in one universe opening up and relinquishing her, while another pair reached out to catch her as she fell.

Chapter Thirty-eight

Maggie tried to move her hands up to block out the intense light searing her eyes but could not.

"Do not struggle," a man's voice instructed. "You will only become more frustrated."

The voice whispered to someone else in the room. A wet cloth dabbed her forehead, then was gone.

"Are you with us now?" the man asked.

Her lips felt rubbery, her jaw pulsating like someone had punched her in the mouth. She tried to bite down, but discovered that her cheekbones and even her gums were sore. Her tongue licked the corner of her mouth and tasted blood.

"You are safe now."

Safe now...safe now...

The reassuring words floated into her brain.

A man with a moustache peered into her face, leaned toward her, and placed a light kiss on her cheek.

"Your moustache tickles," Maggie whispered, attempting to make her lips move in a normal fashion. Her voice was hoarse. "Do I know you?"

The man frowned. "She doesn't remember me."

"She will, in time," the other man said. "They all do."

"And the dream?" the man with the moustache asked. "Will that come back as well?"

"There are no guarantees, though my professional guess is that she has already begun to let it go. Look at her face. She certainly appears to be at ease."

"Yes," the man with the moustache said, leaning over her again. "She does." He placed the back of his hand against her cheek. His eyes told her he was someone who cared about her; someone she could trust.

But then the trusting hand disappeared as he moved out of reach. Her arm tried to follow, but it remained frozen. She listened as the two men held a private conversation.

Maybe I'm invisible, she thought dreamily.

The man with the moustache spoke first. "I am working hard not to blame you, or the pills," he said. "It's obvious you wanted to help her. But I still don't understand how it could have gone this far."

"We may never know," the other man said. "In most cases, the women rediscover happiness within a few weeks of taking the tranquilizers. Your wife is an exception. It continued to haunt her, with or without the pills. I wouldn't believe it if I hadn't seen it myself, the way her lucid dreaming so abruptly evolved into psychosis. A case like this could change the psychiatric field forever."

"So, my wife becomes an interesting anecdote to share with your colleagues over martinis?"

"Sam, you have to understand. Maggie represents more to the scientific community than nominal interest. Dreams are a vital part of our existence. Without them we would go mad, eventually die. They are what help us solve problems, relax after a hard day, give the brain a chance to unwind and regroup.

When a particular problem is left unsolved, or certain fears are not dealt with, whether on a conscious level or otherwise, elements of the dream will sometimes return when we enter the dreamscape again. The ultimate goal of the unconscious mind is to find a solution."

"Then what makes her so unique?"

"Maggie's dream returned every night, each time beginning where she left off the time before, with details in tact, as though she were watching a movie bit by bit. Or, in this case, *making* a movie. It's uncommon but not unsupported throughout history that some people have recurring dreams. Believe it or not, they are usually precognitive—premonitions, if you will. But being a willing participant, having conscious control within the dream, well, let me put it this way: In all the years I've studied the human psyche—and keep in mind, I've counseled hundreds of women—this is the most remarkable case of dream involvement I've ever witnessed."

The moustache man peered into Maggie's half-open eyes. "But the dream is gone now?"

"Ask your wife."

"Won't that upset her?"

"Not if we have eradicated the dream."

The kind man leaned closer. "Who is John?" he asked.

John…

For a fleeting moment she knew the answer, felt as though she must know, otherwise why would he be asking her? She could taste the answer on her tongue, lying just beneath the bitter tang of metal, but both tastes were squashed and replaced by a flood of recipes from her Betty Crocker cookbook: veal parmesan; beef strudel; crêpe Suzette…

"Who is John?" the man asked again.

Fearful she would offend the man with her ignorance, she barely breathed her answer: "I do not know anyone by that name."

Beneath the moustache, the man smiled, and she returned the smile, her lips cracking at the corners. She had given the right answer, even though it felt wrong.

"When will you take off the restraints?" the kind man asked the other.

"When we're sure she isn't a danger to herself. Most likely in a matter of days. We'll keep her comfortable until then."

"Then she can come home?"

"Not until I feel she's ready."

"Will she be…" The man with the moustache placed a gentle hand on Maggie's head. "Like she was before?"

"Of course."

"No more melancholy?"

"She will most likely be the same woman you married before you went off to war. Her spirits should be lifted, her desires like that of any other happily married woman."

"What if—"

"Let's take one moment at a time. See how she does. This type of therapy is used as a last resort, but when necessary, it works on most patients immediately. All of them eventually."

The man said, "I owe you a thank you, Dr. Germaine."

"I must thank you as well, Sam. Not only for your trust, but for your kind donation. It will greatly help with further research. Of course, if your wife hadn't come to me in the first place, I wouldn't have had the opportunity to help. She's a kind woman with good intentions who inadvertently stepped onto a path of self-destruction."

"How many other women do you think are on that same path?"

"Oh, there are scores of others. A few therapists agree that our personal subconscious minds are not separate from one another, but connected universally. A collective thought process. If this theory of universal subconscious is correct, and I believe it is, there will be countless more women looking for guidance as the world continues to change. Like an intuitive domino effect. I'm only glad I was able to help her. Even if you don't believe in everything we quacks have to offer."

"You are beginning to convince me." The man with the moustache leaned over Maggie again. He smiled. "You'll be home soon, my magpie."

Home?

"Back to where you belong. Back to our happy world."

An impressionistic image of a field entered Maggie's mind, the wildflowers swaying back and forth, a warm wind blowing across their blooms. But the painting melted away before she had a chance to imprint the scene.

Her eyelids felt heavy so she closed her eyes. The kind man with the moustache would be taking her to a world of happiness. A world of perfection. A place she knew would satisfy her.

And she couldn't wait to go.

Chapter Thirty-nine

The painful scream of the whistle echoed through the house.

"Hold your horses!" Maggie shouted from the master bedroom.

She finished zipping up her dress, slid into her pretty low heels and, holding carefully to the banister, made her way down the steps. She strode into the freshly painted kitchen, tied the frilly apron around her waist, and removed the kettle from the burner. As she poured the boiling water into the porcelain teapot on the kitchen table, the back door opened, letting in a gush of wet, chilly air.

"Hi-de-ho!" Susan said gaily as she closed the door behind her. "Brr. I don't remember it being this cold last September!" She took off her twill coat and neatly arranged it across the back of a chair revealing a green cashmere sweater and a silk scarf tied around her neck, matching perfectly with her evergreen skirt. "You look wonderful," she told her best friend.

They wrapped their arms around one another in a friendly hug.

"So do you," Maggie said. "Look at your glow! You were made for motherhood."

"Look who's talking!"

They held each other out at arm's length and shared a laugh.

"How's the back?" Maggie asked.

"I've been doing some stretches I read about in this month's *Redbook*. Remind me to show them to you later. How's your sciatica?"

"I've found a cure!" Maggie slid out one of the kitchen chairs and displayed a small square pillow, swathed in a paisley pattern of swirling greens and reds.

"Where did you find that?" Susan asked, picking it up and squeezing it between her hands like a soft accordion.

"I made it," Maggie said proudly. She grabbed a container of eggs from the refrigerator and a mixing bowl from a lower cabinet and placed them on the counter. "Sam bought me one of those newfangled Singer sewing machines. He told me it would fill my days with bliss, creating things for him and me and the house."

"Don't forget little Elizabeth or little Milton."

"Of course. I can't wait to make all those play clothes and pajamas."

"A new sewing machine," Susan said. She placed the pillow back on Maggie's chair. "Hot dog!"

Maggie cracked four eggs into a bowl and added sugar and flour. Within minutes she had mixed the cookie dough, and together the two women placed the sticky balls on a cookie sheet. Once the cookies were in the oven, they sat at the table and prepared their tea, then leaned back and took one another in.

Susan said, "You are one lucky gal, Maggie, I can tell you that."

"I am truly blessed."

"So, you're really fine?"

"I am."

"No more melancholy?"

"Suze," Maggie said, "I asked you never to mention that word in this house again. As far as I'm concerned, that's a four-letter word."

"I just want to make sure that my best friend—who happens to be due a few weeks after me—well, that she's okay."

"I am."

"No more silly talk about being unsatisfied?"

Maggie didn't remember ever being anything less than content, and laughed at the thought. "What woman in her right mind would be unsatisfied with this?" She fanned her hands through the air like a cheery game show assistant. "I have a man who loves me, a home I tend to with my own hands, and a baby on the way."

Susan glanced up at the clock hanging on the kitchen wall behind Maggie.

"Somewhere else you'd rather be?" Maggie asked.

Susan said nothing for a moment, then suddenly spurted, "Oh, gosh, Maggie. You know how awful I am at keeping secrets. But…"

"But what?"

"It was all Sam's idea, really."

"Sam?"

"Just what the doctor ordered." Susan giggled at her own joke but stopped when she saw the blank look on Maggie's face. "You're about to have some visitors."

Maggie couldn't imagine who would come for a visit. She had no friends other than Susan. At least that she remembered. Even Susan had disappeared from her memory until recently.

"Today's your shower, Maggie. Your baby shower. I didn't want to tell you, I promised Sam I wouldn't. But you—I just thought you should get a little prep time, you know, with everything that's happened."

Maggie knew Sam had shared many things with her best friend, though she wasn't sure of the details. He had spoken with some of her past coworkers, had even telephoned her sister up in New York. None of it mattered to Maggie. She felt fortunate to have forgotten whatever it was that had made her sad before, but the thought of strangers in her home caused her anxiety.

"I don't want any visitors," Maggie said.

"I knew you'd say just that," Susan said. "Look. These are friends of Sam's mostly—wives of other doctors. Some of them you've met before. You're going to get presents, and we'll play some fun games. Come on, hon. You're about to have a baby. If ever there was a time to celebrate, it's now."

"When will they be here?"

Susan stood up and opened the back door, pausing to glance at the clock again. "In thirty minutes." She stepped onto the stoop and reappeared with two large grocery bags. She closed the door with her hip and placed the bags on the counter.

"What's all that?" Maggie asked.

"You can't throw a shower without goodies!"

Maggie stood up. "Let me help."

"Hogwash," Susan said, untying Maggie's apron and arranging it around her own waist. "You're the queen today, so act like one. Why don't you go clear off the coffee table? I want to put some hors-d'oeuvres in the living room."

Maggie did as her friend asked. She didn't like to cause waves, especially since the shower was Sam's idea. Sweet Sam. He always knew what was best.

She cleared the cherry wood table of baby magazines and department store catalogs and stacked them on the bookshelf.

She smiled to herself as Susan bustled about in the kitchen, opening and closing cabinets, stacking dishes, pulling silverware from drawers. Within minutes, the smell of Maggie's sugar cookies drifted into the living room.

"When you're through with the table," Susan called, "why don't you turn on a little music?"

Maggie stared at the big boxy radio sitting in the corner of the room, an invisible piece of furniture when Sam was at work or out on the golf course. He preferred that Maggie not turn it on unless he was there to oversee what station they listened to. Evenings were spent together enjoying Milton Berle and other blithe radio shows. And even though Sam took pride in affording the latest in household goods, the state-of-the art television now on the market was something he had decided to forgo. Their old television had been donated to the hospital's lounge. He also kept tabs on the newspaper. Each day, when the *Baltimore Times* hit the door, it remained unopened on the front porch until Sam came home. Later, he'd browse through it while Maggie tidied up the dinner dishes, then he'd throw it in the trash can. Sam explained that keeping negative information out of the home would help Maggie be a better mother while growing the baby, and Maggie wholeheartedly agreed. No news was good news in her delicate condition.

But now, Maggie was embarrassed not to be a part of the everyday world. Susan listened to the radio, read the paper, went to the library alone, checked out books she chose herself.

Maggie clicked on the RCA and waited through the one-minute warm-up buzz, then moved the dial to an old swing station. For a moment she stood there, her arms folded across her chest, her eyes closed as the clarinet and saxophone entered her ears, filling her with long-forgotten pleasure. What harm could a little music do? After all, she thought, as she placed her hands on her roundness, this was *her* shower.

She traveled about the room making sure the couch pillows were fluffed, the cushions smooth, and the curtains open to let in the autumn sun at the best angle. She ran a finger across the mantle, the bookshelves, and the coffee table, looking for dust. Satisfied, she took a seat on the sofa and waited for her friend to finish in the kitchen.

Soon, Susan glided into the room with a platter of cheese and crackers in one hand and a tray of cookies in the other. A small-handled bag dangled from her wrist. "Gouda cheese from the butcher and fresh sugar cookies from your amazing oven."

"I can't believe you've gone through all this trouble," Maggie said.

"Are you kidding? This was a cinch," Susan said as she placed the platters side by side on the coffee table. She took a stack of napkins from her apron pocket and splayed them out next to the platter. She pulled party favors out of the bag—a fanned-out tissue centerpiece which read "CONGRATULATIONS!" in large pink scroll across the front, a small clear box of diaper pins, a short stack of 5x5 index cards, a bunch of pencils—and organized them along the mantel.

The doorbell rang.

"Perfect timing," Susan said gaily as she untied her apron. "Now remember. Act surprised. Sam would have me over a barrel if he knew I told you." She headed back into the kitchen.

Maggie went to the foyer and straightened the headband which held back her thick red mane. Over the last few months, her hair had grown past her shoulders until it hung down in long ringlets. Sam was right—she did look prettier with her hair this way.

In a flash of excitement, the door opened and a half dozen women streamed in, the cool air trailing behind and hovering in the entranceway. Maggie placed a hand against her chest in feigned surprise, offered hugs and cheek kisses, took jackets and stoles and hung them in the hall closet. Each woman gently touched Maggie's cheek or tummy, or took her by the hand and exclaimed how healthy she looked, how beautifully glowing her skin was, how amazing it was that she hadn't gained but a few pounds. The last gal handed Maggie the damp newspaper from the front stoop. Maggie laid it on the hallway table for Sam to read later. After all, she had no need.

Maggie examined each guest's face, women kind enough to step out on a chilly day in honor of her impending childbirth. She thanked them, smiled at them, giggled along with them as they made themselves at home on sofas or chairs, spreading out their tailored skirts, readjusting Sunday hats, observing their guest of honor like an exquisite statue on display in a sculpture garden.

As Maggie sat facing them, she wondered, had she met these women before? Were they part of the past that she had no recollection of and perhaps never would?

She wanted to share her curiosity with Susan, but her best friend was busy imitating Emily Post, gracefully striding from kitchen to living room, filling pretty china cups to the rim with coffee or tea, making sure each gal had her fair share of cheese and crackers and cookies on the dainty dish.

For over an hour, they played baby shower games and listened to baby tales, most having to do with labor, others simply sharing the antics of infants—baby's first smile, first step, first tooth, first word. Maggie plastered a wide grin on her face as the word "imposter" crept into and then settled in her head. With sincerity, the women smiled at their honoree; these doctor's wives sipping tea, nibbling treats, gabbing happily as most women do at baby showers, totally unaware that Maggie didn't have the slightest inkling of who they were.

Chapter Forty

"All the girls at the country club refer to you as the miracle of Baltimore," a bleached blond told Maggie as she dabbed her Passion Red lips with her napkin.

"Oh, that's silly," Maggie said.

"Is it? Getting pregnant when Sam…well, you know. It's like magic."

Maggie listened to this stranger sitting in her living room, speaking of Sam like she was privy to his personal information. How much had Sam shared with his colleagues? How much had they, in turn, shared with their wives? How much did these women know that she didn't?

The blond added, "It's like you both have fairy dust swirling over your heads."

Games continued, hot drinks flowed, baby stories became boring and didactic, and Maggie's jaw throbbed from the incessant smiling. At some point, someone turned up the radio. The volume of chatter increased. Laughter rose for a moment above the music. Someone started singing along with Ella Fitzgerald. The entire room became a choir, harmonized voices escalating, then falling. Someone placed a glittered cardboard crown upon Maggie's head; beautifully wrapped gifts were placed at her feet; flashbulbs popped like firecrackers. One by one, she untied the shiny satin ribbons. From boxes she pulled hand-knitted and crocheted booties, hats, sweaters, mittens. She unveiled pretty crib sheets, soft blankets, lacy bonnets, stuffed animals, a butterfly mobile. One gal gave her a gift certificate for a year's worth of Tidy Toddler Diaper Service. Another gifted a pair of white leather shoes so tiny they fit in the palm of Maggie's hand.

Having a good time wasn't so difficult after all, she thought, even without knowing who these women were. She could see her life in the future as, like an embryo, it grew and took form within her imagination. There were Christmases to look forward to: decorating trees, donning the house in holly, having their little one sit on Sam's shoulders, placing the angel on the tree's top; candles lit and songs sung in choir at midnight mass, sugar cookies and chocolate milk left for Santa; racing to dump out stockings, open gifts, dive into honey-baked ham and homemade mashed potatoes. There were birthdays, with chocolate cake and Neapolitan ice cream, and candles to blow out after making wishes with eyes squeezed shut. There were school meetings, school recitals, school sports. Countless puppies, kittens, goldfish, hamsters. There would be days of training wheels, followed by days without, followed by scraped knees shortly after. Lost teeth would be placed under pillows for the tooth fairy, Easter eggs would be colored and hidden in the wondrous flower garden behind the house, swing sets would be installed, homework would be done nightly at the kitchen table, prayers said in tiny hopeful voices at bedtime, after teeth were brushed, bodies bathed, pajamas buttoned. Lights would go out, except for the little night light that kept away the bogeyman. All of these wondrous moments would be hers to have, hers to keep.

Memories she would keep locked away in her heart, for fear of losing them.

Maggie caught Susan's attention while the group "ooed" and "ahed" over a hand-crafted picture frame. She mouthed the words, "Thank you."

Susan winked and got up to fetch another pot of coffee.

The radio music was interrupted by a stream of commercials, but no one bothered to turn it down. One actor bragged about the smooth flavor of his pipe tobacco, another aimed to convince the audience that their pets couldn't live without Purina Chow. The weatherman offered advice about the autumn's first frost due that night, and a newscaster reminded them there were less than one hundred shopping days until Christmas.

"Let's get some real music in here," one younger woman said as she turned the dial to a modern station. She stood next to the radio, tapping her foot along to the bass beat.

The chatter elevated to a spot above the song, finding rhythm with the music, voices shouting to be heard, until Maggie had to leave the room. She wasn't used to all this commotion; her home was generally undisturbed as she baked casseroles, made the bed, ironed shirts and linens.

Susan stood in the kitchen placing the last of the cookies on the platter. A fresh pot of coffee had just finished brewing.

"You having fun?" she asked Maggie when she saw her. "I am," Maggie said. "I truly couldn't ask for anything more in a friend."

"Ditto."

On the other side of the kitchen door, the women's laughter dwindled to silence. Maggie cocked her head to the side and listened as the radio announcer's deep voice filled the living room.

Susan put the spatula in the sink. "Now what on earth could hush a roomful of hens?"

Together they stepped into the living room, the coffee pot secure in Susan's hand, the platter in Maggie's. The collective smile the women had shared for the last ninety minutes had vanished. Each woman looked down at her napkin or her hands. A few had their eyes closed.

The man on the radio used a less animated voice than when he was announcing the next performer or advising which laundry detergent was best for his listeners.

"—at Eastern Weapons Plant in Baltimore, considered to be the worst serial killing in the East's history. The bodies of—"

Susan rushed across the living room. "We don't need to hear this, ladies," she said, clicking off the radio. She turned to the guests like a stern teacher to a classroom of unruly students. "This is a baby shower."

The air in the living room grew dense without the radio and constant chatter. Susan, barely skipping a beat, resumed her place as hostess, walked around the room, refilling coffee cups.

"What's happened?" Maggie asked from the doorway, gripping the oval edge of the platter, suddenly a stranger in her own living room, her desire to know the answer overtaking the knowledge that what she may learn could tarnish the home she worked so hard to keep polished.

"Oh, hon," Susan said, taking the platter from Maggie's hands and placing it on the coffee table. "We don't need that kind of news getting into our heads. Do we, ladies?" She touched Maggie's arm lightly before strolling back into the kitchen.

Maggie waited for the women to return to their cackle and conversation. She suddenly needed them to be loud, needed their laughter to fill up the corners of her living room, unimportant chatter to burrow into her ears.

Until this moment, Maggie hadn't cared whether or not she had any girlfriends, didn't worry over much in her life really, other than keeping Sam happy and making sure her baby would be healthy. Pieces of rubbish had no right spilling into her world. But she suddenly wanted to know what these women knew. She felt left out. She wanted to hear the news. She wanted to read the paper. The paper that Sam said she shouldn't read because it could hurt the child; could clog Baby Milton's or Baby Elizabeth's embryonic mind with negative elements. He had, over the last few months, even become a Dr. Spock devotee.

Susan's enthusiastic voice cut through the silence: "Let's play Baby Bingo!"

The babble rose like zeppelins into the air, one voice colliding into another; whatever had been heard on the radio moments before again replaced by excited talk of bouncing babies and domestic bliss as Susan handed out little pencils and Bingo cards.

"I'll be right back," Maggie told Susan.

"You okay?"

Maggie lowered her voice. "I need to use the powder room. Seems like I go ten times a day."

Susan laughed. "I know what you mean."

Maggie slipped out of the living room and entered the foyer. There on the table lay the newspaper, filled with a collection of facts and information that had no bearing on her or the baby or their home: obituaries, want ads, political commentary, economic particulars, post-war updates. What did she care of these things? Today's paper was merely one of many that had thumped against the front door and landed on the welcome mat; one of many she hadn't missed reading.

Until now.

Chapter Forty-one

As Maggie slipped up the stairs with the paper tucked under her arm, she heard a woman in the living room say, "We assumed she knew. It's been in the headlines for months."

Susan's response was protective. "Well, she didn't know. Maggie's finally in a good place, and Sam wants to keep it that way."

One night that summer, Maggie and Sam had run into a couple of gals while at the movies. The two perky women pulled Maggie into a hug, asked about her life since leaving the plant, the smell of face powder and perfume spilling into Maggie's nostrils, transmitting flashbacks of grimy fingernails, pinned up curls, grease-smudged cheeks. But the flashes were as fleeting as a lightning bolt, the brightness blinding her for a millisecond, then disappearing, leaving behind nothing but static electricity. Maggie had stood with her hip against her husband's, knowing that these two women—women whose faces and names she could not remember—expected to be introduced to Sam. They waited for what seemed to be an incredibly long time, until Sam finally stuck out his hand, introduced himself, asked their names, then said something clever to make the women laugh. But Maggie saw the way they glanced over their shoulders as they walked down the aisle to their seats, their heads nearly knocking together as they whispered to one another.

Sam was always coming to her rescue. He was her knight in shining armor. Her bodyguard.

Her keeper.

Upstairs in the bathroom, Maggie sat on the closed toilet seat, peeled off the rubber band, and slid it onto her wrist. She placed a flat palm against the soggy newspaper, took in a deep breath, let it out again—

In and out…in and out…slowly now…

—and unfolded it.

The headline stood out in bold letters: "Another arrest made in bizarre murder case at Eastern Weapons."

Below the title, the woman's face that stared up at Maggie seemed vaguely familiar, but then so did many things since she was released from the hospital last spring. The face was pretty in a European way, somewhat exotic. Two thick braids of dark hair matched even darker eyes.

Under the photograph sat a caption: "The only thing I'm guilty of is helping others."

We've shared a lot more around here than casserole recipes…

Gouda cheese and sugar cookies became a clump of wet sand in Maggie's stomach. She placed her mouth under the sink's faucet, drank water until the turmoil in her belly subsided, and sat again. She resumed reading the article.

"Jocelyn Mestrelli was arrested early yesterday morning in the cosmetic department of Macy's while dozens of spectators looked on, charged with intent to sell narcotics. She had been employed as one of a handful of female drill press operators at Eastern Weapons Plant in South Baltimore. Eastern has been plagued with troubles beginning earlier this year when the plant's owner, Charles Sanders, was arrested for the illegal distribution of weapons. Police say that no other Eastern employees have been arrested with regards to the case against Sanders, who was convicted and sentenced last April to forty years in prison. Mestrelli's arrest comes on the heels of the current investigation regarding the bizarre murders of at least a dozen men and two women, also ex-employees of Eastern. The FBI, along with the Baltimore Police Department, have been working together to—"

The article directed the reader to page A7.

Maggie frantically tried to turn to the section, but the wet pages were clumped together like *papier-mâché*. Black ink bled onto her fingers as she painstakingly separated the pages, first A5, then A6—

"Maggie?"

Instinctively, she threw the paper to the floor, her feet making a mad dash to cover the evidence, warm blood rising to her cheeks.

Susan stood in the bathroom's doorway, her hands on her hips. She glanced at the barely hidden newspaper. "I thought you were sick…"

I am sick, Maggie thought dimly.

"You're not supposed to get upset," Susan reminded her. "Sam would die if anything—"

"I want to know."

Susan fiddled with an earring. "What?"

"Everything," Maggie said. "I want to remember."

"You know what Sam told you. You don't need to remember all that stuff. It will only disturb you. And you know we can't let you get—"

"I worked there, Suze."

As Maggie waited for her friend to respond, the smooth and steady tempo of her heart quickened, though why she did not know. Sometimes her pulse would accelerate this way, her palms would grow clammy, her neck would tingle, as if a ghost had just passed through her. But the only ghosts around her now were ones from her own past that she could not remember.

"I know you worked there," Susan said.

"But I don't *remember* working there," Maggie said sadly. She stared at the paper lying on the tile floor between her feet. "I want to remember."

Susan sat on the edge of the tub and took Maggie's hands in hers. "Maggie, you have everything you need, don't you?"

"Yes."

"Everything you want?"

"Yes."

"Then remembering a time in your life when the chips were down, well, what's the point in that?"

"But *you* know," Maggie said. "All those women downstairs, *they* know. I just want the right to know."

"What is it exactly that you need to know?"

"Who was murdered."

"Oh, Maggie…"

"I may not remember working there, but I still want to know." Two thin lines of tears ran down her cheeks. "Aren't I allowed to grieve, even if I don't remember them?"

Susan pulled a starched white handkerchief from inside her sweater sleeve and handed it to Maggie. "If I tell you, then will you let it go? Will you just move on with your life? Raise your baby, love Sam, be a wonderful wife and mother without all that other stuff filling your head?"

Maggie nodded.

Susan paused a moment, then said, "Someone from Eastern was responsible for the murders."

"Jocelyn Mestrelli?" Maggie asked.

"You remember her?"

Maggie blushed and looked at her hands. "No. I read her name in the paper."

"Oh. Well, from what the police say, Jocelyn was just selling drugs to make ends meet. They don't believe she's directly connected to the murders."

"Did I know any of them?" Maggie asked. "The ones who were—"

"I don't know."

An obscure face of a middle-aged man with an ugly toupee drooping over his forehead entered Maggie's mind. "Sanders."

"Do you remember him?"

"He was my boss," Maggie said, surprising herself with this recognition.

"Right."

"That's all I remember."

"He's in jail for selling weapons on the black market," Susan said. "He was arrested last winter. That's why the plant closed. But he's never been a suspect in the murders either. He was just a careless criminal."

Maggie picked up the paper, but Susan took it out of her hands and placed it on her own lap.

"Back in the very beginning," Susan said, "the FBI interviewed dozens of ex-employees to see what evidence they could gather against Sanders. For some reason, a few people couldn't be located. That's what started the search."

"Why didn't they interview me?"

What if Maggie was a larger part of the picture than she

realized? What if she had known about Sanders and his weapons, or Jocelyn selling drugs? What if Maggie actually knew who—

"Your therapist," Susan said. "He got a court order so you wouldn't be questioned. He told the feds that you…weren't of a proper state of mind. That your answers would be of no help."

Maggie could tell that her friend was collecting her thoughts, like a housewife shopping for just the right melon, weighing one in each hand to see which was the better fit for a fruit salad.

"It's believed the murders began within weeks of the plant closing," Susan finally said.

"So long ago."

"Yes. But then, early last spring, they found her. The murderer."

"A *woman*?" Maggie asked. "How could a woman—"

"I knew this would upset you," Susan said. "I can't do it. It's not right. Not when your life is so…"

"Perfect?"

"Yes."

"Then I'll just read the paper myself," Maggie said.

Susan pulled the *Times* close to her chest and crossed her arms.

"As soon as the party is over," Maggie said, "I'll take a nice long walk to the newsstand. Fresh air will do me good." She sounded mean, but she didn't care.

Susan pulled her lips into a thin line. "I hate that you're making me do this."

"Well, I hate that you're treating me like a child."

"Fine. They arrested a woman named…oh…I've forgotten her name." She glanced up at the ceiling. "It's right on the tip of my tongue. Anyhow, she's also the one who ratted on Sanders."

"How did they find her?"

"It all happened back in mid-January when the investigation

began. The police ransacked Eastern and discovered a basement. The door was built into the floor of a broom closet. The building was ancient, supposedly used in the 1800s as a place to sell and trade slaves. The basement at one time had been a holding area. More like a dungeon, from what I gather. Anyhow, they seized illegal weapons, arrested Sanders, the plant closed, and since the FBI had already gone through the place, fingerprints and so on, it sort of left the building on the open market. Anyone could have gone in there. Bums stealing leftover junk. Kids vandalizing the place. The murderer decided to live in there. Like a rat. She got evicted from her boarding house because she couldn't pay the rent. A few months later, the police found her, along with what she had hiding down there in that basement."

"What?" Maggie could barely hear her own voice. It seemed to be coming from far away, transmitted from the other side of the globe.

"The bodies," Susan said. "Bound with ropes and chains. All shot to death. They found guns and ammunition and gallons of lemon citric cleaner. I guess she liked to keep her weapons shiny. Or maybe she used it to clean up after—" Susan stopped to take in a deep breath. "Anyway, they also found a tank load of tranquilizers."

"Tranquilizers?"

"All of the bodies had drugs in their system. That was the only way she could do what she did, slipping them pills like that, especially the men. She was tiny. A little mouse, really." She pointed a scolding finger at Maggie. "I knew those mind drugs were no good. I'm so glad you're over your melan—well, you know. I'd hate to think my best friend could have gone bonkers taking those awful things."

Maggie didn't remember ever taking tranquilizers, and she

could only half recall the time spent floating in and out of consciousness in the sanitarium. She could remember nothing of the events that led up to her admittance and only a smattering of the incredible war everyone still spoke of. It was as if those years of her life had once been written in bold white letters on a chalkboard, then erased until only pasty smears were left behind. With Sam's support and the aid of her psychiatrist, she had worked hard to keep it that way.

"Why did she do it?" Maggie asked quietly.

"The newspaper said she rambled on about women not having their due; that it was time to stop men from ruling the world. She cursed the United States Government, Truman, Sanders. Apparently she was angry about losing her job, but I can't imagine who wouldn't be happy to get away from that God-awful factory work. She supposedly called herself the new reigning supreme. Said that it was time for men to follow. Time for a queen to take control."

An apparition with pink lips and silky white skin wearing a tiara floated before Maggie's eyes, but just as quickly vanished. Scenes like this one often crawled up next to her, so close she believed she could step inside and live within them. But they either disappeared before she had a chance to mark them in her memory, or they remained obscure and elusive, like bands of reflected light dancing twenty feet above her on the ceiling, always there, begging for attention, yet just out of reach.

"Her name," Maggie mumbled.

"What?" Susan asked.

"What was her name?"

"I don't re—"

"Look it up."

"Maggie…"

322

"Look it up!"

"Okay, okay." Susan carefully opened the wet paper. "They've been re-running her picture for months like she's an advertisement or something. Now…let me see…" She pointed. "Yes, here it is."

Maggie tore the paper from Susan's hands and held it up. She stared at the photo. Eyes of anger and derangement and utter hopelessness tried to hide beneath a mass of bristly hair. A long thin scar marked the woman's chin. With her pallid skin, tiny beady eyes, and almost nonexistent lips, she was the antithesis of a queen. Susan was right: She looked exactly like a mouse.

…this is my dream…you just happened to stumble in…

She pushed the nonsensical phrases from her head and silently read the name underneath the picture: *Persephone (Percy) Madeline Harper.* Maggie's eyes scanned the article. The chill started at her spine and traveled quickly up the back of her neck, into her skull, behind her eyes, and down her throat. Her tongue grew cold and numb.

"Maggie?"

"The rest of the page is dedicated to—"

"Yes, I know. They've shown those photos nearly every week. They're hoping someone will come forward with more information, offer names of missing loved ones. People who worked at Eastern, even those who didn't. Hard to know if there are any more bodies out there with so many of our fellas MIA. Holy mackerel. The whole thing is enough to give even a normal person nightmares."

"*Normal?*"

"Oh, hon, you know what I mean," Susan said.

Maggie continued to scan the photos.

"Come on, Maggie. Haven't you seen enough?"

Hadn't she?

She tapped a finger against the flat faces as she read their names to herself: *Roberta Ann Michaelson; Ada May Latham; Charles (Chuckie) Michael Taylor; Antonio Lewis Dwyer; Marcus Scott Southerland; Nelson James Johnson; Kirby Thomas Biddle; Nathan Ellis Fairchild; Richard Frederick Stevens, Jr.; Tobias (Toby) Gunther Sidney Averette; Garrison Wilbur Burns; Norman Prescott Waller...*

Her finger hovered a moment over the man's photo.

Norman...Norman...

Her finger kept sliding, like a divining rod trying to locate water beneath bedrock. Every photo had its own caption, encapsulating each life in a one or two-line blurb: *Riveter. Smelter. Dock worker. From Ohio. New York. Baltimore. Washington. Eldest daughter. Youngest son. One of seven. Age thirty, forty-one, thirty-seven, twenty-two. Father of four. Father of twins.*

She recounted the photos, her finger taking its time to circle each and every face. Two women, ten men. When she got to the end, she picked at the top corner of the soggy paper and turned it. Two more photos waited to be viewed. *Perry Washington Sinclair: Truck driver. Twenty-eight years old. Baltimore native. Father of two...*

When Maggie's finger inched its way to the last photo, it halted, her pink polished fingernail landing just under his chin. With her eyes squinted, she examined the face, much in the same manner Dr. Germaine would examine hers from time to time, searching beyond the pupils to make sure her mental health was still in check; that she hadn't suddenly floated off to Mad Hatter Land. Even though the man's grainy picture was black and white like all the others, she knew those eyes staring up at her were filled with swirls of brown, like warm fudge mixed with chocolate ice cream. She knew he loved whiskey, dancing, and comic books. That he was kind and sincere. How she knew any of these things, she did not know.

Perhaps electroshock therapy makes one a mystic, she thought.

Silently, she read the name below the photo, moving her lips but stopping the words from entering the air: *Jonathan Dean Smith*.

Jonathan. Dean.

JD.

Assistant Manager. Thirty-two years old. Baltimore native. Only son.

Maggie traced the photo with her eyes as if by examining it the man would somehow become real.

I am real…if you leave, she will kill me…

A lump filled her throat. Tears threatened to come. Surprised by the sudden feeling of despair, she took a deep breath and read aloud the rest of the article, keeping her focus on the words: "'Renowned psychotherapist and author of the anticipated book, *Dreams and the Women Who Own Them*, Dr. Randall Germaine was questioned last week by reporters while entering the sanitarium where he runs a depression clinic for women: 'Percy was a patient of mine for a few weeks prior to Eastern's closing, but she stopped coming to her sessions shortly after being fired from her factory job. Like so many other women after the war, she was depressed and showed signs of extreme confusion. I felt she should be admitted and given full-time care until her depression was under control. Unfortunately, she disappeared before that could be accomplished.' When asked if Percy was mentally fit to stand trial, he responded, 'In my medical opinion, she is not. The court has placed her under my complete supervision, and she will remain so until after the trial, regardless of any plea or outcome.' When asked how Percy was able to obtain so many pills, and whether or not it was the tranquilizers that caused her to become delusional, Dr. Germaine told reporters, 'I'm sorry. That is all I can say at this time.'"

Susan said, "She obviously had a sick fascination with blue collar boys. Though no one knows why she killed the women. Maybe it was a jealousy thing. They had worked together in nuts and bolts. She was a nut job, all right. When the cops found her, she was high as a kite, sitting in the cellar beneath that filthy broom closet, a brass whistle in her hand. And she was emaciated, like she hadn't eaten in weeks, and she was wearing a crown on her head made of twigs. When the police questioned her, she babbled like a wild woman. She told them that her other world was still waiting for her, where she was the ruler, and how she had to get back there. And all that hogwash about women getting their due. Talk about having rocks in her head."

Maggie scanned the article a second time, hoping for another flicker of recognition, of something, anything. But as hard as she tried to rip through the fog that clouded her memory, the fog that somehow seemed cruel and safe at the same time, she could never get the thoughts to stick, their shapes melting away as quickly as butter on a hot skillet. Once the shapes were gone, relief filled her, as did the knowledge that everything she desired already belonged to her; that allowing disturbing news to permeate her protected world was dangerous.

Maggie closed up the paper, folding it twice.

Perhaps you will find your perfect world elsewhere…

Girlish laughter from her living room floated up the steps and into the bathroom.

Maggie removed the rubber band from her wrist, absently rubbed the indentation it had left behind, wound it around the paper, then wound it again, as if by tightening the band she could strangle the photos and captions and thoughts of death into oblivion. Maggie was done with the newspaper. Done with anything and everything that could contaminate her flawless future. Her life which lay before her was as flat and stiff as one of Sam's starched collars. No creases to trip over. No surprises to knock her off her lovely new heels. No upsets that could send her back to that dismal sanitarium. What did it matter if she had known any of those people before? What did it matter if she could or couldn't remember the woman she used to be?

Now is the time.

Susan was asking a question.

"What?" Maggie said.

"Do you know her?"

But Maggie understood that Susan was masking the real question: Did Maggie remember *any* of them? Did she remember *anything*?

Maggie stood up and placed the wet folded paper on the vanity. Beneath the faucet, she scrubbed her ink-marked hands with a bar of soap, dried them on a towel, and looked in the mirror. The woman gazing back was beautiful, a goddess even, with those long red curls and decorative freckles. As she and her reflection adjusted their headband, the woman in the mirror spoke to her: *Did you even have a life before Sam? Was there really a war? Did you actually run a drill press?*

That last thought nearly made her laugh as she looked down at her beautifully manicured nails.

Had she been diagnosed with depression? Had she been confined to that awful ward for over a quarter of a year? She had long ago surrendered trying to dredge up the truth in any of these things. Life was so much lovelier this way. She would not allow a news article to overshadow the shining moments in her life. No news was good news. Sam really did know best.

"No," Maggie finally answered, handing Susan the newspaper as they stepped out of the bathroom and made their way to the top of the staircase. "No," she said again, as if by saying it twice the word would be set in stone.

Susan linked arms with Maggie as they descended the stairs together. In the hallway, Susan placed the newspaper back on the marble table.

A collection of pretty smiles turned toward the two women as they appeared in the archway of the living room. Maggie felt like a princess about to offer the masses everlasting riches. There was such hope in their eyes. Such desire, as if they, too, yearned for the perfect world with which Maggie had been blessed.

"I'm so relieved," Susan whispered, squeezing Maggie's arm. "What woman needs that kind of stuff spinning around in her head? That would truly be crummy."

As they stepped into the living room, Maggie rested her hands on her round belly. A wondrous tap from a miniature foot or fist sounded from deep within.

"Yes," she told her best friend, beaming like the perfect expectant mother. "It certainly would."

BOOK DISCUSSION QUESTIONS
(Spoiler Alert: Do not read these questions before reading the book!)

1. Have you ever had a repetitive dream, or a memory of a dream that has stayed with you for a long time? How has it affected you?

2. There is a specific reason I placed *Maggie's Dream* in post-WWII America. Why do you think that is? What difference would it have made if the story took place in today's world?

3. Can you relate to Maggie's earlier frustration? How so?

4. Most women are familiar with America's Rosies. If you have any real-life stories of Rosies that you have known, please share with the group.

5. What would have been the most difficult part of living in post WWII America as a woman? As a man?

6. Do you think Sam is a terrible husband? Do you think he is calculating in the way he treats his wife, or is he a product of his era?

7. Years of research went into the writing of *Maggie's Dream*. Were there some facets of the post-WWII era you did not know before reading the book? If so, what?

8. Keeping in mind the era, what are some choices Maggie could have made besides using tranquilizers? Could she have left Sam and gone out on her own?

9. Based on the novel's ending, what kind of life do you see in Maggie's future? Is she happy? Does she have many children? Will she stay with Sam? Will her memory ever come back?

10. Electroshock therapy was commonly used from the 1940s through 1960s, most often on female patients. Why do you suppose this was?

11. How do you feel about dreaming in general? Do you believe as Carl Jung did, that the dream is the window to the soul? Or do you believe something different? Explain.

12. Who was your least favorite character and why?

13. Do you like Dr. Germaine? Why or why not? How did he help Maggie? How did he harm her? What could he have done differently to help her?

14. According to the Foundation for a Drug-free World (2005), in the US alone, more than 15 million people abuse prescription drugs. This is more than the combined number who reported abusing cocaine, hallucinogens, inhalants, and heroin. How do you feel about prescription drugs in general? If Maggie lived in our world today, would she have to find her drugs on the black market?

15. Were you satisfied with the story's ending? Explain.

16. Keeping in mind that the novel has elements of magical realism, explain what you believe is the portal Maggie uses to enter Percy's drug-induced world.

17. Do you understand Percy's angst and ultimate desire to have a world she could call her own? What leads her to this point?

18. During Maggie's era, women were considered spinsters if they did not marry before a certain age, or ever. How have women's views of marriage changed since then? How have men's views changed since then?

19. I discovered that electroshock therapy is still used today for mental illness, though it is used sparingly, and the patient is better managed while undergoing treatment. How do you feel about this? Is this an archaic treatment? Is it better or worse than taking tranquilizers or other prescription medications?

20. Did Maggie really suffer from depression? Or do you think it was something else?

Acknowledgments:

I will forever and always begin my list of thanks with my husband, Jay Kenton Manning. You are the sole reason I have not escaped to an island where there are no such things as computers, social media, or deadlines. Your laughter at the end of each arduous day, your warmth while trudging across the publishing tundra, and your unyielding faith in my work are vital to the mental health of any writer, wife or not! Of course, there is an extra-special appreciation for my incomparable book covers.

Speaking of which, the original artwork for this book's cover was designed by Johnny Linder, whose illustration is exactly what I imagined before stumbling across it on Pixabay.com. So a HUGE *danke* is sent to you, Mr. Linder, all the way to Germany. I am honored to have your talent grace my cover.

A larger-than-life thank you goes to Uwe Stender, my agent, who has believed in me since that first submission long ago, in another life it seems. Without your eyes and heart, Uwe, my writing would only be seen by the walls of my file drawer. Thanks for sticking with me. You don't have to, you know.

Thanks to all of my early readers, some of whom took time away from their own writing schedules to offer their sage advice, listed here for the world to see in this alphabetical marquee: Anne

Barrington; J.D. Cortese; Padgett Gerler; Olwen Jarvis; Denice Josten; P.A. Moed; Scottica Rapp; Katherine Sartori; Valerie Pacheco-Schalow; Peggy Supinski; and Kate Wernersbach.

Special nod goes to Jason and Marina Anderson at Polgarus Studio, not only for being professional and prompt, but for showing kindness and patience with every book you touch. Because of your expertise in formatting, my readers have choices!

A big bear hug goes to Mary Jo Buckl, owner of The Next Chapter Bookstore in downtown New Bern, North Carolina. Your genuine support of local authors goes so much further than you will ever take credit for.

Additional thanks to Sandra Ferguson, Angela Maurer, and Jennifer Argenti, the best beast-sisters a writer could ask for; and Amanda Edwards, for always taking the time and offering support no matter how busy you are.

Maggie's Dream would not have been filled with such detail if not for the following organizations and websites, listed here respectively, which helped to keep me from meandering outside historical facts: The Michigan Medicine Department of Psychology; History.com; and PBS.org.

Finally, thanks to Edward Madden for the lyrics to his and Gus Edwards' beautiful song, "By the Light of the Silvery Moon," first published in 1909 and later made famous by Fats Waller, Doris Day, Little Richard, Etta James, and so many other greats.

Author's Note:

I hope you enjoyed *Maggie's Dream*. Feel free to leave a review on *Amazon*, *Goodreads*, *Twitter*, *Facebook*, or any other site that makes you happy.

Other books by Leslie Tall Manning

Women's Fiction:

GAGA: *Self-e Library Journal Selection Recipient*

Young Adult:

Upside Down in a Laura Ingalls Town: *Sarton Women's Literary Award Recipient*

Leslie Tall Manning is an award-winning author of Adult and Young Adult Fiction. A frequent visitor at schools and libraries, she loves connecting with readers of all ages. She resides in the Southeastern United States with her artist husband.

To buy or review books, please visit Amazon or other online retailers.

Get to know Leslie better:
www.leslietallmanning.com

Feel free to follow:
Goodreads:
www.goodreads.com/author/show/8118702.Leslie_Tall_Manning
Facebook: www.facebook.com/pages/Leslie-Tall-Manning-Writer/236448826562926
Twitter: twitter.com/LTManningWriter
Instagram: instagram.com/leslietallmanning
Pinterest: www.pinterest.com/leslietallmanni/